THE LAST PEARL FISHER OF SCOTLAND

Brodie McBride is having a tough time. The last expert in the ancient art of pearl fishing, he's on a quest to track down the pearl that will complete a necklace for his wife, Elspeth — convinced that the love token will save their marriage. But Scotland's rivers are running out of mussels, Elspeth is running out of patience, and their ten-year-old daughter Maggie is running wild with her moustachioed pet rabbit, Frank. And when Maggie takes matters into her own hands, determined to keep the family together, the McBrides are soon at the centre of an international commotion that will change everyone's lives forever.

SPECIAL MESSAGE TO READERS

THE ULVERSCROFT FOUNDATION
(registered UK charity number 264873)
was established in 1972 to provide funds for
research, diagnosis and treatment of eye diseases.
Examples of major projects funded by
the Ulverscroft Foundation are:-

- The Children's Eye Unit at Moorfields Eye Hospital, London
- The Ulverscroft Children's Eye Unit at Great Ormond Street Hospital for Sick Children
- Funding research into eye diseases and treatment at the Department of Ophthalmology, University of Leicester
- The Ulverscroft Vision Research Group, Institute of Child Health
- Twin operating theatres at the Western Ophthalmic Hospital, London
- The Chair of Ophthalmology at the Royal Australian College of Ophthalmologists

You can help further the work of the Foundation
by making a donation or leaving a legacy.
Every contribution is gratefully received. If you
would like to help support the Foundation or
require further information, please contact:

THE ULVERSCROFT FOUNDATION
The Green, Bradgate Road, Anstey
Leicester LE7 7FU, England
Tel: (0116) 236 4325

website: www.foundation.ulverscroft.com

THE LAST PEARL FISHER OF SCOTLAND

JULIA STUART

ISIS
LARGE
PRINT

First published in Great Britain 2016
by
Vintage

First Isis Edition
published 2017
by arrangement with
Penguin Random House UK

A catalogue record for this book is available
from the British Library.

ISBN 978–1–78541–343–8 (hb)
ISBN 978–1–78541–349–0 (pb)

Published by
F. A. Thorpe (Publishing)
Anstey, Leicestershire

Set by Words & Graphics Ltd.
Anstey, Leicestershire
Printed and bound in Great Britain by
T. J. International Ltd., Padstow, Cornwall

This book is printed on acid-free paper

For my father and late mother

The greatest happiness of life is the conviction that we are loved; loved for ourselves, or rather, loved in spite of ourselves.

Victor Hugo

CHAPTER
ONE

1998

It didn't get much better than this. Brodie gazed at the sun flashing bronze on the scurrying river, trimmed with a million shades of green. Today was the day all right. He, Brodie McBride, the last full-time pearl fisher in Scotland, was going to find the largest pearl in living memory. The one that was going to save his marriage. This stretch of the Tay had been good to him in the past. It couldn't let him down now.

He ran back to his car and hauled from the roof rack his home-made boat, a square wooden box with a canvas bottom that he used for deeper rivers. Inside was his long hazel stick, the end of which he'd split in two and whittled to resemble an old-fashioned clothes peg. Opening the boot, he grabbed his glass — a tin jug with a glass bottom that a smith had made about a decade ago when his old one started to leak. Mouth dry, he placed it carefully inside the boat, and hurried with it to the river. There was one last thing he had to check. His fingers reached inside his jeans pocket. There it was, the old aspirin bottle in which he would put Elspeth's huge pearl.

There was a bigger wobble than usual as he sat astride the lying board, the wooden plank that stretched across the top of his vessel. He pushed himself away from the bank with his pearling stick, then paddled with it to the bend, thrusting against the water on alternate sides. He'd try here. Water splashed against his chin as he tossed the stone anchor over the side. As he lay face down on the board, he could feel his heart thudding against it. Through the water's fractured surface he pushed the glass, and lowered his face to it. Holding it with his teeth so as to have both hands free, he peered at the riverbed. Patches of sand emerged between weeds fluttering across the riverbed like green ribbons. He couldn't see a thing with them in the way.

There! *Margaritifera margaritifera* — the only word Dad had taught him how to spell. Partly buried in the sand, the pearl mussels stood tips ajar, like black hands in prayer. The old, ugly ones were always the best, with a line — often a parallel pair — running to the shell's edge from where a pearl might be. But you could find a decent pearl in a shell without any markings at all, which meant any amateur weekender could come along with no clue what to look for and find something.

Brodie shifted his glass this way then that as he stared at the nodding mussels. Which one? Which one? Not that one. Nor that. They were too wee. What about that one there, by the rock? It must be about ninety years old, given the size. This was it, surely. Arm drawn back, he plunged his stick towards it.

He'd been convinced that the day had finally come moments after waking this morning. Mouth against the pillow, he listened for the cheerful song thrush. Nothing. It was the evil hour again — that no-man's-land between one day and the next when his mind would conjure up a carnival of catastrophes that would last until dawn. He tried to slip back to sleep, but it was hopeless. It kept coming at him in capital letters. Underlined. Forty-three next month, and he still hadn't found the largest pearl for Elspeth's necklace after nineteen years of searching. He'd be the same age Dad had been when he died and left him without even a goodbye.

He turned towards the soft sleeping shape of Elspeth, fingers curled in front of those lips that had once sought his. It hadn't always been like this. They used to be like sea otters, holding hands as they slept so they wouldn't drift away from one another.

Then it came to him, like a whisper from God. Today he was going to find it. He tossed aside the bedding, toes searching for the comfort of his slippers. From their huddle on the chair he grabbed yesterday's clothes, and felt in the drawer for his cosy underpants, the nearest thing he had to lucky ones. Down the landing he slunk, past a door covered with unicorn stickers. Mustn't wake Maggie. Nose pressed against the cracked bathroom window, his heart lifted at the first glow of a tentative sun following days of ruinous rain. He'd spent his working life being subjected to the indignity of catastrophic deluges that rattled his skull and sneaky horizontal drizzles that shimmied down his

3

collar. Snow often twirled merrily towards him as if he'd be pleased to see it, then lie in wait for him in obese heaps along the riverbanks. Hail, as sharp as glass, would aim straight for him. When the sun finally deigned to toss out a ray, he'd be ravished by Highland midges, that most demonic of species. He risked everything — including his life — hunting for nature's most exquisite gem. But today he would return home not only dry, but a hero. As he began to dress, he caught himself in the mirror. He didn't look like one, mind. Hair as wild and grey as a donkey, and just as stubborn.

Down the cottage stairs he fled, missing the two that creaked. In the living room he threw apart the awful pink velvet curtains, the only thing he'd inherited from Aunt Agnes. A watery light hit the red sandstone walls built from the plundered remains of Nether Isla's once glorious abbey. But it still wasn't bright enough to see the bottom of a river. Couldn't the sun get a move on? He had to find the pearl.

Foot swinging, he sat in his armchair, eyes fixed on the sky. Unable to bear the waiting any longer, he got up to perform his secret ritual. He paused, listening to make sure that neither of them was up. Silence. Beyond the bookshelves, stacked with history, he knelt in the corner furthest from the fire. Another pause, just to be certain. He then lifted the loose floorboard, reached into the hidey-hole that neither wife nor thief could find, and grabbed it.

Settled on the settee, the tin resting on his ruined knees, he ran a finger along the raised lettering: *Dr*

Foster's Rain Pills – A Cure for the Deleterious Effects of the British Weather. It had belonged to James, his great-great-grandpa, pearl fisher to the Prince of Wales. Apparently, the future king had been just as besotted with Scottish pearls as was his mother, Victoria. Dad had given him this tin just before they left the house that very first day he took him pearling. Must have been about five. He could see himself now in those brown trousers that were too big for him, standing on the riverbank feeling sick with excitement at the prospect of finding something.

With a slight tug, the lid opened. Even after all this time, he still felt a thrill. Seventy-two white pearls as round as moons with the hint of a pink sky. They shifted on their cloth bed as he tilted them towards the window. Nothing compared to the misty beauty of Scottish pearls. Nothing. You couldn't fake it.

He'd better rinse the pearls again before he left, otherwise they might crack. Leaving the tin on the coffee table, he went into the kitchen for a bowl and some distilled water. As he returned, he stopped. Maggie. Sitting on the settee, her blonde hair in uproar, and the bottom of her left pyjama sleeve hanging empty. She hadn't spotted the tin, had she?

He stood in front of it. "Did you have another nightmare?"

"Why haven't you given all those pearls to Mum to sell to Mr McSweetie?"

He couldn't believe it. The pearls had been his secret for nineteen years, and now Maggie was leaning around his legs to get another look at them. She'd seen thousands of his pearls over the years, but they'd always been a variety of colours and shapes: buttons, barrels and drops in anything from white to gold, silver and blue. She'd never seen a collection like this before — all round and the same exquisite white with tender pink overtones. No one had.

"It must have been that cheese sandwich you had last night that woke you," he said.

She lifted her face, as pale as a snow bunting. "Mr McSweetie would buy all of them."

"I blame that English Cheddar your mother bought. I told her to stick to the Orkney stuff. It's the cows. They get all depressed stuck down there in Somerset when they could be up here, kicking their hooves in paradise."

"Has Mum seen those pearls?"

"On no account mention them to your mother. Come on, back to bed. I'll smuggle you a monk biscuit. I've found out where Mum hides them. You'd think she'd have more imagination than the airing cupboard. It was the first place I looked."

"Why can't I tell Mum about the pearls?"

He didn't have time for this, he had to get his stuff together. "It's a secret."

"I won't tell anyone."

She was still just sitting there.

"If you go back to bed I'll let you watch *Columbo*."

"Two biscuits, *Columbo* and the secret."

It was like negotiating with some power-crazed despot, not a ten-year-old girl in pyjamas with penguins

6

all over them. Outside, it was getting lighter. He had to get out of here. "Promise you'll keep it to yourself?"

She nodded.

"They're for your mother. Been collecting them ever since we were married." Now he felt all exposed. "Right. Up you go."

She frowned. "That was ages ago."

See. That was the point. His mum had told him that Dad took fourteen years to collect the pearls for her necklace, and Brodie had been at it for nineteen years and he *still* hadn't finished Elspeth's yet. "They have to be the same colour and lustre. And be the right size and shape. Takes years." He jerked his head toward the door. "Bed."

"What do you mean, the right size? They're all different."

Why wouldn't she just go back upstairs ? Stifling a sigh he glanced at the clock on the mantelpiece, then swiftly arranged the pearls on the table until they formed a perfectly graduated necklace. "See how they start off small, get bigger and bigger, then become small again?"

"There's a gap in the middle."

"That'll be the biggest one. I'm about to find it." He strode to the window and looked up. He had to be first on the river. Couldn't bear someone else scuffing up the water before him.

"Why is it a secret?"

"Because it's a love token," he said, his mind drifting with the river waiting for him. "All McBrides give their wives a pearl necklace. Family tradition." Why was he telling her this?

Now she was standing in front of Mum's tiny black-and-white photograph on the wall. Elspeth had found it in a dusty taped-up box in the loft, got it framed, then hung it next to her parents' pictures. It was meant to have been a surprise. A nice one. He'd avoided looking at that photo for years.

"Like that one?" she said.

Silently he stood next to her and stared at Mum's cream pearl necklace. He could still remember her gripping his hand as they walked back home from Dad's funeral, and pointing out a woman who she insisted was wearing it.

Maggie looked up at him, eyes blue and clear like her mother's. "Will everything be all right again when you've found it?"

"What do you mean? Everything's all right now, isn't it?"

Silence.

"What happens if you don't find it?"

His stomach shrank.

"Dad?"

He didn't know what to say.

"What happens if you don't find that big pearl?" Her voice was higher, more worried.

He jerked his head towards the stairs. "Bed."

The pearls back in their hiding place, and finally alone again, he returned to the kitchen. There was no time for breakfast or to make a sandwich. As he started to fill his water bottle, the stairs creaked. Who was that now? He had to go. It was a Saturday. Some of the weekenders might be out trying their luck.

"Was it your back?"

Elspeth. Standing in the doorway tying her dressing gown across that slim waist of hers, dark hair ruffled past her shoulders. Thirty-two years after first seeing her barefoot on a riverbank and he still couldn't look away.

"Is that what woke you?" Her voice had an early-morning croak to it. "You should let the doctor have a look at it. All that bending. It's no good for it. Did your father suffer with his?"

"We've run out of Orkney Cheddar."

Why was she sitting down? He had to get out of here. A part-timer might try their luck at that bend in the Tay near Meikleour where he just knew the pearl was.

"I used it all up." She yawned. "Last night."

"Must have been hungry."

"Didn't say I ate it," she said sleepily. "Said I used it." She got up and flicked on the kettle.

"What for?"

"Fancy some tea?"

"Used it for what?"

"It's like what Michelangelo said. When they asked him how he sculpted David."

"What did he say?"

"He said he looked at the stone and removed everything that wasn't David."

"So?"

She slid back onto the chair. "So I looked at the cheese and removed everything that wasn't the Taj Mahal."

There was a pause as he tried to take it in. "Maggie's modelling clay. It's in the fridge. You could have used that."

"She's finished it."

"Already? I only just bought it."

"She's made a surprise for you."

"Don't like them."

Silence.

"What was it?"

"A birthday cake. With your name on it and everything."

He didn't get it. "Out of modelling clay? And anyway, it's not until next month."

"She said she didn't know whether you'd be here to have it, and was worried it would go off if she made you a normal one."

Now he got it. It was because of last year. He'd fished the Tay, then had a hunch about the Evelix, four hours north. Instead of coming home for his birthday supper, he'd driven up there and spent the night in his car so he wouldn't lose any time in the morning. He didn't find anything. Tightening the lid on his water bottle, he headed into the hall.

"You do know how to get there, don't you?" she said, following him. "It's that funny little road off the high street."

What was she on about? He screwed his feet into his shoes. Thankfully his stuff was already in the car. "I'll be back later," he said, unlocking the door.

"You can't go without Maggie. And anyway, it's not even six. Come on, I'll make you some eggs."

He wasn't taking Maggie to the shells. Not today. Not when he had to find that pearl.

"For God's sake don't let her see the puppies." She sat down on the bottom step. "I've told her, but you know what she's like."

He blinked. The goldfish. But the pet shop was in Perth, half an hour away. He'd have to wait for the damn thing to open. "I'll take her in the week." He opened the door.

"You promised her that fish for the start of the summer holidays," she said, getting to her feet. "That was a week ago."

"Like I said, next week."

"It's her first pet. You know how much she wants one."

Didn't she see? He was going to make it all better. By the end of today everything would be sorted. Neither of them would be disappointed in him any more.

"I'd go myself, but she wants you to take her."

"Me?"

"She's got it into her head that you're some kind of goldfish expert."

He gazed at the worn carpet. Expert? The only thing he knew about goldfish was that you flushed them down the loo when they died. How could Maggie think he was an expert at anything? He felt a shift inside. There was something about that bairn that got him in the guts. Always had.

"I'll take her before I go to the shells, and pick up some more cheese once I've finished. Be back for supper." He'd come home a hero. On all fronts.

"Everyone else has got a dog," said Maggie in the passenger seat next to him, fingering the edge of her sunflower shorts.

The handbrake squealed as he hitched it up as high as it would go. "We're not everyone else."

Head lowered, he peered through the windscreen at the purple facade dotted with black paw prints. Pet shops gave him the heebie-jeebies — all those trapped animals desperate for love. He wound down his window to get some air. The deserted street was just as ugly as the store with its tossed fried-chicken boxes and beer cans. You'd have to put a gun to his head before he'd ever live in a city.

"How long do we have to wait?" She was flicking the little finger of her prosthesis, the way she did when she was anxious about something.

"Forty-three minutes." He tapped on the clock. "Got a feeling that's fast, though."

"Why didn't we just come when it opens?"

"The early bird catches the goldfish."

He leant back. All he could hear was the plastic ticking of the clock as if a bomb was about to go off.

"Samantha Grey's got one," she said.

He scratched at something on his trouser leg with his thumbnail. "Got what?"

"A dog."

"Why don't you get some sleep? I'll keep a lookout."

"Not tired."

She wanted that fish. Big time. Before they'd left, she showed him the spot she'd cleared on her dressing table for the bowl, pointing out that its occupant would have views of the garden. What it must be like to want only a goldfish.

"Alice's goldfish used to look at you like that." She widened her eyes with her fingers.

"They get that vacant look after a while. All that swimming round and round does their heads in. We'll teach it some tricks. Get it to jump through hoops like a dolphin."

He stared at the door, willing it to move. Couldn't they open early for stock taking? A hamster head count?

"Thought about what you're going to call it?"

"Rover."

She was looking ahead of her, seeing the wonder of it all. Then something happened and she frowned.

"It won't die, will it? Alice found hers floating on top of the water. Her mum said she must have fed it too much."

He shook his head. "We'll pick a clever one. One that knows when it's had enough to eat."

"What do they look like, the clever ones?"

"It's all in the shimmer."

There was a pause.

"Dad?"

"Yes?"

"When will my freckles go?" She was still worried about them.

"Never, hopefully."

"Is it true what you said? Ages ago."

"What did I say?"

"That there was a shower of gold when I was born and that's why I've got them."

"How else would you account for them?"

She turned to the window, unbrushed hair obscuring her face. "Once we've got Rover you can go and find that pearl and give it to Mum with the others when you get home. She's going to love them, I know it."

Staring ahead of him, all he could see was nineteen years of failure. He was going to find it today, wasn't he?

"They're opening!"

Something was stopping him from getting out of the car. He still had his stupid seat belt on, that was why. Once he'd finally released himself, he hurried towards the shop. As he advanced, a man in an over-stuffed black T-shirt appeared on the horizon like a pirate ship. The numpty wasn't going in, surely? Not after they'd been staking the place out for forty minutes. As he started to run, the man broke into one of those astonishing sprints normally performed by hedgehogs. As Brodie reached for the handle it was seized by a doughy fist, an inked swallow caught between the thumb and forefinger. Once inside, he tried both over- and undertaking, but the way to the counter was irrefutably blocked. Stiffly, he trailed after him down a gauntlet of horrors — lunatic budgies talking to their reflections in mirrors, wild-eyed gerbils trying to gnaw their way to freedom and suspiciously silent vivaria in which evil lurked.

When, eventually, they arrived at the counter, he attempted to catch the attention of the assistant, a pale-skinned woman with hair as black as her lipstick. But she was staring at Maggie's prosthesis, as stiff as a doll's arm. Couldn't she just look away embarrassed like everyone else did?

He tapped on the counter. "I'd like a goldfish. For my daughter."

Both the assistant and the man looked at him.

"The other customer was here first." She fiddled with her gold nose ring.

The man nodded, then pointed to the canaries. "I've got witnesses." He scratched at his stomach with his thumb. "I'm after something for my wife."

"What about a hamster?" said the woman. "Great sense of humour."

"Be a waste. She hasn't got one."

"How about a mouse? Very loyal."

"Too small. She's short-sighted."

"A parrot. Something to talk to."

He shot out a warning finger. "Wouldn't want to encourage that particular aspect."

Brodie tapped again. "While the gentleman's deciding, may I have a goldfish?"

"One of the clever ones," said Maggie. "It's all in the shimmer."

"Run out, I'm afraid. Next delivery is due on Monday. But don't take my word for it. You never know with head office."

"Run out?" Brodie said, incredulous. "How can a pet shop run out of goldfish? It's like going into an off-licence and being told they've run out of whisky."

The assistant shrugged. "Everyone loves a goldfish. There was a run on them yesterday. Try your luck and come back on Monday."

"Excuse me, I was here first."

"Monday? I can't come back on Monday." His voice was starting to rise. "The bairn needs one now. I promised."

"What about Tuesday? Though between you and me, you're probably better off trying on Wednesday."

He couldn't stand the smell in here. It was getting down his throat. "I've got to get her one today. Don't you see?"

"Or next Saturday to be certain."

"What's that?" Maggie pointed to a cage behind the counter.

The assistant followed her finger. "Snowball."

"Looks like someone's had a wee on that snow," said the man.

"I love him," said Maggie.

Brodie peered. "Why is it reduced?"

"A customer brought him back," she said. "Haven't been able to shift him since."

"I love him."

"But what is it?" said Brodie.

She looked at him like he was dim-witted. "A rabbit."

"A rabbit? It could fly with those ears. Shouldn't they be sticking up?"

"Just what I was thinking," said the man. "Like Bugs Bunny."

"He's a lion lop," she said. "They're meant to do that."

There was something about pet rabbits that gave him the creeps. They were all teeth and no brain.

"I love him."

Maggie was staring at it like she was bewitched. It reminded him of those furry things on a stick you used to get rid of cobwebs. "Can it see through that fur?"

"I wouldn't stick your finger in to find out," said the man. "With teeth that size it'll take your arm off."

Silence. Even from an upside-down parrot.

Maggie's cheeks were so flushed she looked as though she'd just been slapped.

"We'll take it," said Brodie, swiftly taking out his wallet. "Snowball."

For a moment the assistant didn't move. "Never thought we'd get rid of him." She reached up to the latch. "At least you won't need a hutch. He's a house rabbit."

"What's that?"

"Lives indoors."

"We'll take a hutch anyway." He snapped down his credit card on the counter. "Best one you've got. Snowball might like a summerhouse with garden views. Isn't that right, Maggie?"

She still hadn't taken her eyes off it. "He's not called Snowball. His name's Frank."

"Well, let's get Frank into the car pronto. And I'm driving."

The day had started to die as he walked silently into the kitchen on his return from the Tay. Slices of chicken suffocated underneath cling film on a solitary plate on the empty table, a drop of congealed gravy spoiling the place mat below. Maggie, with her back to him, was pouring tea into the sink from the family pot. It was the one commemorating Queen Victoria's Diamond Jubilee which had belonged to his great-great-grandpa. For some reason Mum had given it to him when she sent him a hundred and fifty miles south to live with Aunt Agnes for what was supposed to have been a few months. Elspeth, in a floral cotton dress and bare feet, was washing the dishes next to Maggie. There, on the wall, was the print of the Battle of Culloden he'd bought last week from a charity shop. He'd just driven along the enormous beech hedge said to grow heavenwards as the men who planted it had been killed in that battle. The heroes.

"That's a lot of teeth for a goldfish," said Elspeth as she turned, water dripping from her yellow gloves onto the tiles.

He said nothing.

She raised her eyebrows. "Did you get the cheese?"

Silence.

"Did you find anything?" Maggie was looking at him like it was the most important thing in the world.

A swallow.

"Dad, did you find anything?"

He couldn't say it. Just couldn't say it. He shook his head then flinched as the teapot slipped from her hand,

and china five generations old smashed into thousands of brittle shards. No one moved during the even louder silence that followed. Fear stirred his stomach as he heard the voice again. The one always whispering that he was going to lose them both.

CHAPTER
TWO

Mum couldn't hear her, could she? She'd want to know what she was up to, and there was no way she'd let her go if she found out. As quietly as she could, Maggie slipped inside the cupboard under the stairs and pulled the door behind her. It smelt of winter in here. The torch made a loud click as she turned it on. There was Dad's grey anorak, a big empty ghost. Against the wall was the ironing board, all silver and shiny like snails had crawled up it. She winced as she stubbed her bare foot against the vacuum cleaner. Still hadn't cleared up the mess on the living-room carpet. There was the spot she usually sat, back against the wall as the electricity meter made that whirring noise. Nobody could find you here. You could sit eating an entire packet of sultanas and not hear anyone arguing the whole time.

They must be in here somewhere. She shone the light at the far end and there they were, stuck between the Christmas tree stand and the suitcases. Stepping closer, she reached for the dusty pair of pink Wellingtons. They'd protect her feet if there were any skeletons.

Back in the hall, she held each boot upside down and shook it. You always had to check that nothing had crawled inside before putting them on, like earwigs. If they got into your ear they ate your brain, everyone knew that. Hopefully they were all inside Samantha Grey's wellies and they'd eat her silly head off.

As she crept to the front door she found that her toes were squashed up at the ends. There was no way they'd fit come winter, and she might not get another pair so she'd have to keep wearing them. A sudden squeak of a floorboard made her turn. Two feet were standing at the top of the stairs. Now they were coming down. It was all going wrong already.

"Wellingtons in this weather?" said Mum, standing in the hall with a mug in her hand.

"We're going to look for tadpoles. Alice and me."

"It's the summer, they'll be frogs by now."

She reached for the doorknob.

"Have you vacuumed up that glitter on the living-room carpet?"

"Guard Frank," she said, pulling the door behind her.

Her rucksack bounced uncomfortably as she began to run. Mum said it was rude to look into people's houses, but how would you know what they were doing if you didn't? She turned her head. Next door's white cat was picking its way over the ornaments on their windowsill. The next house had such thick net curtains the house looked like it was filled with fog. And there was Mr Cruickshank from number 27 sitting on the sofa wearing white underpants up to his armpits. Normally they were flapping on the washing line. If he was ever stranded on a desert island he could use them as a sail, Dad said.

She bent her head and picked up speed. If she ran fast enough they'd let her compete in the Olympics, which meant she'd get to fly in a plane for definite.

Her feet were all horrible and sweaty by the time she clumped down the last row of terraced cottages, and headed towards the Tolbooth. Tall and narrow, it had a clock on the top in case you dropped your watch in the bath, and had to wait for your birthday for a new one. Mum said it was built ages ago and sometimes prisoners had been locked inside, which was why it had a massive keyhole. Now everyone was locked out of it.

There was Alice, waiting with her back against it. What happened to her wellies ? She was wearing flip-flops.

"You still haven't told me where we're going," said Alice, tucking her straight brown hair behind her ears as she approached.

"In there." She jerked her thumb towards the Tolbooth.

Alice's eyes became even bigger behind her new glasses. "But we're not allowed!"

"The petrol station in Blairgowrie has been robbed. They might have hidden the money inside. We could share it."

"Why would they put it in there?"

It was obvious. "Because no one's allowed in."

"It's stealing."

She shook her head. "Doesn't count if someone else stole it first."

Alice glanced doubtfully at the door. "But we haven't got a key."

"The wood's been pulled away from the window at the back. I saw it yesterday when I was exploring. It must have been the robbers. We can get in there."

"But it's haunted, everyone says so."

"Ghosts don't come out on a Sunday."

"But they might get the day wrong."

"Ghosts *always* know when it's a Sunday."

She frowned. "How?"

"God tells them."

The brambles scratched Maggie's thighs as she led the way round the back, pushing aside the branches with her prosthesis. Underneath the window, she stood on a stone and peered into the darkness. It wasn't going to be easy. She'd have to grab the far edge of the window ledge and try and pull herself in with only one hand. At least it was wide enough to rest her tummy. Eventually she slithered down the other side, ignoring the scrapes to her knees.

"What's it like?" called Alice.

"It smells horrible." Her voice sounded all echoey.

"What of?"

"The boys' loos."

After what seemed like ages Alice crawled in, then dropped down beside her. "I can't see anything! Let's get out of here!"

"Get my torch from my rucksack, it's in the front pocket."

Alice didn't move. "Everyone says there's skeletons chained to the walls."

"You don't have to look at them, just search for the money."

There was an unzipping sound, and Alice handed her the torch. Holding her breath, she swept the white beam across the floor. An old trainer, some beer cans and the remains of a fire. Was that it?

Alice clutched her arm. "What was that noise?"

They froze.

There was a gust of air as something passed over their heads, making a horrible whirring noise. Screaming, they bolted for the wooden staircase.

"I've just lost a flip-flop!" wailed Alice as they climbed.

"Keep going!" It was going to get them, they should never have come.

Eventually, there was nowhere left to run, and they stood, catching their breath. Maggie looked around. There was a huge bell hanging above them so they must have made it to the room right at the top.

"Is it still following us?" whispered Alice.

She listened. "It's gone." With the heel of her boot she scraped at the floorboards. "There's poo everywhere. Must be rats up here."

"That's not from rats. One of my cousins has one. They have wee black poos, some with a curl."

"Look at all these feathers," she said, turning round. "It must have just been a stupid bird downstairs." Poo, feathers and a smelly old sleeping bag — there wasn't any money up here either. Back against the cold wall, Maggie sank down in the corner.

"We'd better go soon," said Alice. "My mum will kill me if I get caught."

Rummaging in her rucksack, Maggie pulled out the box of fairy cakes she'd made especially for Alice. They were now all squashed, and the buttercream icing was stuck to the lid. "Want one?" she said hopefully, offering them to her.

Alice shook her head.

The cake Maggie bit into was lovely and vanillary. "Thought you said you were going to wear your wellies," she said, mouth full.

"Couldn't. They're at my mum's." Alice sat down next to her. "I'm with my dad this weekend, and he doesn't like me going home when I'm staying at his."

Maggie wiped her lips, her appetite gone. Mum and Dad couldn't divorce. Where would her bedroom be if they did?

"Did you get your goldfish?"

"My dad bought me a rabbit instead."

"What's its name?"

"Frank."

Alice smiled. "Can I come and see him?"

Slowly she shook her head. "Won't come out from behind the sofa."

"Why not?"

"He's having a think about things."

"What was that noise?" said Alice, her eyes all big again behind her glasses.

She listened. There were footsteps coming up the stairs.

They got to their feet.

"It's the robber coming back for his money," wailed Alice.

Her chest was hurting. "But there isn't any money."

"Maybe he's hidden it, and he's coming up here to get his sleeping bag. He might have a gun!"

As the pounding got closer, they both backed up against the wall. Maggie looked around for somewhere to hide, but it was too late. A man appeared, eyes as small as spiders, wearing a big coat even though it was sunny. She could smell him from here. A scruffy black dog was pulling at its lead by his side.

"What are you girls doing here?"

He wasn't going to shoot them, was he? "Would you like a fairy cake?" she said, offering the box to him.

He just looked at them.

"You could scrape the icing off the lid and put it back on. It won't matter."

"What's wrong with your arm?"

"Nothing."

"You've got a false one."

"Born like it."

The ugly dog was trying to sniff her.

"Are you that robber?" she said.

"What robber?"

"The petrol station one."

"No idea what you're on about. What are you doing here? This place isn't safe for children."

They were trapped. They should never have come. The man was going to kill them both and it would be all her fault. She nodded at the sleeping bag. "Why don't you go home to sleep if you're not the robber on the run from the police?"

"I've nae got one."

Where did his children sleep if he didn't have a house? Maybe he never even saw them.

"Scram!" the man shouted, taking a step forward. "Or I'll set my dog on you."

They fled down the stairs, and scrambled back through the hole. Maggie's heart was thumping in her ears as they ran towards the park. How would she stop Mum and Dad from arguing now that she didn't have any money to give them?

As he hurried through the trees to the scurrying South Esk, the tiny blue pearl he'd found in the Naver yesterday rattled in his aspirin bottle like a solitary penny in a collection box. It had taken him almost five hours to get to the northern Highlands and that was all he'd found. Spending the night up there in his car after a pie and beer in a pub hadn't exactly helped his back either. At least it had saved him thirty quid on some grotty B&B, and he hadn't had to listen to the thudding of the headboard from the next room. How long had it been since he and Elspeth . . .? Ages. Couldn't they go back to when she'd suggest having an early night, those blue eyes of hers telling him she had no intention of sleeping?

The bacon sandwich he'd just eaten in Brechin began to give him heartburn as he strode into the river. He'd driven straight here as soon as he'd woken, which had taken more than six hours with the traffic. He had to find something. Elspeth had been staring out of the kitchen window gnawing the side of her little finger when he'd left yesterday morning. What had she been thinking about? Life without him?

Stick in one hand, he tipped some water into his glass so it wouldn't steam up, held it in the river and lowered his face to it. He hadn't been to these lower reaches for ages. That was the magical thing about pearling: he could strike it lucky any minute. There were those God-awful days when he found nothing. Others when he found something worth between ten and four hundred pounds. Strike it lucky — as he was going to do today — and he'd be looking at a few thousand.

Several paces later he stopped, horrified. A dark brown sediment was swirling around his feet. He took three hesitant steps, stirring up more of the cloudy filth. Through the murk he could make out some mussels by a rock. It couldn't be. It was horrible. Just horrible. Shifting his glass this way, then that, he moved closer. They were gaping open. All of them. Like corpses' mouths.

No longer certain of his legs, he grabbed a couple and clambered out. Water wept from his pointless hessian bag, streaming down the side of his waders. As he slowly opened his fingers the shells flopped apart. Dead. Both of them. It was bloody pollution again. Fertiliser and soil from farmland had been washed into the river, producing this hideous dark sediment full of algae that had smothered the mussels. Pollution had also ruined the Ythan, that glorious pearl river said to have thrown the largest pearl in the Scottish regalia. It was so terrible that no one had bothered to fish it after the 1970s. The River Ugie had been wrecked in the same way. And now here.

Arm drawn back, Brodie hurled one of the mussels. The tiny coffin soared into the air, spun furiously, then smashed down into the water. He tossed the other hopeless one onto the grass, raised his foot, and crushed the sodding thing with his heel.

Elspeth leant closer towards the hall mirror. She didn't look desperate with all this make-up on, did she? She tugged down the sides of her dress. It was the red one Brodie unzipped before they'd even got out of the door to go to dinner. How long ago was that? Last year. She fingered the ends of her hair skimming her right breast. Maybe it was time to get it cut. It might make her look younger — would he touch her then?

She could still remember their first intimate moment. It was the winter when it had snowed a month early and they ran to the fisherman's hut after school, flakes studding their hair like blossom. As they lay together on their coats, his fingers worked their way up her thigh, her breath shorter with every inch. When his hand went even further she let out a gasp, no longer feeling the cold sliding in under the door.

From her reflection she turned and reached for her handbag to check that it was still there. She was being ridiculous, she knew: things didn't just jump out of your bag. Sure enough there it was, the old Nivea pot that contained the button-shaped grey pearl. It was a beauty all right. She closed her eyes. Dear God, or anyone else who happened to be listening, please let Mrs Campbell buy it.

As she ushered Maggie out of the front door and closed it, something gave way. One of the screws in the handle had worked loose. The wood must be too rotten to hold it, too rotten to even go on the list of things that needed fixing.

"When will Frank come out from behind the sofa?" said Maggie, her mouth full of doughnut.

"Soon."

The bairn squinted in the sun. "But what's he doing?"

"Planning his next novel." She reached for the bairn's hand and started walking.

"Will he come out before Dad gets back?"

"I'm not sure when either of them will appear, I'm afraid."

A man in tailored shorts and tanned legs was standing at Mrs Wallace's door on the other side of the street. Most blokes' calves round here were so white they'd scare the birds from the trees. He turned to face her and she looked away as quickly as she could. It was Cameron Wallace. Alpina had said he was finally moving back from the Middle East. She must look a right state trying to walk in these shoes. He was still staring at her. She lowered her gaze to the pavement as the sound of her ridiculous footwear filled the silence between them.

Several minutes later she noticed a dull thumping sound. Maggie was wearing her Wellingtons again —

with a sundress. Why hadn't she spotted them before they left the house? There wasn't time to go back now. She was going to be late for work as it was. At least Alpina had said she'd cover for her. That was what sisters were for, even if they did resent you. "Why have you got those on? Your feet will get hot."

"Just like them," said Maggie, sugar glimmering on her chin. "Did you know that Wellingtons were invented by the Duke of Wellington?"

"Who told you that?"

"Dad. And the Earl of Sandwich invented sandwiches."

As they passed the General Store, Nessa was slumped at her empty counter eating a Cornetto and listening to country music. Her roots needed doing. It couldn't be easy bringing up Alice on her own. The poor thing must have been expecting an ice-cream rush with this weather, but everyone was still going to the Co-op, lured by the bargains. It would be awful if the store closed down. They'd already lost half the shops in Nether Isla. She pressed on. There was no time to stop for a chat, she had that pearl to sell. Besides, she'd only feel obliged to buy something. Not with those prices.

"Did Earl Doughnut invent doughnuts?"

She glanced at her watch. They'd have to walk faster. Mrs Campbell had said she was going on holiday in the afternoon, so it was this morning or not at all. How long had it been since she'd last visited her? About four years. It had taken that long for Brodie to find another grey button that matched the three she'd already bought for her son's waistcoat.

"Did he?"

"No."

"Who did then?"

"Maggie, you've got jam down the front of your dress." She took out a handkerchief and rubbed at it. "God. I've made it worse. I should have bought those American ones."

"Why American ones?"

"They've got a hole in the middle." She took Maggie's sticky hand and started to hurry. What would Mrs Campbell think, turning up with Maggie in a dirty dress?

"Why do American doughnuts have holes in them?"

Her stomach clenched. Had she put the pearl in the pot? She should have checked while she was in the hall.

"Mum, why do American doughnuts have holes in them?"

"I don't know. So their policemen can carry them more easily?"

"What do they do with the middles?"

Of course she'd put the pearl in the pot. She remembered fetching some cotton wool to protect it. What was wrong with her? She wasn't normally like this.

"Mum?"

But would Mrs Campbell buy it? She was one of her best private clients, and always paid much more than Mr McSweetie in his shop. But you never knew with the rich. They had some funny ideas.

"Mum? What do they do with the middles?"

The problem was that the pearl was from the wrong river. Mrs Campbell only collected pearls from the

Spey. She had a thing about it as her family used its spring water to make that whisky of theirs.

"Mum?"

"The middles?" She paused. "They leave them out on Mars to see if there's any life there."

At the remains of the ruined abbey they stopped to cross the road. If Mrs Campbell offered her as much as last time, there would be a bit left over after paying the gas and electric. A tenner, perhaps, towards a new prosthesis for Maggie, one that moved. She hadn't told Brodie about it. He wouldn't think the bairn needed something so fancy. But that was because it hadn't been his fault.

The doctors had told her it wasn't hers either. They kept shaking their heads each time she suggested a reason — a cleaning product she might have inhaled when she was pregnant, or even the odd glass of wine. After a while they began to look at her like she was off her head. All she'd wanted was a reason, while they just kept insisting it was nature. But why would nature make her daughter unable to tie her own shoelaces?

It was Brodie who'd saved her in those very early days. Once they'd got back from the maternity unit, she'd stood in Maggie's room, freshly painted in that ridiculously happy yellow, seeing everything that was wrong with herself as she stared at the stranger in the cot. She couldn't even bring herself to touch the bairn whose life she'd already blighted, and who was screaming as if she knew it. At the end of that blistering first day, Brodie went out to buy some bottles and formula. For a week he fed that baby, and she'd watch from the living-room door in a filthy dressing gown as the inseparable pair slept in his armchair.

He never once abandoned her in her darkness. Each time he finished telling her it wasn't her fault, he'd cup her cheeks and insist that the bairn would grow up and be loved just as fiercely as he loved her, his wonderful wife. He'd hold her close and whisper that what mattered in life wasn't how many hands you had, but the size of your heart. And he'd kiss the top of her head, and tell her that this daughter of theirs would make her mark on the world, and no one would stop her. Eventually he caught her drifting soul, and one morning she lifted her most precious thing out of the cot, held her to her breast and fed her.

"Where do they put the jam if they haven't got a middle?"

Silence.

"Mum?"

"Why don't you ask Mrs Campbell? She's flying to America this afternoon."

"Is she going on holiday?"

"I expect so."

"Can *we* go to America?"

"One day."

"That's what you always say, but we never go anywhere. Why can't we go now? In a plane."

She looked up, searching for an answer, the television aerials like scars against the irrefutably blue sky.

"Because we need to be around when Frank comes out from behind the sofa."

34

Their feet grated loudly on the gravel as they walked up the drive, making her feel like a trespasser. With its bay windows overlooking the lawns, the red sandstone house was still as imposing as ever. The conservatory was new. Bet that was where Mrs Campbell sipped her afternoon tea with her feet up.

She pushed the large black bell, with its cracked paint, and waited. How many times had her great-grandmother scrubbed these steps? Each generation was supposed to better itself. She'd got her degree all right, the first in the family to get one. And yet, despite her education, here she was, standing at Mrs Campbell's door feeling like a pedlar. She'd had a proper job the last time she was here — people looked up to her. There'd been none of this anxiety about whether she'd get a sale or not.

"Mum?"

Maggie was looking worried for some reason. "Yes?"

"Why don't some people live in a house? Like tramps."

"Tramps? I suppose they might have lost their job, and haven't got enough money."

"But why don't they live with their family?"

"Sometimes things don't work out how you want them to."

"But if you've got a wife and children you should stay with them."

"Doesn't always happen that way." Had they heard the bell?

"Does that mean they don't see their children?"

She'd definitely got the right time. She'd written it down on the pad by the phone.

"Mum? Does that mean they don't see their children?"

"Probably not."

The door opened and the housekeeper, a short, soft-edged woman in a white blouse and black skirt, stepped back to let them in. Silently she led them across the hall to the drawing room, where Elspeth settled on one of the crimson silk sofas facing each other in front of the fireplace. Staring at her from the walls were several generations of Campbells who'd made the family fortune from that huge distillery next to the Spey. Meanwhile, her Brodie was risking everything — his job, his family, their future — by drinking so much of that very same whisky. It wasn't like this a year ago. Now she was playing second fiddle to the grottiest pub in Nether Isla. It was the rejection that hurt the most. Brodie had always put her and Maggie first. Always.

Maggie picked up a paperweight from the side table.

"Careful," she urged. "It's expensive."

"What's it for?"

"You put it on a piece of paper to stop it blowing away."

"Why doesn't Mrs Campbell just use a book?"

"She collects them. They're old."

"Why are they expensive if they're old?"

Elspeth reached into her bag. Better check the pearl was definitely there.

"How did they get the stars inside?"

It was there. Thank God.

She turned to answer. What was Maggie up to now standing next to that Chinese cabinet? Its doors, inlaid with mother-of-pearl, were wide open, and she was reaching into one of the drawers.

"Come and sit down." She patted the sofa.

Slumped down next to her, Maggie started flicking the little finger of her prosthesis. What was wrong with her? She usually liked coming to see her private clients.

The door opened and Mrs Campbell strode in wearing a straight beige skirt that was tight across her pot belly. Her hair, swept back into a chignon, was too dark to be natural, given the looseness of her neck.

Elspeth's dress stuck to the back of her legs as she stood to greet her. "You remember Maggie."

"She has your eyes."

Maggie lifted them towards Mrs Campbell, and gave her a tight smile.

That wasn't like her.

Knees together, Mrs Campbell sat down opposite them. "Such beautiful weather we're having. It must be a relief for Mr McBride after all that rain. How romantic to spend your day looking for pearls. At least he's not having to work in that jam factory in this heat."

"Pearling's very chancy, Mrs Campbell. Very chancy. He could open over a hundred and fifty mussels and not find a pearl good enough to sell. And he knows what to look for."

"You said on the phone that you had some good news. Has your husband found the fourth pearl?"

Elspeth took a square of black velvet from her handbag and spread it out on the low glass table between them. She opened the pot, and placed the flat, grey button on the cloth. Sitting back, she slid her palms down her thighs.

Mrs Campbell put on her glasses, reached for the pearl, and studied it. From a small box she took three others, and lined the pearl up next to them on the table. Her lips pursed as she examined them.

Dear God, please let the pearl be the same as the others.

The mouth suddenly relaxed into a smile. "It's a perfect match — the colour, the size and the lustre. I can't tell you how thrilled I am."

She'd have to tell her, she wouldn't be able to live with herself if she didn't. "I know you only collect pearls from the Spey. I should tell you that my husband found this one in the Laxford."

"The what?"

"The River Laxford."

She sat back. "All the way up there in the northwest Highlands?"

"Aye."

"Has he stopped fishing the Spey?"

She shook her head. "No, but this is the only grey button of the right size and lustre he's found since the last time. There's no guarantee he'll find another one in the Spey."

"But he's already found three."

"It took years, and he's found none since." She nodded at the pearl. "That might well be the last of its kind he'll ever find."

"Things aren't that bad, surely." Mrs Campbell gestured towards the window. "Scotland has half the world's population of pearl mussels."

"Brodie's the only full-timer left."

"Which means he's got the pick of the crop."

"They're dying out. Overfishing and pollution. It's been in the papers." If Mrs Campbell ever bothered to read one. "That's why the others gave up. They couldn't make a living."

Mrs Campbell peered again at the grey button.

"I came to you first as I know you want four of them for your son's vest in time for his wedding." Elspeth nodded at his photograph on the mantelpiece. The poor sod had the Campbell nose all right. "A good-looking man like that, he's not going to be single for long."

There was a clicking sound as Mrs Campbell fiddled with her necklace. After a moment she dropped her hand, and the jet fell back against her chest with a final clink. "While I appreciate your honesty, Mrs McBride, I think I'll take my chances. The Spey's always meant so much to my family."

All this way for nothing. Wasn't even offered a cup of tea. Forty minutes here and forty minutes back. In this heat. No juice for Maggie. Not even a measly glass of water. She put the pearl back in the pot, and got to her feet, pulling her dress away from the backs of her thighs. Silently Mrs Campbell followed her through the hall.

"Do come to me first when your husband finds another one in the Spey," she said, holding open the front door with fingers throttled with diamonds.

Standing on the step, Elspeth faced her. He wasn't going to. Couldn't she see? "It's finding the last one that's always a nightmare."

CHAPTER
THREE

"You're late," said Brodie, nodding at the clock above the empty bar. He'd been sitting here since eight trying to forget the state of the South Esk this morning.

Mungo settled two pints on the battered wooden table. He'd just had a haircut, making those ears of his look even more like satellite dishes.

"Only by twenty-eight minutes. You're not technically late unless it's more than half an hour."

"Says who?"

"Me."

He sat back. "You're always late."

"Am not."

"You were even late for Maggie's christening. I'll never forget Rev Maxwell standing at the font tapping his fake Rolex asking where the hell the godfather was."

Mungo shrugged. "Was trying to miss the bit when I had to renounce the Devil."

Brodie pushed away his empty glass and reached for the full one. "You must drive Alpina nuts."

"She was already nuts when I married her." Mungo looked around. "Where are the others? You said team training started at eight."

"I wouldn't worry about them if I were you." He leant forward. "They knew that gynophobia is an irrational fear of women. Even Stugly knew that, and he's the thickest man alive."

"It was a good guess."

"Why didn't you just write down what the rest of us said? That's what you're supposed to do. Majority consensus. Pub quiz rules."

Mungo put his Guinness back on the table, and wiped his mouth with the back of his hand. "Overruled you. Thought I was right."

"I still don't know why Alan had to ask for silence before reading out our answer over that stupid microphone of his. Fear of vaginas? You were kidding, right? Fiona looked as though you'd asked to see hers."

Another shrug. "Like I said, it was a good guess."

Brodie snatched up his quiz book, and started leafing through it. They couldn't come last again. The humiliation of it. Fiona knew a thing or two, but then there were the others. The only reason he'd let Stugly join the team was because he'd given Elspeth a job. And as for Mungo, it was like picking each other for their football teams at school. You always played with your best pal, no matter how useless they were.

"Can't we just have a drink?" said Mungo, raising his eyebrows, coupled together like railway wagons. "Play Cluedo like we normally do."

"It'll be Colonel Mustard in the library with the lead piping. It always is." He selected a page. "Art and literature. Which novel starts: '1801. I have just returned from a visit to my landlord — the solitary neighbour that I shall be troubled with'?"

"*Nineteen Eighty-four.*"

"Incorrect. *Wuthering Heights.* According to the King James Bible, what swallowed Jonah?"

"Come on, that's too easy."

"What's your answer?"

"A whale."

"Incorrect. A great fish."

"What, like a giant turbot?"

Eyeing him, Brodie turned a page. "How many lines are there in a limerick?"

"There was an old man with a beard, who . . . er . . ." He tapped the table as he hesitated. "There was a young lady from Spain, who something, something . . . There once was a bloke from somewhere-I-can't-quite-remember-where, who la, la, la, la, la, la, lah . . . Seventeen."

"Incorrect. Five." He paused. "Which is the best method to lure a rabbit out from behind a sofa?"

"Pickled onion crisps."

"How do you know that?"

He rolled his eyes. "Everyone knows that."

"Science and technology. Which extinct creature got its name from the Portuguese word for stupid? You should get this. Inside knowledge."

Mungo frowned at the ceiling as if the answer were up there in the inscrutable handwriting of a doctor. Still waiting for a reply, Brodie glanced around. Alan, with his castaway's beard, sat eyes closed behind the bar, looking as though he was either in communication with

God or asleep. At least the beer was cheap. That was the only saving grace of the Victoria. That and the fact that you could spend the entire evening alone here without having to endure someone going on about their ex-wife. Or football.

Mungo sat back in defeat. "Why don't we ask Cameron to join the team? Then we'd win. He knows everything. He's just done some MBA."

Cameron. Now he was a dodo if ever there was one. How Mungo could have a brother like that he'd never know. "Considering he lives in Bahrain, it'll be a bit tricky."

"He's back," said Mungo, taking a swig.

"Team's full. Anyway, he only ever comes home for a week or two." Thank God.

"Back for good, I mean. He's moved in with Mum while he finds his own place and his shipment arrives. Got his old bedroom back."

Brodie's glass knocked against his teeth as he raised it to his lips. Cameron Wallace was back for good. He couldn't believe it. On top of everything else. Did Elspeth know?

Stugly was going to kill her. Alpina had told her he'd come in yesterday morning while she was at Mrs Campbell's. That was the trouble — you never knew when he was going to turn up. And now it was twelve minutes past nine and she still had to get changed. It would have been quicker if she'd put on her uniform before leaving the house, but she didn't like Maggie seeing her looking like a maid in that vile black polyester dress and white apron. God forbid she'd grow up thinking that her mother was only fit to serve.

It was Brodie who'd found her the job. If it hadn't been for him, she'd still be in her nightie thinking her world had come to an end. Three months after she'd lost her teaching position, he'd gone to every business in Nether Isla and asked if they had anything for her. It had been more to do with helping her get back to her old self again than anything else, though God knew they needed the money now. That was what Brodie was like, always looking out for her. So why wouldn't he listen to her whenever she brought up the fact that there weren't enough pearls to make a decent living any more?

She started to run, but didn't have the right bra on. Stuff it. As she slowed to a walk, she glanced into the empty butcher's with its piled-up post. All these abandoned shops with their rusted signs wheezing like consumptives in the breeze. This place used to be known as the Jewel of Strathmore because of the red sandstone buildings. Victoria and Albert had once stayed a night on their way back from Balmoral. Never mind the fact that the Queen noted in her diary that the women got much better-looking further into the Highlands.

The weatherman on the radio was going on about continuing high temperatures and scattered thunderstorms as she shoved open the cafe door. She should have been standing behind the counter by now, serviettes folded, pad in hand and a smile slapped on her face.

Her uniform was still in a heap in the cupboard where she'd dumped it yesterday. She grabbed it, bolted the toilet door behind her and pulled down her jeans. The dress squeezed her thighs together like dough as she yanked it up. There had to be a better way of making a living than this. When she was teaching she could look after Maggie in the holidays. Now she had to ask her friends and neighbours if they could have her, and not all of them were ideal. Shona from next door sometimes gave the bairn little jobs to do at the salon, but she was the sort of hair-dresser you could only trust with a pair of scissors in the morning — by lunchtime she'd hit the white wine. Then there was old Mrs Wallace over the road with her stuffed buffalo head in the hall. Loved her to bits, but she was certain she was starting to forget things.

As she took up her position behind the counter, Alpina burst through the kitchen swing doors carrying a fistful of forks, her chef's hat pitched like a yacht on her tempest of grey hair. She was getting as round as those teacakes she always cremated, which wasn't something Elspeth was going to point out, even if she was her sister. Something was up, she could tell by that look on her face. Sure enough, the kitchen doors opened again and there was Stugly, chest hair coiled like copper wire at the neck of his grey T-shirt.

"Who do you expect to serve the customers if you're not here?" he said.

You could drive the number 57 bus through that gap in his teeth. "There aren't any, Stugly. And there were only two when I wasn't here yesterday. Alpina served them."

"It's Mr McShane, I've told you."

She wasn't calling him that. For two years she'd sat next to him in maths trying to stop him from copying her answers.

"Do you know why we're getting through so much sugar?"

"The customers are putting it in their tea?"

"More sugar than we should be. Given the takings."

What was he trying to say? "I'm not putting it in my handbag, if that's what you mean."

He glanced at Alpina, who held up both hands.

"Don't look at me. I'm on a diet."

"How I am supposed to run a business when the staff don't turn up and the sugar disappears?"

That was it. She'd had enough, and it wasn't even ten o'clock. "It would help if people actually wanted to come in here, Stugly. Why don't you put your hand in your pocket and spend some money on the place for a change?" She pointed. "Get rid of the pine panelling and those photographs of Scottish castles with fake blue skies." It was all coming out. "And I've already told you about the tea policy. It should be one bag per customer. Tea rationing finished in 1952."

He looked furious, but she couldn't stop. It was like falling into a hole.

"You should just be honest about it and put up a sign calling it 'The Worst Cafe in Scotland'. Give it a USP. They'd flock in their thousands just to see how bad it is. And I'm telling you, they wouldn't be disappointed."

"I'll let you know tomorrow." He moved towards the door in his grey trainers and jeans with the collapsed backside.

"About doing up the place?" He'd listened. Maybe now they'd get some customers, and she'd be able to save more tips for Maggie's prosthesis.

"Whether you've still got a job."

Fingers tapping the counter, she watched as he crossed the road. What had she done? She needed this job. She reached into her apron, and handed Alpina an envelope. "Yesterday's tips," she said, filling the silence. As paltry as they were, she always halved them. "Someone left tuppence under his plate yesterday afternoon. I almost gave it back to him."

"Still," said Alpina, stuffing the envelope into her trouser pocket. "Every bit helps the running away fund."

"What running away fund?"

"Don't tell me you haven't got one. Most women start theirs as soon as they come back from their honeymoon."

"What's it for?"

"Just in case."

"Just in case what?"

"You married the wrong man."

"What can I get you?" she said in the direction of the customer as she gazed out at the distant hills. She shouldn't have spoken to Stugly like that. They'd already threatened to cut off the phone, and Brodie hadn't exactly given her many pearls to sell over the last

48

few weeks. Mr McSweetie wouldn't cough up much for that tiny blue one with the hopeless lustre.

The man turned. Cameron Wallace. After all this time. He'd started to go grey, but those brown eyes were just the same, looking at her like he couldn't see anyone else. Over the years she'd spotted him about town when he came to visit his family, but they'd never talked. She could feel herself going red. How ridiculous. They'd married other people.

"Heard you'd moved back. For good."

"The place hasn't changed much. Nor have you. But that's a good thing." He smiled, wide like before.

"There's a Co-op."

Silence.

She knew what was coming next.

"I thought you were teaching history."

"They closed the secondary school last year. You must have heard about that."

"Didn't fancy teaching elsewhere?"

"Nothing's come up locally. If we moved, Maggie would have to settle into a new school. She's had enough problems with the one she's at. Brodie's not keen either, what with wanting to be near the Highlands for the pearls."

She'd done the right thing agreeing that they should stay in Nether Isla. That was what you did when you loved someone — you put them first and trusted them when they said that everything would be all right. So how come she felt like she was about to fall off a cliff?

"What else is Brodie up to?"

"Just pearling."

"How's that going?"

She paused. "The handy thing about the Co-op is that there's a post office at the back. They closed the main branch."

The door opened and a woman wearing sunglasses came in with a boy she used to teach. With any luck he wouldn't recognise her.

Cameron was still watching her. She could feel it.

"Did you ever finish writing that book about the history of Nether Isla?" he said. "Something to do with the monks, wasn't it?"

There hadn't been time since the school closed. The cafe didn't pay enough, so she'd started cleaning some of the big houses in the evenings. And then, of course, there was the issue of wanting to. Somewhere between cleaning other people's lavatories and folding paper napkins she'd lost the will.

"Taken up pottery instead."

"Any good?"

"Got one of those rare talents. So rare no one's yet spotted it."

"Let me know when you've finished the book. I'd like to read it." He looked past her. "Who owns this place?"

"Stugly."

"Stugly? Is he still around? I can't even remember what his real name is."

"George McShane. He keeps insisting I call him Mr McShane."

"Is he still stupid as well as ugly?"

"The wheel's turning, but the hamster's escaped." She glanced at his hands as he smiled. Those wide knuckles. Funny how they were still so familiar.

"So Brodie's only pearling?"

There were customers waiting to be served. "What is it you'd like?" He was still looking at her. "From the menu," she added, just to be clear.

He picked it up. "How's the tea?"

"Depends how thirsty you are."

"I'll risk it."

She moved towards the kitchen, then turned. "So why did you come home?"

"My marriage. It didn't work out. The kids have moved back to Blairgowrie with their mother. I wanted to be near them."

He was fiddling with the edge of the laminated menu. It needed wiping.

"They're fragile things," she said.

He raised his eyes. "Children or marriages?"

"Both."

You were meant to tell your best friend everything, but she wasn't going to tell Alice what she'd done at Mrs Campbell's yesterday. No one could know about it, not Mum, not Dad, no one.

As she pushed open the door of the General Store, she quickly tugged down the sides of the green-and-white-checked tea towel covering the contents of her basket. It was private.

"Is Alice here?"

Her mum looked up from the tower of jelly packets she was building on top of the counter.

"She's dusting the canned fruit. I hear you two are going to make a cake together."

"At my house. I've got all the tins." Alice would come with her when she told her where they were really going, wouldn't she? She was going to give her a special treat in case she didn't want to be her friend any more after what had happened in the Tolbooth.

"Your house? It's nae bother, Maggie. I've got cake tins upstairs."

"We're using special ones."

Holding a feather duster, Alice appeared from behind the shelves. "Special ones?"

"For a mermaid cake. I've just bought all the ingredients."

"You shouldn't have spent your money," said Alice's mum. "I've got a shopful."

She started for the door. "Come on, Alice."

"Will someone be with you? I don't like the idea of you two girls operating an oven on your own."

"Dad."

The tower collapsed.

"Let's hope you're better at baking than your Auntie Alpina, Maggie. I'd like a slice of that mermaid cake, whatever it is."

"Why are we going this way?" Alice looked up and down the street. "I thought we were going to yours."

Clutching the basket closer to her, Maggie quickened her pace. "We're not."

"Then where are we going?"

"Edinburgh."

Alice stopped. "Edinburgh? We can't go there, it's miles away! It'll take hours."

"We have to. I've got a surprise for you," she said, continuing to walk.

"I'll have to ask my mum if I can go."

"She won't let you," Maggie called over her shoulder.

"But I haven't got any money. We'd have to get the bus and then a train. It'll cost loads."

She stopped and tapped her dress pocket. "I've got my pocket money."

Alice frowned and tucked her hair behind her ear. "What sort of surprise is it?"

"It's your favourite. If you don't like it, I'll let you have my set of nail varnishes."

"You can't give me that. Your mum gave it to you."

"Won't need to. Come on."

"But what about the last time we went somewhere we shouldn't? That smelly man in the Tolbooth could have killed us."

Alice was still just standing there. She wasn't going to come. "He was just some silly tramp. I told you. Come on, or we'll miss the bus." She started to run. "We can try on all the perfumes at Jenners. It's free!"

"But you're carrying all the ingredients," shouted Alice.

"That's not ingredients. It's Frank."

Sitting on the back seat with the basket on her knees, Maggie felt her pocket to make sure that it was still there. Thankfully Alice had been standing behind her when she paid the driver, and hadn't seen inside it. There it was. Her bead purse with the huge bundle of twenty-pound notes she'd found in Mrs Campbell's cupboard, and pushed down one of her wellies. It was three hundred and twenty pounds. She'd counted it out on her bed four times to be sure. It was wrong to steal, but sometimes you had to when something was very important, like helping Dad find that pearl. God would understand. You were meant to stay together if you were married, they made you promise it in church. And anyway, Mrs Campbell wouldn't miss the money. She had so much it wouldn't fit in her purse and she had to keep it in a cupboard.

"Where are you two off to?"

Fiona, the woman who ran the B&B, was looking round from the seat in front. Maggie could smell her cigarettes from here.

"Perth. I've got to buy my mum a birthday present. It's a secret."

"How lovely. Won't mention a word."

Alice leant towards her. "Won't your dad wonder where we are?"

"He's at the shells."

"My mum would kill me if she knew we were going to Edinburgh."

"So would mine. She thinks I'm at Mrs Wallace's."

"If you're bad, your parents get divorced."

54

Who would look after her if Mum and Dad got divorced? The rumble of the engine underneath her thighs suddenly made her feel sick. "I know."

"What happens if we get lost in Edinburgh?"

"We won't. I've been there loads of times for the hospital." She lifted the edge of the tea towel and held it against her forehead. "You can't stay in Nether Isla all your life, can you, Frank?"

Alice put her cheek against hers and peered inside. "How did you get him out from behind the sofa?"

"Pickled onion crisps."

Gripping a twenty-pound note, Maggie raised herself onto her tiptoes at the ticket office. "Two child returns to Edinburgh, please."

The man behind the window ran his tongue back and forth against his top teeth as if checking they were still there. "Children aren't allowed to travel on trains unaccompanied."

"Mum's in the toilet."

He glanced at Alice standing next to her. "Then why aren't you buying your mother a ticket as well?"

The note felt all hot in her hand as she pushed it towards him. "She's already got hers."

His tongue was stroking his teeth again.

"Your mother will have to buy them herself."

She rose even higher. "Can't. I told you. She's in the toilet." He still wasn't going to give them the tickets. She leant towards the glass and lowered her voice. "Diarrhoea."

The tongue disappeared and fingers covered in silver rings pushed the tickets and change through the gap underneath the glass. "Green-banana sandwich. Tell your mother. Works like cement."

"Only just made it," said the woman with the silly pink hair, easing herself into the two empty seats opposite them.

Why couldn't she sit somewhere else? As Maggie drew the basket across the table towards her, the tea towel started to move.

"Hope that's not a cat in there," said the woman, clutching her throat. "They bring me out in hives."

"It's Frank."

The woman shot out a hand and hoisted up a corner of the cloth. "It needs a haircut."

Maggie pulled it back down. "It's rude to look into someone's basket. You have to ask permission. And anyway, rabbits don't have their hair cut. That's sheep. Everyone knows that."

She frowned at the houses flicking past, then felt a nudge.

"The ticket inspector's coming," hissed Alice. "He'll see we're on our own and call the police."

Maggie grabbed the basket. "Come on. Quick!"

Down the swaying carriage they staggered, and bolted the toilet door behind them.

"It stinks even more than the Tolbooth in here," wailed Alice. "This was meant to be a *nice* surprise."

There was a bang on the door and the train lurched to one side.

"Tickets, please."

"We're having a wee," called Maggie.

"Who's in there?"

"Two ladies."

The light dimmed as the train shuddered through a tunnel, making her ears go all funny.

"Come on," she said when the noise stopped. "He's gone."

Alice drew back the lock, and they stepped out. The inspector was staring at them from underneath the brim of his cap.

"Tickets please, girls."

Slowly Maggie put down the basket and reached into her pocket.

"Not travelling on your own, are you?" He studied their tickets.

"Mum's in there." Maggie pointed to the carriage. "The lady with the hat."

"Can't see anyone with a hat."

He was going to call the police any minute. They'd find all that money in her purse, and she'd get into really big trouble. Mum and Dad would take Frank back to the shop. "She must have gone to the buffet to get us some crisps."

He looked at them in silence. Frank was about to jump out and run down the corridor, she just knew it.

"Don't forget that basket." He gave it a kick with his boot. "You wouldn't believe what some people leave on trains."

It was beautiful in Jenners. You could spend all day in here and always be happy. It was like someone had set out the nicest things in the world for you to sniff and touch. And all the assistants had to be really nice to you, even if you were a child. It was the rules.

After spraying themselves with perfume, they headed off to the lift. Up and down they travelled, taking it in turns to press the buttons.

"We'd better get out," said Maggie eventually. "Frank might get travel-sick. And anyway, it's time for your surprise."

The knickerbocker glories made a horrible sliding noise on the tray as Maggie carried them to their table. She'd had to balance one end on her prosthesis. It was really, really heavy. Any minute now she was going to drop it. Everyone in the cafe would stare at her and Alice wouldn't get her treat.

"You should have got the woman at the till to help you," said Alice, jumping up and taking the tray from her.

"Didn't need any help."

She lifted Frank out of the basket, settled him on the seat next to her, and positioned a small bowl of salad in front of his nose.

"These are the best knickerbocker glories in the world," she said, pushing one towards Alice. "Me and Mum always have one after we've been to the hospital."

She snatched up her spoon and took a mouthful. Lovely.

"Excuse me, ladies."

58

A man in a suit with a drop of blood on his shirt collar was standing next to them. "Is that your rabbit?"

Maggie took another spoonful. "Wha' rabbit?"

"The one sitting next to you eating the Salad of the Day."

She glanced down. Frank was going mad with the grated carrot.

"I'm afraid rabbits aren't allowed in Jenners."

"If rabbits aren't allowed, you have to put up a sign like 'no bombing' in the swimming baths."

"I'm going to have to ask you to leave the cafe."

She loaded her spoon with vanilla ice cream, and sucked it staring straight ahead of her. Wasn't going anywhere until Alice had finished her knickerbocker glory. She'd bought it with her pocket money.

"It's Frank's birthday," she said, meeting his gaze. "He doesn't eat birthday cake, so I got him a salad. They've let me out of hospital specially so I can celebrate it with him."

The man scratched an eyebrow.

"The doctors said it might be the last time I get to see him."

Everyone was looking at them. He was going to call her a liar and Mum and Dad would find out.

He cleared his throat. "Seeing as though it's Frank's birthday, on this occasion I think we can let him stay for two more minutes. Provided he remains in the basket."

As the man walked away, Alice picked up her spoon and smiled. She looked like she'd just been given all the nail varnish in the world.

"Is it really Frank's birthday?"

"Every day's Frank's birthday." Maggie stood up. "Just going to the loo."

Her hand skimmed the black shiny rail as she hurried down the stairs. Once out of Jenners, she stood still, suddenly confused. It was here somewhere, down one of these streets. She'd walked past it loads of times with Mum. She ran down the nearest lane, but it wasn't there. Try the next one. It wasn't here either. Just as she thought she was lost, she spotted the jeweller's straight ahead of her.

The door wouldn't open. Stuck to it was a sign telling her to ring the bell. Why did she have to do that? The door should be open so anyone could just walk in. There was a buzzing sound as she pressed the button, and she pushed the handle again.

Standing behind a desk was a lady with bosoms wearing a lovely dress. She'd look like that one day. All golden.

"Are you on your own, lassie?"

The clocks on the walls ticked loudly in the silence.

"My dad's sent me in to buy something. A surprise for my granny."

"Isn't that lovely." She smiled as if she was really pleased to see her. "And there was I worrying you were lost. What is it you're after?"

"A pearl."

CHAPTER
FOUR

Dad still hadn't come back from the shells. Maggie pushed her forehead against the cold living-room window to get a better view of the street. He would be home soon, wouldn't he? There was something she wanted to ask him and he had to say yes, he just had to. Otherwise it was all going to go wrong. She glanced back at the clock on the mantelpiece. Only eight minutes had passed since the last time she looked. Why was he taking so long?

Dad was meant to have come home yesterday. Then he called Mum to say he wasn't coming home for the night as he was going to try a nearby river today. After that Mum started cleaning out the kitchen cupboards, and made such a racket Frank hid behind the sofa again. Then disaster struck this morning when he finally emerged, and now she was in deep trouble just when she needed to ask Dad something really important.

Eyes on the dusty lampshade above her, she lay like a starfish on the floor. Bored, she turned her head. A pile of library books, all finished. A jigsaw missing two pieces of lost sky. Her old dolls, their toenails freshly painted with Sangria Shimmer. She raised her feet and examined her own. Beautiful. The dead television in the corner, which was why Frank was shut in his hutch in disgrace and she couldn't play with him.

Dad would agree, wouldn't he? He was always on her side — last week he'd even gone round to tell Samantha Grey to stop calling her names, and she'd had to promise in front of her parents not to do again.

There must be something to do upstairs. She wandered into the hall, and paused at the bottom of the stairs. It would be against the rules to touch the worn patches of the carpet. On her right leg she hopped all the way up, managing to avoid them. Now she had to land on the bare bits. With a switch of legs she hopped along the landing, hitting the threads. She paused at the airing cupboard, but her tummy felt too funny with all the waiting for monk biscuits.

The door to Mum and Dad's room was open, and she leapt in, landing on both feet. Mum hadn't made the bed. She should have done it before going to work instead of sitting on the back step, reading a letter. Afterwards she'd just stayed there staring at the fence, but there wasn't even anything interesting on it, like a butterfly.

From the floor she picked up a white bra, and held it against herself. Would her boobs ever get that big? She couldn't imagine it. What would happen if they *did* ever grow, and she'd have to wear a bra? She wouldn't be able to do it up behind her back like Mum did. Maybe they'd have different bras by then. Or hands. Ones that you could do everything with, like tie your hair back when it was getting on your nerves.

She laid the bra on the bed, fastened it, then reached inside. Sitting up, she pulled it down over her yellow T-shirt, and looked in the dressing-table mirror. The cups were hanging down like empty pockets. That wasn't right. From the drawer she took some woolly socks and stuffed them inside. Two lovely moons.

Next to a box of tissues was the brown eyeshadow Mum had put on to go and see Big Nose Campbell. She rubbed some on her finger, raised her eyebrows like Mum did, and covered both lids. Now she needed some lipstick. It didn't matter if you went over the edges a bit. Once she'd finished, she leant towards the mirror. She looked just like the lady in the jeweller's yesterday.

The pearl. Sock boobs bouncing, she darted into her bedroom, and lifted the lid of the jewellery box she kept on her chest of drawers. The little ballerina used to pirouette when you opened it, but she'd broken it off after Fatty McEwan told her she'd always be useless at ballet even if she had two real hands. She lifted out the compartment full of tiny seed pearls she'd found, and peered inside. Still hidden at the bottom, between the colourful rings from Christmas crackers and Mum's old bracelets, was the grey drawstring pouch.

Pushing aside her heaped penguin pyjamas, she sat with it on her bed. Alice had to take her pyjamas back and forth between her parents' houses. What would happen if Mum and Dad divorced? She might forget them! Would she be allowed a pair in each house, how would Alice know which one to call at and what about

Frank? What if she was at Mum's, and Frank felt like being in his summerhouse but it was at Dad's place?

It wasn't going to happen, not with what she'd got planned. She took the pearl out of the little bag, letting it roll back into her cupped palm. Look at it. It was huge, almost as big as one of Dad's boring marbles. You could see the pink shimmering through the white. Her, Mum, Dad and Frank. Together. Always.

As Brodie headed for the house, he pulled out the useless sprigs of bog myrtle he'd stuffed down his collar as defence against the midges. It never worked. He didn't know why he kept trying it. From the fridge he fetched a beer, and held the cool can against the back of his neck to stop the wretched itching as he wandered into the living room. Maggie's library books were in a pile on the floor. A nearly finished jigsaw, some dolls. Wasn't she too old for dolls? He paused. There was still no sound of running feet to greet him. She must have gone to play with Alice. If she wasn't back in fifteen minutes, he'd give Nessa a ring and check that she was there.

The stairs seemed steeper than usual as he clambered up, taking a swig of beer. As he waited for the bath to fill, he sank down onto their unmade bed. His fingers reached for Elspeth's soft white nightie and, breathing in, he held it to his face. He'd just spent two days at the shells, and found nothing decent. That was how it was sometimes, feast or famine. It had been for years. But he needed to find the big one now, before Elspeth realised what a mistake she'd made and went off with someone else. A better man than him. More successful. What had happened to that feeling that nothing would ever come between them? He'd walked back down that aisle feeling they were invincible.

Suddenly realising, he stood up. The ledgers in his hut. They might tell him where he would find it. Of course he knew every pearl river in Scotland, and which colours they tended to throw. But the thing about the ledgers was that his great-great-grandpa had started them, listing the colour, size, shape and lustre of every good pearl he'd found, as well as its precise location. Each generation had continued them. He hadn't looked at the old ones for years. They might mention a river or burn he'd given up on decades ago, or never even tried because the yield had been so poor — and now, all these years later, any young ones buried below the surface would have become adults. Why hadn't he thought of the ledgers before?

Down the stairs he slithered in his socks, and ran across the lawn to his hut, the private place he'd built for sorting his pearls. The old handle rattled in its socket as he grabbed it and threw open the door. Maggie. Sitting on his chair, staring up at the map of Britain on the wall. She turned like a startled grouse. What had she done to her face? There was brown stuff all over her eyes, and red smeared on her lips. And what the hell was she wearing over her T-shirt? A white bra stuffed with hiking socks.

"What are you doing? You know you're not allowed in here on your own." He jerked his head. "Out."

"Can I come with you to the shells tomorrow?"

She'd slow him down. Get in the way. "Not tomorrow."

"*Please.*"

"They're predicting a storm." He stood to one side to let her out.

She didn't move. "I don't mind them any more."

"Why don't you invite Alice round tomorrow?"

"She's going to her gran's."

"You could read your library books."

"Finished them."

"What about the marbles I got down from the loft for you? I used to play with them for hours. You're never alone with a box of marbles."

She shook her head.

"Frank. You could take him for a walk round the park. We'll get him a lead in case the dogs take a fancy to him."

Her gaze fell to the table. "He's in detention."

"Already?" He put his hands on his hips. "What for?"

There was a pause.

"Chewing through the TV aerial cable."

That was all he needed. Something else to pay for. "That slack-eared turncoat."

"He didn't know!"

"I rescued him from the bargain aisle when no right-thinking member of the public wanted him. Offered him the run of the house."

"Maybe he thought it was liquorice."

"I went out and bought some pickled onion crisps for him especially. Had to drive all the way to Blairgowrie as no one had any."

Her brow wrinkled. "He won't do it again. *Promise.*"

"And look how he repays me — munches through the TV aerial cable with those vile fangs of his in the middle of a new series of *Columbo*. You couldn't make it up."

Silence.

"The cheek of it."

She was just staring at him with all that make-up on her face.

"Like he thinks he's doing *us* a favour by having him around." He held out his hands. "As if we should be honoured that he deigns to drag those ears of his across our floors."

A swallow.

"Are you sure you're feeding him enough?"

Slowly she nodded. "Just likes the TV aerial cable."

"A goldfish wouldn't have eaten through that cable."

"He says he's sorry."

Her shoulders were hunched as if she were bracing herself for something, and her bare toes were gripping the chair rung so tightly they'd turned white. She'd painted her nails. Badly. She was still just a kid.

"If you're not up by half five, I'll have to go without you."

All smiles, she stood up. Swiftly, he closed the door and they crossed the lawn without a word. It would take him twice as long now. As he stepped into the kitchen, he could see Elspeth standing stock-still in the hall staring ahead of her. An untouched raspberry ripple ice cream was dripping red tears onto her hand. She blinked at Maggie as if she couldn't understand what she was seeing. Turning to him now, like it was all too much to take in.

"There's water running down the stairs."

The landing carpet sank like moss as he groped his way down the landing in the feeble morning light. He should have studied the ledgers last night, but there'd been no time after all the fuss with the bath overflowing, then going to the Victoria to forget all about it. No one would remember the flooding fandango when he came home this evening. He could see the huge pearl now, sitting in the middle of the others in Mum's red leather necklace box, and the look on Elspeth's face when he gave them to her.

The kettle seemed far louder than usual as he crept around the kitchen making tea, the soles of his feet studded with crumbs. Clutching a mug, he stepped out into the tepid dawn. A perfect drop of silver illuminated the garden, a good omen if ever there was one. Mussels opened during a full moon so that pearls could develop their lustre. At least that was what Dad had once told him as he'd sat on his knee, willing his four-year-old legs to grow longer so that he could go with him to the shells.

An empty whisky bottle rolled across the hut floor as he sat down at the table. It was the one he'd finished the night before last after Mungo told him Cameron had moved back. There'd be no more drinking like that again. He was always telling himself he'd stop, usually the morning after the night before, but this time he'd actually do it.

From the table drawer he took out his matches and lit the lantern. A thin glow seeped up the wall to the newspaper cuttings, some aged to the colour of mustard. Most of them showed him either scanning a riverbed with his glass or holding a handful of pearls towards the camera. Journalists had always been fascinated by how he made his living, especially since he'd become the last full-timer. There was something about the wintery beauty of Scottish freshwater pearls that stirred the heart. Much more than diamonds. They didn't need to be cut and polished by man to make them beautiful, they were already perfect. And they were all there for the taking — *if* you knew where to find them.

Careful of the leather spine crippled from wear, Brodie pulled out the oldest volume from the shelf. Thankfully he'd managed to rescue them, along with Dad's pearling stick and tatty tweed cap, when Mum starting throwing out all of his stuff after that hideous wake, attended only by the next-door neighbours. All those trays of curling sandwiches and sausage rolls left untouched. He glanced at the stick, propped up in the corner, and saw the time when Dad had taken him to the woods to find that piece of hazel, and then shown him how to whittle the end so that it resembled a clothes peg.

On the inside cover, written in a fancy black script, was the inscription: *James McBride, Pearl Fisher to His Royal Highness the Prince of Wales.* His great-great-grandpa had learnt everything he knew from Scottish travellers, experts in the art, who spent their summers at the shells. Mum had told him it was James who'd first given his wife a pearl necklace as a love token, starting the family tradition. Travellers never wore their pearls, believing them to be unlucky. How could pearls bring bad luck? He had a tin full of stunning ones for Elspeth, collected over nineteen years, and nothing terrible had happened to him.

His eyes lifted to a cutting on the wall from the *Scotsman* showing the Queen being presented with a freshwater pearl brooch while she was opening a hospital wing in Edinburgh. James wasn't the only McBride with royal connections. The pearls in that brooch were definitely his. All of them. He remembered finding each one.

The musty scent of history engulfed him as he snatched through the pages searching for each mention of a white pearl with pink overtones. Once he'd finished James's ledgers, he tugged out Great-Grandpa's, followed by Grandpa's and then Dad's. As he scanned the columns, it came to him. Each one of them had found a really good white pearl with a pink hue in the Isla. Grandpa had even found one there that weighed twenty-one grains. The huge pearl was in the Isla, just down the road. The irony of it. He'd proposed to Elspeth along its banks, picking the spot — underneath a rowan — specially. Rowans were known as travellers' trees as they were said to save those on a journey from getting lost. He could still see Elspeth gazing up at him, eyes as blue as harebells saying yes long before she actually spoke.

The sky. He scrambled to his feet, the chair toppling over behind him as he placed both palms on the window. The whole of the sky was streaked with rose. Dad had said that it was during stunning sunrises like this that pearls got their pink tinge. It was the same way that pearls ended up white if mussels opened their shells when it snowed. His nose touched the dusty pane. Finally the universe was listening to him.

The grass was still damp as he hurried back to the house. They'd need to take some sandwiches with them. Halfway to the bread bin he stopped. Elspeth. Sitting at the kitchen table, a mug clasped in her hands. She was wearing that white cotton nightie. Why on earth was she up at this hour? She must have been worrying about the carpet.

"I'll get someone round to look at the hall ceiling. It probably just needs to dry out."

"The drinking, Brodie. You promised."

That. He yanked open the fridge. "Did you get any more of the Orkney Cheddar, or did I dream it?"

"Another phone bill came yesterday. A red one. They'll cut us off if we don't pay. What if Maggie were ill or had an accident? We wouldn't be able to call an ambulance."

He nodded towards Dewi and Shona's. "We'd go next door. Use their phone."

"I didn't get a first-class honours degree in history to do that."

It was all about to change for the better. She'd see by this evening. "Have you heard today's weather forecast?"

"You're going to have to find some other work, Brodie. There aren't enough pearls left."

The sky was the same pink as the tint of her white pearls. This was the day, he'd show her what he could do, and she'd realise she'd married the right one. He searched again behind the eggs. "Have you been sculpting the Orkney?"

"It's been getting worse. You know it has. Why do you think the other full-timers gave up?"

He moved aside a lettuce, just in case. "They weren't good enough."

"They couldn't make a decent living out of it, that's why. They were warning about the mussels dying out in the nineteenth century. We found the newspaper cuttings in the library, remember?"

"That was when there were still fisheries on the Tay. Whole families were at it. It's just me now. I've got them all to myself." Surely she could see that?

"You and all those amateurs who slaughter thousands of mussels at the weekends as they don't know what to look for. I've listened to you often enough going on about the piles of shells they leave behind on the banks."

He shut the fridge door. Her engagement ring didn't seem to fit any more. The tiny diamond had slipped round her finger.

"She'll just have to have a banana sandwich."

"I'm worried," she said, still gripping the mug. "You know how badly the cafe's doing."

He hated her working there. It was the only thing he'd been able to find for her.

"How many did you find yesterday?" She wasn't going to drop it.

"There's only the three of us."

"And what's that supposed to mean?"

"We should have had another one." It had taken him years to agree to try for a baby, and now that they had Maggie, he knew he'd never be able to live if they ever lost her. "Maggie . . . It was a mistake."

"What was a mistake? Having Maggie?"

"How could you possibly think I meant that? I meant we made the wrong decision not having another." Elspeth had been worried about passing on some kind of defective gene, believing something was inherently wrong with her, which of course the doctors had said was rubbish. Nothing he'd said had convinced her otherwise either. A movement caught his eye. The bairn was standing in the doorway. She hadn't heard them, had she?

Why did they have to argue? Maggie looked at Dad, his hair like a wizard's. "When are we going to the shells?"

"Are you taking Maggie pearling?" said Mum.

He opened the bread bin.

"You're not taking her to the Spey, are you, Brodie? Not with that current. She still can't swim very well."

She frowned. "I can."

"We're going to the Isla. I've never seen it so low."

She fingered the stiff paint drips on the door frame. Everything would go back to normal with what she'd got planned. Normal like when they used to eat together every night. Not Dad making that funny food when Mum was out cleaning.

Mum stood up. "What would you like for breakfast, Maggie? Toast?"

Her tummy was fluttery, like there was a bird inside. "I'm not hungry."

"You'll have to eat something before you go. What about some porridge?"

She shook her head.

"You can't go pearling all day on an empty stomach."

"French beans from the garden."

Dad opened the back door. "I'll get some."

She looked at Mum. "When's Frank out of detention?"

"This evening."

Sitting down, she pressed a finger into a spill of sugar on the plastic tablecloth. This evening, when everything would be all right again. She raised her finger to her tongue and tasted salt.

Brodie scrabbled the key into the ignition. He was trying to make as much money as he could. For her. For Maggie. For both of them. Couldn't she see the hours he was putting in? He usually left home as soon as it was light, and didn't come back until it was too dark to see the riverbed. Often soaked. Then he had to clean and sort the pearls in his hut, and fill in the ledger. And if she was out on one of her cleaning jobs, he did the cooking. And he was very good at it, Maggie always said so.

He'd better double-check he had everything. There on the back seat were his glass, Maggie's smaller one, two hessian bags, lunch, water and his waders. His pearling stick was on the roof rack. Where were his tongs? He'd made them from a pair of electrician's wire-strippers when the law was brought in making it illegal to injure or kill a pearl mussel. A turn of the handle parted the two valves up to a centimetre, which was wide enough to see inside before returning the shell to the water. Some of the part-time professionals had also made a pair, equally as determined as he was not to harm the mussels. That law had been introduced in 1991, and now, seven years later, those idiot amateurs were still not using tongs. He'd seen so many mussels split wide open and left to die on the banks he could weep.

He moved aside the bags. There were his tongs. With any luck, Maggie wouldn't ask for the extra pair, which he'd left behind on purpose. She'd figured out a way of using them by holding the shell between her feet. It had made his day the first time he saw her do that. If only Dad had been there to see her. The problem was she always took ages, and there'd be no time for her to open anything today.

"Ready?" He started the car. They were going to remember this day forever.

She nodded.

As they pulled away, Maggie pushed a cassette into the player. It would be "Take It Easy" again. He knew it. Sure enough, the familiar strumming filled the car. She was as mad about the Eagles as he was. The breeze was already warm against his cheek, and he ducked his head to survey the sky. They'd still been going on about storms on the radio. No sign of anything yet.

Right on cue Maggie started to sing as he turned up the volume. It got him every time she did that. He didn't know why, it just did. She probably didn't even know why someone would have seven women on their mind. The breeze was whipping her hair as she nodded in time to the beat, her fingers tapping against her denim shorts. It wasn't half as loud as she usually sang, but that didn't matter. She'd got up early. He'd join in, like he always did. The two of them together, singing their hearts out. Here it came, the bit about standing in a corner in Winslow, Arizona. Head back, he started belting it out.

As soon as Brodie realised he was singing on his own he stopped. Maggie was staring straight ahead, her mouth set in that tight way of hers. Something was up.

"Don't worry, Frank'll be dragging those ears of his around the house again by the time we get home."

No reply.

Was it the banana sandwiches? He'd explained it was all there was.

Once out of the car, he led her by the hand onto the bridge to show her just how glorious it all was. "There's something special about being the first to see a river in the morning," he said, leaning against the stone wall. "It's like God's painted the scene specially for you."

Fields of raspberry bushes, studded with garnets, were stretching out on either side of them. In the

76

distance rose heather-covered hills, flushed with mauve. Every year the same miracle. Below, the timid glow of early sunlight shone like gold dust on the water. The place was just as magical in the winter when wisps of mist hung over the Isla like the ghosts of herons.

"Dad said all rivers smell different. Reckoned of all the ones in Scotland this one smelt the best." He breathed in. "Meadowsweet and pewter."

No wonder the monks had chosen this area to build their abbey. When he and Elspeth had carried out all that research for her book, back when they still did things together, they'd found a sixteenth-century woodcut of a monk holding up his cassock as he stood in the Isla. In his other hand was an open mussel cradling an enormous pearl.

"Let's get going," he said, striding back to the car. "Make sure you put on some suncream. It's in the glovebox."

Once he'd tugged on his waders, they staggered down the grassy bank. It was just here that he'd first told Elspeth he loved her. Well, not exactly told. He'd been too shy for that, being only fifteen. He spelt it out with stones on the riverbed. As they crossed the bridge the following day he lowered his head in case she just laughed at him. She came to a sudden stop, after which was a terrifying silence. Then her soft, warm hand reached for his and held it all the way to her house. No one had stood by his side like she had. Since she'd come back to him after those awful five months with Cameron Wallace she'd saved his life every single day.

His eyes didn't leave Maggie as she stepped into the river, holding out her arm and stump as she tried to keep her balance. She never wore her prosthesis when she was at the shells as she had a thing about getting it wet. The hessian bag slung across her shoulder was so long it was almost touching her pink boots. She could still reach the mussels there. Any deeper and she'd need a pearling stick, and for that you had to have one hand to hold it and another to pull the mussel off the end. She still hadn't got round that one.

"Keep to the edge," he called.

"I know."

The pressure of the water was comforting against his legs as he strode towards the middle. Holding the glass steady by its handle, he began to search the stony bottom. Nothing. As he moved forward, he raised his head. Maggie was sensible enough not to get out of her depth, but kids were kids and you had to watch them. Properly. He'd known two pearlers drown in pools, spots in rivers where the water suddenly deepened. One moment they were caught up in the thrill of the chase, the next their feet would have been thrashing below them as if they were being hanged while water poured over the top of their waders, dragging them down. There was no coming back from that, no matter how well you could swim.

For a few minutes he continued upstream, then checked on her again. She was just standing there, looking all forlorn.

"Dad, there aren't any!"

78

He thrashed through the water towards her, making furious waves in the glossy surface.

"We're too close to the bridge. It's where the weekenders park. They must have taken the lot. Let's walk for a bit."

In sun-soaked silence they continued along the bank, his eyes on his feet whipping through the grass. There was something about bridges. One of those nineteenth-century articles he'd found in the library had claimed that the building of bridges was reducing the number of pearls in Scottish rivers. That was the time when some people thought pearls were produced by cattle injuring mussels as they crossed rivers.

She slipped her hand into his. He loved it when she did that.

"We'll try up there," he said, jerking his head. "At the third bend."

Eventually they eased themselves back into the water.

"Keep to the edge, Maggie."

"Dad! I know!"

Through the water he pushed his glass, then lowered his head. There should be a colony here somewhere. His heart tightened. There. Behind that rock. Loads of them, huddled together like nuns. As he straightened, Maggie smiled and waved a shell at him. It was a good one, he could tell from here. It was old and ugly, just the kind he was always telling her to look for.

There were more by his feet, partly buried in the gravel. Drawing back his arm, he aimed his stick.

Eventually, his bag was full, and he called over to her. "Let's open these and have a drink."

Sitting on the bank, he turned the sodden bag upside down. The mussels, some as big as hands, rattled as they fell. Please God, let the pearl be in here somewhere. From his pocket he drew out his tongs.

"Where's the other pair?"

Maggie. He'd almost forgotten she was here. "I left them at home."

"Oh, Dad!"

He selected a shell with a pair of parallel lines running to the edge. His mouth was dry. It was going to be a good one, he'd put money on it.

"Can I borrow yours when you've finished?"

"Not today." As he pressed the tongs into the join, his stupid hands started to shake.

"But I want to open mine."

This was going to be it. The torment was going to be over.

"Dad?"

The two halves began to open as he turned the handle.

"Please, Dad. I really want to open some."

He raised the mussel to his eyes. He couldn't believe it. Couldn't bloody believe it.

CHAPTER
FIVE

Not the slightest bump in the flesh. Brodie began to feel sick as he tossed the shell onto the grass.

"Can I?"

"Can you what?"

"Open mine."

She was still going on about that. He chose another mussel with a crooked back. It was this one, for sure. "Next time."

"But you always let me."

Jamming his tongs against the seal, he worked the handle, then let out his breath. Not a sodding thing.

"Dad!"

The edge in her voice made him turn. She was looking at him as if he'd just ruined her life. "We'll go pearling next week and you can open them then. Bring some of those doughnuts with us and see how many we can eat in three minutes without licking our lips. Bet I win."

In bitter handfuls, he returned his mussels to the Isla. Settled next to Maggie again, he reached over to her pile.

"Got some good ones here. Best pearl fisher I know."

She looked away.

The nearest shell fitted snugly in his hand, and he gazed upstream as he started to turn the tiny handle. They'd almost reached that stretch where Grandpa found a pearl weighing twenty-one grains. Elspeth's was here all right. Once he'd finished opening Maggie's, they'd move on and find it.

As he peered inside the shell his stomach flipped. There was a bulge in the mantle. He'd never thought the pearl might be in one of Maggie's. From his jeans pocket he took out his matchstick, and carefully moved aside the flesh. Something dropped into his palm, startling him. It was green and wee with it. So much for *that*.

"Do you want to keep it?" he said, offering it to her.

She inspected her pink boots.

"You like the green ones."

Still ignoring him.

"Thought they were your favourites."

She stood up. "You can sell it to Mr McSweetie."

She wasn't usually like this. Silently he finished opening her mussels, then dropped them back into the water, watching them plunge like knives towards the riverbed. She probably wanted to be with Alice. Or Frank. Couldn't it last a bit longer — the bit before she grew up and left him?

As they returned to the river, he scanned the bank. They'd gone past Elspeth's rowan. On the way back he'd point it out to Maggie, and tell her about the time he got down on one knee and they'd promised to stay with each other forever. It would make up for her hearing them argue this morning.

His bag finally full again, he thrashed his way to the bank, eyeing the steel sky. He tossed his tongs on the grass next to his sopping bag. "I'll be back in a minute. Stay out of the water."

He paused as she kicked her way out. Once she was safely on the grass, he hid behind an oak. She would do as she was told, wouldn't she? Usually did around water, but there was always the first time. It only took a couple of minutes for a bairn to drown. The horror of it.

Quickly he pushed down his waders, and fumbled with his flies. What would happen if he came home without the pearl? Couldn't bear to think about it. When he'd finished, he stood for a moment looking to the hills for courage.

As he came out from the trees Maggie was lying on her back, arms outstretched.

"Can I have a sandwich?" she asked, sitting up.

She was suddenly all smiles. What had brought this on? He reached into the pocket of his waders, and passed her one. "It's banana."

"I know." She pulled off her boots.

There were her toes again with nail polish all over the sides.

"Just going for a paddle. It's boiling."

Knee-deep in the water as she ate her lunch, she smiled at him through her messed-up hair. She'd certainly changed her tune. Kids. You never knew where you were with them. One moment they made you feel like you were the best dad in the world, the next you didn't even feel worthy of picking up their school shoes.

"Don't go any further in. It gets deep there pretty quickly."

She nodded, all freckles and dimples.

The shells skidded out of his bag as he emptied it. Sensing something, he raised his head. The low, sooty clouds had dulled the leaves of the alders to unpolished emeralds. It couldn't rain now, for God's sake. He hadn't found it yet. The pearl could be in any one of these shells — nineteen years of hunting would finally be over. He glanced at Maggie. He didn't like her being in the water on her own, even if she was just in front of him.

Someone was laughing. He turned. Two men in shorts were coming along the bank towards them carrying hessian bags. The shorter one looked familiar. It was Mungo walking in that way of his, like he had someone else's legs. There was something about the man next to him. His stomach clenched. It was him. Cameron. The competition.

Both their bags were full, he could tell from here. They must have already fished this section of the river, and be on their way home. So he and Maggie weren't the first to see the Isla this morning after all. As he dragged the back of his hand across his forehead, a breeze, infused with foreign scents, unsettled his hair.

"Dad, aren't you going to open your shells?"

Maggie was coming towards him, drops of water as bright as quartz clinging to her white legs. A frown formed as she looked towards the two men. She grabbed the tongs and handed them to him.

"Come on," she urged, kneeling down next to him.

Eyeing the mussels piled on the grass like plump black purses, he reached out a hand.

"Brodie!" called Mungo, approaching.

He lifted his head. "Thought I'd see you in the pub last night."

"Family dinner. Cameron's back."

"So I see," he said, his eyes not leaving Mungo.

"Teaching your dad pearling, Maggie?" There was a clatter as Mungo lowered his bag to the ground and sat down. "About time he found something."

Half a smile, as if she wasn't sure whether he was teasing.

"Thought you'd given up," said Brodie.

"It was Cameron's idea. He's got all nostalgic since coming back."

The wet hessian was straining over the lumpy contents of Mungo's bag. "Must have started early."

"I stayed over at Mum's and got woken at three in the morning by someone making a cup of tea. Couldn't get back to sleep."

"Jet lag," said Cameron, smiling as he joined them on the ground.

There was a faint whiff of something expensive. Cologne or whatever men like Cameron used to scent their patch. He looked at him then with his suntan and bank manager's hairdo. Cameron Wallace. His name still had that annoying ring to it. He'd been a year above him and Mungo at school, and had always tried to look cool in his uniform. That low-slung tie with its convoluted knot, like he was attending a school for sailors. He was one of those balloons who'd blown up some frogs in biology. Theirs was the next class to use the lab and he and Mungo had had to sit there with the glistening guts stuck to the ceiling above them. Some of the other jokers were in prison now. Or worse — the jammie.

"What brought you back?"

Cameron crossed his brown ankles.

What were they? Deck shoes. He didn't have a boat as well, did he?

"You get island fever after a while."

Brodie mopped his forehead on his shirtsleeve. It was the one with the stains from painting the hut a few years ago. What a wreck he must look.

"Cameron's just bought one of those new houses with a view of the Isla," said Mungo. "All right for some."

They'd stood empty for more than a year. No one round here could afford them, and the developer had become a laughing stock.

"We should have gone to Bahrain too, Brodie, and earned ourselves a nice, fat tax-free salary. Had our own pool and a maid. Cameron hasn't swum in someone else's wee for years. Apart from mine when I visited him last year."

Brodie leant back on his hands. "Not much engineering in Nether Isla." With any luck, he'd push off somewhere else to find a job.

"I wouldn't worry about me," said Cameron. "What about you? Last man standing, I hear."

"Doing great. Aren't we, Maggie?"

A reluctant nod.

She could have looked a bit more convinced.

"Where's Bahrain, Dad?"

"Next to . . ." He frowned. How the hell did he know? He'd left school as soon as he could in order to go to the shells full-time. He'd read. God knows he'd read. Books had filled the empty space between him and Aunt Agnes, each last page feeling like another grief as he raised his head and found himself back in the real world. But you could never catch up with people who had a degree. People like Elspeth and Cameron.

"In the Middle East somewhere." He flapped his hand, as if the precise location was irrelevant.

"You were always rubbish at geography," said Mungo. "Thought you were meant to know things seeing as though you're pub quiz team captain."

"It's an archipelago near Saudi Arabia," said Cameron.

"That's right," said Brodie quickly. "In the Persian Gulf."

"Which these days, of course, is known as the Arabian Gulf," said Cameron. "You'd love it, Maggie. Loads of pool parties."

"She wouldn't," said Brodie. "Be too hot."

Cameron leant forward and raised his eyebrows.

They were plucked. Definitely.

"Think of all those pearls, Maggie. Six hundred square miles of oyster beds. Anyone can go and dive for them. The Bahrainis stopped harvesting them commercially when oil was discovered. Back in the 1930s."

Maggie was looking at that numpty like he'd just offered her the keys to Magic Kingdom.

"They're oyster pearls," said Brodie dismissively.

"And meant to be the best in the world. Something to do with the sea's freshwater springs. You should get over there. Buy a boat and set yourself up in business. I could put in some capital if you need it. You'd have to learn how to scuba-dive."

"Brilliant idea! I'll drive the boat," said Mungo. "Get me out of that stinking chippy. There's only so many sausages a man can batter in a lifetime."

Brodie nodded at the Isla. "Nothing beats the beauty of Scottish river pearls."

"Like I said, everyone says Bahraini pearls are the best in the world. It's the lustre."

"I live in Scotland." He raised his chin. "Die here too."

"Have a think about it. At least you wouldn't have to stand in freezing cold rivers all year finding next to nothing. And it would get Elspeth out of that dump of a cafe. What the hell's she doing waitressing anyway?"

He felt a stab. "She'd hate it over there."

"You're wrong, Brodie. She'd love it. Fascinating history. Entire fields of Bronze Age burial mounds."

The idiot was trying to make out that he knew Elspeth better than he did. He turned to Mungo. "Found anything yet?"

"We haven't opened any. It's about to chuck it down, big time. I thought we'd better find some shelter."

The sky was now looking like it had been pummelled black and blue. How the hell was he going to find the pearl with it pouring?

"Cameron wanted to wait for it to start," said Mungo. "He hasn't seen rain for ages. I give him until the end of the month before he runs back to the desert."

There was an urgent tap on his leg.

"Come on, Dad. You've got to open these."

Cameron took a Swiss Army knife out of his pocket, then emptied his bag.

"What the hell is that knife for?" said Brodie.

He chose one of the blades. "To open the shells."

"You can't use a knife. It's illegal to injure or kill a pearl mussel. Mungo, give him a pair of tongs."

Cameron was looking at him as if he were some halfwit.

"I'm happy using a knife."

"Not in my company you won't be."

"Keep your hair on, Brodie," said Mungo, handing Cameron a pair.

"It's not as if anyone would know." Cameron glanced around. "There's no one for miles."

"I'd know."

A silver vein flashed across the sky.

"Bloody hell," said Mungo. "Did you see that?"

Something landed on Brodie's cheek. Dark drops were now blooming on the shells like weeping sores. There was a bellow of thunder, then the pummelling started. He got to his feet, squinting against the rain.

"Let's go. Maggie, help me put the shells back into the river."

"No! We've got to open them." She was still in her bare feet and her scuffed hair was darkening as it began to stick to her head.

"There's no time." He raised his voice over the roar of the downpour. "You're getting soaked."

"No!" She was grabbing at the mussels and stuffing them into his bag. "We'll take them with us. Open them under a tree like we always do when it rains."

"Not with the lightning. It's too dangerous." The back of her white T-shirt was already pitted grey.

"Dad, we've got to!" She was almost screaming.

The sky cracked open again with a flicker of electric white. A much louder boom sounded several seconds later as if someone had blown up the world. She jumped, then started scrabbling at the shells again.

He'd just have to help. It was the fastest way of getting her out of here. "We'll open them under the bridge," he shouted. "Come on, quick. Cameron, pick up your shells. It's illegal to leave them to die on the bank."

Rivulets were running down Cameron's forehead as he looked at him like he'd gone mad. "For fuck's sake," he said, stooping to reach for them.

The rain was coming down so hard Brodie could barely see what he was doing. Once all the shells were gathered, he slung his and Maggie's bags across his shoulder, and helped her into her boots. Her hand felt as fragile as a bird's wing as he grabbed it and started to run. After a moment he glanced back. Her eyes were closed against the lightning to stop her going blind, and her little arm was clamped against her ear so she wouldn't go deaf. She always did that during storms. The fears of a girl who didn't want anything else to go wrong. He pushed on faster along the bank, his breath rubbing against his lungs like crushed glass. Blinking madly against the rain, he hurried on, gripping her tiny bones even tighter.

If only Stugly would just tell her. It was the waiting she couldn't stand. He'd been in and out of the cafe all morning, something clearly on his mind, and not once mentioned his threat from yesterday about sacking her. She gazed out of the window as she waited for Rev Maxwell to make up his mind. The pendulous clouds were the colour of dirty washing-up water. Something was about to happen out there.

"What can I get you?"

"Just some tea," he said, moving aside his *Telegraph* crossword and lacing his fingers. There was dried glue on the top of his thumb. He must still be making those Airfix model airplanes.

"Anything to eat with that?" Stugly had told her to always ask, especially the ones who suffered with temptation. She offered him a laminated menu. All of them needed wiping again. The bore of it.

"Not for me, thank you." He patted his stomach.

As if it needed pointing out. She lingered, studying the dark strands of hair trained across the moon of his head. There was the tip to consider. "Busy?" It was all she could think of.

A shake of the jowls. "People just want to be outside during a heatwave."

"All those Judases worshipping the sun." She nodded towards the window as she headed for the kitchen. "Seems like your luck's in. It's going to bucket down."

When she returned with his order, Fiona was sitting next to him. You had to keep an eye on her. She might look all innocent with her Joan of Arc haircut, but she had a habit of slipping an entire bowl of sugar sachets up her sleeve and walking out with them for that B&B of hers. Not that anyone ever stayed in it.

"Happy birthday," said Fiona. "Is Brodie taking you somewhere nice?"

"It was four months ago. Stayed in."

She frowned. "I bumped into Maggie earlier in the week. Said she was buying you a birthday present."

"Must have misheard." She set down Rev Maxwell's tea, and reached for her pad in her apron pocket. "What would you like, Fiona?"

"Did you hear Cameron Wallace is back?"

That. She headed towards the kitchen. "I'll get you some coffee."

"Must be nice to have him back."

Hand on one of the swing doors, she stiffened. It had been over between them for years. Even if she did wonder whether Brodie still loved her, it was definitely over, no matter how often Cameron looked at her like that. "Why would that be?"

"Nice for Mrs Wallace. I'm lucky if I see my son once a month and he only lives fifteen minutes away."

"Aye. Nice for Mrs Wallace."

As she came back in, Rev Maxwell was licking his fingers. Not him as well. She was sick of this. The pensioners smuggling in their own food she could understand. But him? She strode over and picked up his empty cup. A constellation of sugar shone from his cheek and there was a drop of jam on the table. It must have been one of those doughnuts from the Co-op still on special offer. "Anything else I can get you?"

"Enough is sufficient for the wise," he said, leaving some coins on the table.

"Dodge," she said as he headed towards the door.

He stopped.

She pointed to his newspaper. "Ruse. Second down. Five letters."

As he fled, he almost bumped into Stugly, the swell of his chest visible through his soaked white shirt. Stugly's nipples. That was something you didn't want to see.

He snatched a napkin from the nearest table and dabbed his forehead. "Where's Alpina?"

"In the kitchen."

"Better get her."

As they joined Stugly at the table, he removed his tie and slung it on the table where it lay like a clubbed snake.

"They . . ." His voice slipped.

Silence.

"I thought . . ." He swallowed, then raised his eyes. "I'm sorry about the sugar, Elspeth. I hope you'll forgive me."

She did, a grown man about to cry.

With bitten fingernails, he fiddled with the button on his cuff, then cleared his throat. "I've just been to the bank."

Alpina leant forward with a smile. "Are we finally going to get that second oven?"

He stared ahead of him as if suddenly interested in the pine panelling. "We're closing down. Tomorrow."

A slash of rain hit the window. Everything seemed muted, as if the world had turned out the lights.

Finally the smudged edges of the bridge came into view. Brodie dipped his head again to keep the rain out of his eyes as he continued to run. It wasn't until they were safely under the brick archway that he released Maggie's wet fingers. Hands on his thighs as he caught his breath, he watched the embers of the storm. "At least the thunder and lightning's stopping."

He turned when she didn't reply. She was standing with her hand clutched under her chin, hair clinging to her head like treacle.

"You're freezing. I'm taking you home. We'll put the shells back in the water. Somewhere we'll remember. Then we'll come back tomorrow and open them."

"No!" She bent down, tipped up his bag and started groping through the pile. "Someone will find them. Come on, Dad. Open them. Then we'll go home."

She was in one of her moods, he could tell. They always made him feel utterly useless.

"You're not cold, are you?" said Cameron, sitting next to her. "Not after all that brilliant running.

Whenever it rains in Bahrain, all the expats stand at their windows to watch it."

"Why?" she said, still searching through the pile.

"It only rains a few times a year. I don't know how you stand it, Brodie, getting soaked all the time."

"His brain rusted over years ago," said Mungo.

"Some of us are more resilient than others." Brodie sat on the other side of Maggie. They'd have to be quick, she was wet through.

"Open this one, Dad." She passed him his tongs, smiling like it was Christmas. He could see why. It was so ugly and crooked he could kiss it.

"Who made these, anyway?" said Cameron, inspecting his pair.

"I did," said Brodie. "For Mungo."

Cameron grabbed a mussel from his bag, and pressed the points into it. "Not as easy as it looks."

"You have to force them in. Like this." He pushed against his own shell. It was going to be in this one, and Cameron would be here to see it.

"Then turn the handle, I presume?"

"It separates the shells so you can look inside without harming the mussel."

"In Bahrain you take the oysters home in a bucket. Open them with a knife on your patio with a few beers while your maid's making you a nice little curry."

"You could always go back."

She tugged at him. "Come on, Dad, open it."

"What happens if there's something inside?" said Cameron.

Brodie reached into his pocket. "Just poke it out with a matchstick. Watch."

"Can I borrow it a sec?"

"He'll need it back," said Maggie. "Right away."

Cameron worked the matchstick inside his shell, then shook it over his cupped hand. A huge pearl silently dropped into his palm.

"Bloody Nora!" shouted Mungo.

Something happened at the back of his throat. It was exactly the same colour as Elspeth's pearls. Nothing that size had ever come out of a Scottish river, he was certain. It was about ten millimetres by the looks of it. Ten point five even. And it probably weighed around thirty grains. Not only was it perfectly round, but the lustre of the thing. It was incredible, even from here, and in this terrible light.

"Look at that, Brodie!" said Mungo. "It's enormous!"

He watched the rain piercing the Isla, feeling each stab wound. A whimper sounded, and he looked round. Maggie's chin was trembling like a caught white mouse. Then, all the way from the hills, came the warring rumble of unspent thunder.

CHAPTER
SIX

Even her knickers were soaked, she could tell. There were goose humps all over her legs as if someone had pricked her with a pin. The rain was hitting the windscreen so hard the wipers were making a horrible screeching sound. Why couldn't Mungo hurry up in their stupid car in front? She had to get home. Tell Frank what had happened. It was terrible. She pinched the side of her thigh, hard until it really hurt. Hopefully it would stop her from crying.

"Mungo couldn't go any slower in reverse," said Dad.

He was pitched forward against the steering wheel like he was trying to touch the glass with his nose. He hadn't even put on the Eagles. Each time he got too close to them he'd jab at the brake as if stamping on a spider that wouldn't die.

"We could've driven to Edinburgh and back in that time," he said, as they finally reached home.

Rain, with its nasty taste of suncream, crept into her mouth as she stood on the pavement watching Mungo and Cameron disappear into their mum's house.

"Maggie! Get inside." It was Dad, sounding like he was about to tell her off. "You're soaked to the skin."

She took a step towards Mrs Wallace's house. She'd tell Cameron he'd picked up one of Dad's shells by mistake and ask for the pearl back. Mungo would be on her side, godfathers were meant to help you, otherwise what was the point of them? There was no way she'd tell him she'd put that pearl in the shell. Nor that it was cultured.

She started running, but two hands grabbed her as she reached for the bell.

"You can see Mrs Wallace another day," said Dad. "Let's get you dry."

His wizard's hair was all flat and soggy like his magic was gone. With the back of her hand she wiped the rain from her lips. "Why did Cameron have to find it?"

"Come on. Before your mother gets home and sees the state of you."

"But why wasn't it you?"

"My luck ran out."

He grabbed her hand and started tugging her back home. His fingers felt wet, as if all of him was crying.

"Where's Frank?"

Mum didn't turn from her bedroom window where the rain sounded like it was trying to come in. "What were you wanting at Mrs Wallace's?"

"Did you let him out of detention? I can't find him. He's not even behind the sofa."

"You need to take off those wet clothes," she said, still looking out. "You'll catch your death."

Her voice sounded funny, like she had a cold.

"I'll run her a bath."

Dad was standing in the doorway with all his clothes stuck to him. He must have rubbed his hair with a towel as he looked like Tom when Jerry put his tail in a socket.

"You're back early," he said.

"Stugly said I could."

He smiled. "Things must be looking up over there."

Finally Mum turned round. "He's closing down. Couldn't make enough."

But that meant they wouldn't have any money. Why wasn't Dad saying anything?

"Any joy at the shells?" said Mum.

Only his Adam's apple moved.

"Look at it," said Mum, turning back to the window. "Still chucking it down. It was just like that when we got married. No one could take any pictures outside the church. Do you remember?"

He said nothing.

"Funny how some people think rain brings good luck on your wedding day."

"Blimey. The state of you. Didn't you hear the forecast?" said Alan, looking up from a copy of the *Scotsman* lying on the bar. Sawdust was caught in his tatty red beard like flies in amber.

"Pint, please."

"Find some nice pearls while you were out there?" Slowly he folded up the paper.

He just wanted to have a few drinks on his own and forget about what had happened earlier.

"Can I have my pint?"

Alan reached for a glass and held it underneath the tap. Behind him, through an open door, was a row of unvarnished coffins. Somehow he'd managed to corner the market for escapism, both the temporary and the ultimate. "Bring on another storm," he said, folding his arms. "Extremes of temperature, always good for business."

"My beer." It was just sitting there underneath the tap.

Alan leant towards him. "Summer sale starts today. Handcrafted, remember. None of that factory rubbish. Handles extra."

"Extra? For the handles? How are you meant to lift a coffin without handles?"

"Exactly. And you'll need six of them. Solid brass. Very expensive." A pause. "I'd recommend oak for you. Suit your complexion."

He slid some coins through a puddle of beer. "Can I have my drink?"

"I've got a beauty out the back," said Alan, jerking his thumb over his shoulder. "On offer. Someone made one of those annoying miraculous recoveries. You might have to bunch your legs up a bit. Not that you'd know about it at the time, of course. Want to see if it fits?"

He pointed to his glass.

"You could use it for storage in the meantime. It would make a lovely blanket box. Come on. Don't be shy. Everyone needs one eventually. Think how much it will cost by then. I'll give you the regulars' discount on top of the sale price."

"I'd get that anyway."

"'Fraid not." Alan tapped at a sign on the wall behind him. "Says there. In the small print at the bottom. 'Regulars' discount not be used in conjunction with any other offer.'"

Couldn't he just drink his pint in peace, for God's sake? Not talk to anyone. "There are other pubs in this town, you know."

"Purple lining. Not many people can carry that off. I can see you in it now. Very regal."

He reached over the bar and grabbed the beer. "Over my dead body."

Sitting with his back to the world at a table in the corner, he raised the glass to his lips. Should have left earlier this morning, then they'd have been the first to reach the section of the Isla where Cameron had found the pearl. He'd have spotted that shell, no doubt about it. If only he'd looked at the ledgers last night when he'd planned to, instead of going to the pub. But there was all that palaver with the carpet — if he hadn't left that sodding bath running, none of this would have happened. He'd be home watching Elspeth open Mum's old necklace box, seeing her face as she gazed at the pearls, knowing she'd made the right decision nineteen years ago.

As he stood to get another pint, the door opened.

"Drinks all round," announced Mungo. "Cameron's buying."

The dodo sauntered in behind him, looking like a bank manager who'd refuse to extend your overdraft.

"Drinks all round?" Alan shrugged. "What's the point of that? There's only Brodie and Fiona here. And she's on orange juice."

Fiona lowered her knitting. "Double vodka and Coke since you're asking. And a packet of nuts. Dry roasted."

"What's the occasion?" said Alan.

"Show him what you found in the Isla, Cameron."

Eyes lowered, Brodie approached the bar with his empty glass.

"Good God, look at the size of that," said Alan. "Have you seen it, Brodie?"

"Same again," he said, nudging his glass towards him.

"We can't celebrate a find like that on our own. We need some company." Alan picked up the phone. "Dewi, it's me. Get down here, pronto. Cameron's buying. Tell everyone who works at the jammie . . . Yes, all of them. And ask Shona to tip off her customers from the salon. There's always room on the pavement — the rain's almost stopped."

"My pint, Alan."

"Pint?" he said, incredulous. "This isn't the time for beer, Brodie. We need champagne. It's not every day someone finds a pearl like that. You've never found one of that size and quality, have you?"

Silence.

"Thought not. And how long have you been pearl-fishing?"

All Alan had to do was shove a glass underneath that tap and turn it on. It wasn't too much to ask.

"All your life, if I'm not mistaken. How old are you? Fifty-odd?"

Brodie tugged the *Scotsman* towards him.

"He'll be forty-three next month," said Mungo.

"Really?" Alan was looking at him like he must have forged his birth certificate. "Anyway, the point is Brodie here has been pearl-fishing for decades. Dedicated his entire life to it. Not only that, but he's the last full-timer in Scotland. And he's never found anything like this one. See, you can tell by his face. Not a sausage. Then Cameron blows in from the Middle East and hits the jackpot straight away. Got to be worth at least half a dozen bottles of Moët. Thankfully, I have them chilling."

"Let's see that pearl," said Fiona, standing next to them.

Brodie turned a page.

"For God's sake, Alan, open that champagne," she said.

"Hear you're buying, Cameron. Your birthday, is it?"

It was Dewi, who'd almost rutted his way through their bedroom wall last night. If there was one thing he never wanted to hear again it was Dewi and Shona at it.

"No, but it's Brodie's next month," said Alan. "Insists he's going to be forty-three."

"Forty-three ?" said Dewi in that South Wales accent of his, which made him sound as if someone were tickling his inside leg. "Come off it, Brodie. I've seen younger-looking walnuts. So what are we celebrating? The others are on their way. Shona's just telling the Co-op lot."

"Show him, Cameron," said Mungo.

"Jesus wept. Where did you find it, Brodie?"

Unable to read the words, he turned another page.

"Wasn't Brodie," said Fiona. "Cameron found it."

"Cameron?"

"Beginner's luck," said Alan. "Which is why we need to mark the occasion properly. Pass these glasses round. Plenty more where that came from. I've just put some more in the fridge. Here we are, Brodie."

"Can't I just have a beer?"

"Where the hell did you find that?" said Rev Maxwell, taking the glass of champagne Alan was offering Brodie.

"In the Isla," said Cameron. "I couldn't believe it. We'd just filled our bags, and had started to head back as it looked like there was going to be a storm. Then we bumped into Brodie and Maggie."

"At least you can say you were there, Brodie," said Alan.

He kept his eyes on the paper. It was as if someone had rearranged all the letters so that nothing made sense.

"Then the storm broke. We could have been hit by lightning any minute. You should have seen the rain."

It would be stair rods next.

"It was coming down like stair rods. So we collected up the shells as you're not allowed to leave them on the bank any more. It's illegal to kill them."

Like he knew the law.

"So we ran all the way to the bridge while the river was getting higher and higher, almost to the top of the bank. If we'd fallen in, we definitely would have been goners it had risen so much. I've never seen a storm like it."

Except in Bahrain.

"Apart from some amazing ones in Bahrain. Anyway, so we finally got to the bridge, and started opening our shells."

Making out that it was his idea.

"So we were sitting there, the rain still lashing down, and I was opening this mussel, hoping that it wasn't going to be battered sausage and chips again for supper, when I saw this lump inside."

Silence. He glanced behind him. The place was heaving. Everyone was watching Cameron.

"So I got a matchstick, and poked it around. And guess what happened then?"

Playing them for all they were worth.

"This stonking great pearl dropped into my hand! It was like an egg falling from the sky. I couldn't believe it. Still can't."

Nor could he. Nineteen years he'd spent hunting for that pearl. It was his. He couldn't even bear to look at it.

"Christ! Get a load of that. How much is it worth?"

That was Shona from somewhere in the crowd.

"How much do you think it's worth, Brodie?" said Alan.

"How much do you reckon, Brodie?"

Mungo.

"Oh, come on, you must have some idea."

Fiona.

"You'd know better than anyone."

Mungo again, nudging him with his elbow.

"Depends." He pushed his empty glass further towards Alan.

"What on?" shouted Stugly. He was right up against the far wall, the place was so full.

"The size."

"Humongous," called Alpina.

"The colour."

"White with a beautiful pink shimmer."

Fiona.

"The shape."

"Round as a snooker ball."

Nessa.

"The lustre."

"Rev Maxwell could comb his hair in it," said Alan. "If he still had any."

"Imperfections."

"Absolutely none," said Cameron.

"And what type of pearl it is."

"It's a Scottish river pearl, you dummy," said Mungo. "Fresh out of the Isla."

Silence.

Everyone was staring at him. It felt like he was pushing through water as he struggled to get to the door. Once there, he turned. It was as if he'd forgotten how to breathe.

"About eighty thousand pounds."

Brodie groped for the glass on his bedside table, and gulped down the stale, dusty water. It was just after ten thirty. What the hell was wrong with him? He always shot out of bed to go to the shells on a Saturday morning, no matter how much he'd drunk the night before. In this case it had been the rest of a new bottle of whisky in his hut. At least that was all he could remember. He hadn't even been aware of Elspeth getting up for her last day at work. He'd just lain there, drifting back to sleep, hoping that it wouldn't be true the next time he woke up. But each time the memory of that perfect pearl dropping into Cameron's hand had kicked him in the guts even harder.

He listened. Nothing but the perky ticking of the clock. Maggie must be playing with a friend. At least the bairn wouldn't see him getting up so late. What a disgrace. He pushed back the covers and hauled on his dressing gown. Maybe if he ate something his stomach would stop moving. A fried-egg sandwich with lots of coffee would do it. He snatched open the door. Maggie. Sitting on the floor, knees clutched, looking up at him.

"Is Frank in there?"

"I would have heard those ears of his dragging along the carpet." Down the boggy landing he trailed and headed into the bathroom. "Have you had your breakfast?" he called, his mouth full of toothbrush.

"Where do you think he's gone?"

He dabbed his lips on the hand towel, then started down the stairs. "Sleeping off all that cable he ate."

"Maybe he didn't like it here," she said over the banister, "and that's why he left."

"He's probably too ashamed to show himself now that no one can watch the television any more. Not even the news, for Pete's sake."

"Do you think he went back to the pet shop?"

"Not him. He'd have to hitchhike, and no one in their right mind would stop."

"Then why can't I find him?" she said, following Brodie into the kitchen as he opened the fridge door.

"Who ate all the eggs?"

"Wasn't Frank."

"Someone must have had them. They didn't just roll out." He flicked on the kettle, pulled open the drawer and started scrabbling through instruction manuals for gadgets that had broken decades ago, an unravelled ball of string that would come in useful one day, and screwdrivers that were always a Phillips when you needed a flathead, and a flathead when you needed a Phillips.

"Where's my aspirin?"

"Will you help me look for him?"

He closed the drawer. "Must have finished them."

"Please?"

It would have to be Marmite on toast. He wasn't even going to investigate the cheese situation. "What did you have for breakfast?"

Silence.

He reached into the cupboard for the jar of coffee and put four spoonfuls into a mug. "You've got to eat something."

"Do you think it was me?"

"Who ate all the eggs?"

"Why Frank left."

He pointed at her. "Frank has not left the building."

"Probably didn't like me. That was why."

She was looking up at him with a Ribena moustache as if it were the end of the world.

"We'll lure him out. That's what we'll do. What's his favourite food?"

"The TV aerial cable."

"Apart from that."

"The laundry basket."

"Now we're talking. The laundry basket. Anything else?"

She raised her eyebrows. "Your slippers."

"Worth the sacrifice. Anything else?"

"The kitchen chair legs."

"Good. Anything else?"

She paused, like she didn't dare say it.

"What?"

Still not looking him in the eye.

"Let's hear it."

"He quite likes nibbling your underpants when they're on the clothes horse."

"My underpants? Which ones? Don't tell me it's the white pair. The cosy ones with lots of slack."

Slowly she nodded.

"The cheek of it. They weren't long for this world as it was. One munch and it could all be over."

Crouched behind the sofa, clutching his fishing rod, he began to feel the evil prelude to pins and needles on top of everything else. Now he couldn't move, even if he wanted to. He stared at his forlorn underwear, hanging from the end of his line several inches off the carpet. How had it come to this?

"We've been waiting ages," whispered Maggie, huddled next to him. "When's Frank coming?"

"Any minute now we'll hear those huge furry feet of his. I just know it."

"Is it all right if I go out once he comes back?"

"Where to?"

Silence.

All he wanted was a cup of coffee. Why was life so difficult?

"What happens if he doesn't come out?"

"That rabbit will show himself, believe me. Let me know the minute you spot him, so I can whip away my lure. Teeth marks trouble me."

Eighteen minutes passed and still nothing had happened, apart from the torture in both his feet, which had almost blown his head off.

"Why don't you jiggle them so he knows they're here?" she said.

The doorbell sounded.

"I'll get it." She was up before he had the chance to volunteer. He could have put the kettle on while he was at it. Made some toast.

Voices, followed by the front door shutting, then silence. He started jiggling. He jiggled for Maggie. He jiggled for Frank. He jiggled for the whole of Scotland.

"There's a lady here to see you," said Maggie from the doorway.

"Don't bring her in here." He waggled the rod even faster. "I'll be there in a minute. Think he's on his way."

After a moment something caught his eye. A young woman was standing next to Maggie, slowly taking in the stuff piled on the floor — his half-digested slippers, the kitchen chairs with their ravished legs, and the wicker laundry basket with its missing corners. She then stared at his underpants hanging from his rod like a white flag shredded by mortar fire.

She smiled. Like it was always summer. "Are you Brodie McBride?" she said in an English accent.

He stayed behind the sofa so she wouldn't see him in his pyjamas. "Aye."

"I'm Ailsa Brown from the *Perth & Kinross Chronicle*. May I have a word?"

He hadn't even combed his hair. "What about?"

"That pearl. The one Mr Wallace found."

CHAPTER
SEVEN

The woman was eyeing his white Y-fronts again. Actually they were a rainy grey colour if you looked at them as hard as she was. He stood up. "I think the kettle might have just boiled."

Tightening the belt of his dressing gown so it wouldn't flap open, he led the way to the kitchen. What must she think of him, still in his pyjamas at this time of day? He came to a halt in the doorway. The bottom cupboards were open, and pots and pans were scattered all over the floor. Not only that, but everything had been dragged out of the washing machine, and was now slumped in a weeping heap in front of it. Just looking at it made his head hurt even more. It must have been Maggie hunting for Frank when he went to find his fishing rod.

"Spring-cleaning," he said, with a dismissive flap of the hand. "Slightly early. Or late, depending on how you look at it. Let's go outside."

The garden furniture was still soaked, including all the cushions. It would have to be his hut, even though only Elspeth and Maggie were allowed in it. After offering her the chair, he stood against the wall, feeling the roughness of the cheap wood. From her large red

112

leather handbag she drew out a notepad and pen. Her eyes, much paler than Elspeth's, lingered over the press cuttings, then slid to Dad's pearling stick propped up in the corner, on top of which was his tweed cap.

Maggie was loitering half hidden in the doorway. He couldn't ask her to make them some coffee. She wouldn't manage carrying both cups, and he didn't want to put her through the ordeal of bringing them out one at a time in front of a stranger. Why did whatever-her-name-was have to come round anyway? The last thing he wanted to talk about was that pearl. He glanced at her sandals. Those neat toes. He shouldn't be looking. Elspeth liked hers being sucked — at least she used to.

"I understand you were there when Mr Wallace found the pearl?"

Even her voice had a kind of glow to it.

"How did you hear about it?" he said.

"Someone called the paper."

Cameron after some glory no doubt.

"People are saying it's the largest river pearl found in Britain in living memory. Is it?"

Maggie stood in the doorway. "Dad, is it all right if I go out?"

The reporter was going to put it in the paper. Now everyone else was going to know how useless he was.

"Is it? The largest?"

He looked away. "Never saw it close up."

"Mr Wallace said both you and your daughter were with him under the bridge when he opened it."

"The light wasn't good. Wasn't even sitting next to him."

"Come on, Mr McBride," she said cheerily. "You're the expert. Is it the largest?"

"Dad, I have to go out."

The woman dragged a strand of pale hair from her eyes. "Apparently you told everyone it was last night."

He could still see it dropping into Cameron's hand. Something collapsed inside him, and his eyes fell to the floor. "I've never seen anything of that size and quality."

"How long have you been pearling, may I ask?"

He hesitated. "First went when I was five. My dad took me. It was in the spring. The daffodils were out. Found a white teardrop." He almost believed it.

She looked up from her pad. "How did you feel when you first saw Mr Wallace's pearl?"

Like someone had ripped out his insides, thrown them on the bank and set fire to them. "Shall I make us some coffee?"

"Since you were five?" She titled her head to one side. "I'd have been gutted."

He pointed at her. "Don't put that in. Surprised. Put that down. Surprised."

"What do you think his chances were of finding it? A million to one?"

There was a tug on his arm.

"Dad! I really need to go out. Now."

He could hardly bear to say it. "More."

"Apparently you said it was worth eighty thousand pounds. Seems a hell of a lot just for a pearl."

"Alison, you said your name was?"

"Ailsa."

"Mind out." He tugged open the table drawer and picked up the amber-coloured pearl he'd been keeping for years in case of an emergency. "Look at that." He cradled it in his palm. "It's a Scottish river pearl. You'll never see anything like that anywhere else in the world. See how the light plays on it."

They gazed in silence.

Returning it to the drawer, he tapped on the wall. "See this?"

"It looks suspiciously like a map of Britain."

"One of the reasons Julius Caesar invaded in 55 BC was to get his hands on our pearls."

She seemed intrigued, then picked up her pen.

"By the twelfth century there was a market for Scottish pearls across Europe."

Her head was bent, writing it down.

"Royalty have always loved them." He started pacing the tiny space. "A huge pearl was found in Aberdeenshire in 1620 and presented to James VI. Lo and behold, the following year the Privy Council of Scotland issued a proclamation that pearls found within the realm belonged to the Crown, and conservators of pearl fisheries were appointed in several counties."

Her pen was still moving, but he couldn't stop. "Thankfully in 1642 a Royal Charter granted Scottish commoners the right to fish for pearls." He tapped on the table. "It still exists. Make sure you put that in. That it still exists."

"Would you mind slowing down?"

Back and forth he strode. "For their third wedding anniversary Prince Albert gave Queen Victoria a brooch with Scottish pearls as a reminder of their first visit to Scotland in 1842."

She flipped over a page. "Just a minute."

"So what's the situation now? England, Wales and Ireland." He pointed to them on the map. "I don't bother going much any more. Ireland's not bad, but there's only one river in England and Wales with healthy reproducing populations. Which leaves Scotland." He slapped his palm so hard against the country she flinched. "We've got half the world's freshwater pearl mussels."

"Half?" She lowered her head again.

"And what travesty is taking place here?" he said, already feeling himself losing it. "Weekend amateurs with no idea what to look for are slaughtering pearl mussels in their thousands. They're picking up shells more than a hundred years old with no sign of a pearl inside them."

He rested a hand on the table to steady himself. "Murdering them when they yank them open with knives and leave them on the riverbank to stink the place out for everyone else. It's illegal to kill or injure a pearl mussel. You should know. It's been in the paper enough. Not that these idiots take any notice."

Another page flicked over. Maggie sat down in the doorway with her back to him.

"I remember picking up mussels with my hands there were so many."

"You're going too fast."

116

His headache was getting even worse. "Now there are people fishing the pools and lochs with scuba equipment. What kind of perversion is that? Scuba-diving?" He raised his hands, seeking an answer from someone. Anyone.

He tried to breathe, but the frightful tirade just kept coming.

"And then there are engineering works in rivers killing the mussels."

"What do you mean, engineering works?"

"Building weirs and deepening pools. And if that's not enough there's the pollution." He prodded himself in the chest. "I'm the only full-timer left. Everyone else has given up. They couldn't find enough pearls to make it work. See those books?"

He grabbed one and slammed it down next to her on the table, making her flinch.

"They're records reaching back to my great-great-grandpa, James McBride, pearl fisher to the Prince of Wales." He could hear the sense of injustice in his voice, too loud for the hut, but it kept spewing out. "Every pearl of note that five generations of us has ever found is written down in these ledgers. None of us has ever found anything to match both the size and quality of that pearl, from what I saw of it. You might find bigger, but not of that quality. There will never been another find like it. Not with the state of things now. Collectors would sell their own children to get their hands on it." He held out his arms to Ailsa. "Name your price."

She was looking at him, mouth open, like she didn't know what he'd do next.

"Now do you see why that pearl is worth eighty thousand pounds?"

Silence. Apart from his ragged breath.

"It should have been you who found it."

He held her gaze, then slumped back against the wall. Why was she, a total stranger, the only one who could see it?

It was definitely a cup of tea situation. Brodie reached into the cupboard for a bag and dropped it into Elspeth's favourite mug. She'd be home any minute, distraught because she was out of a job. Which was why he'd also made supper — macaroni cheese, just the way she liked it — despite the fact that his head was getting even worse as the day progressed.

Not only that, but he'd gone to the barber's after the reporter left. Too many husbands assumed their wives were blinded by love and failed to see they'd let themselves go. The comfort clothes. The gut. The disregard for protruding ear and nasal hair. No wonder their wives no longer wanted to sleep with them. He'd heard all about it while standing behind two stout ladies in the queue at the Co-op.

Seven minutes late. He went into the living room and peered out of the window. Still no sign of her. She was probably tied up at work. He stayed where he was, watching. Eleven minutes now. Maybe he should call the cafe and check that she'd left, just in case something had happened to her on the way home.

Twelve and a half minutes. Some people round here drove like maniacs. What if she were lying in the road, waiting for someone to ring for an ambulance, and he was at home folding paper napkins into stupid shapes?

He'd give her another two minutes. If she wasn't back then, he'd go and look for her.

As he was putting the salt and pepper on the table the front door opened. That was her keys landing on the hall table. A pause to kick off her shoes. She'd be round the corner in a second, looking all depressed.

She was smiling. And wearing that red dress — the one he always wanted to take off. It was a bit much for work, wasn't it?

Her face fell. "I haven't seen your ears since the seventies. Actually it's just one ear."

"Got a discount."

She tilted her head to one side the way people did at modern art when they didn't get it.

"I picked the apprentice. He was sitting there all on his own. Felt sorry for him." He held out her tea, waiting for that smile to come back. "Just made it."

"Thanks. Have we got any wine?" She opened the fridge door.

"I've made supper." Triumphantly he gestured to the table where he'd put out forks as well as spoons for pudding. Strictly speaking, you didn't need a fork for Angel Delight, but that wasn't the point. The napkins certainly looked like swans. If you were being pedantic, you might say they more resembled camels, but at least one of them was still standing. And they were certainly nice and jolly considering the only napkins he could find were the holly ones left over from Christmas. "It's macaroni cheese. Your favourite."

She seemed surprised, like it was news to her.

Bending down, she peered into the oven.

What was that he could smell? She'd been drinking.

"Looks lovely. We went out for a long lunch. I'll have some later. Might need a little lie-down."

"Lunch?"

"That new posh French place in Perth that everyone's going on about. I had to come home and change."

"So Stugly decided to go out with a bang. Good for him."

"Cameron took us all. To celebrate."

"Being unemployed?"

"He's bought the cafe. Asked me to manage it. I won't have to wear that uniform any more." She smiled again.

Silence.

"Will he be there with you?

"Where?"

"The cafe."

"Who?"

"That man."

"Which man?"

"Cameron."

"I expect so. Until we're on our feet."

The candle in the middle of the table made a singeing sound as he pinched the life out of it.

120

"Alpina will do her back in if she carries on doing the Highland fling like that at her age. Everyone at the bus stop was looking at her as we were waiting for a taxi home."

He shoved the packet of Angel Delight back among the currants in the cupboard. It was butterscotch, his favourite. He'd been looking forward to it.

"I'm sorry you didn't find that pearl. Cameron told me all about it. Several times actually."

He froze, his back still to her. There was the sound of tiny feet running down the stairs.

"Is it ready yet, Dad?" said Maggie. She sniffed. "What's that weird smell?"

Christ. The macaroni. He yanked open the oven door, then closed it again and stood in front of it, arms folded.

Elspeth picked up something from the windowsill. "By the way, is this anyone's?" Hanging from her fingers was a tiny grey drawstring pouch. "I found it in the washing machine. Must have come out of someone's pocket."

"Not mine," said Maggie, darting out and running back up the stairs.

"Mum! Who are all those people?" She pushed her cheek against the living-room window to get a better look. There were loads of them standing outside Mrs Wallace's front door. "Some have got poles with fur on the end."

There was a lovely smell as Mum stood next to her. It was that new perfume she'd bought.

121

"Journalists, by the looks of it. The furry things are microphones. I don't know why they're there. Cameron's at the cafe pulling up the carpet."

"But he was in the paper yesterday." His big stupid smiling face and the pearl had been all over the front page of the *Chronicle*. It should have been Dad on the front. They'd stuck a tiny photo of him inside. An old one.

Mum looked closer. "Some of them must be from the nationals."

"What's that?"

"The bigger papers."

"Bigger?"

"They tell you what's happening all over the country. Not just round here."

Everyone was going to know.

"See that van over there?" She tapped the pane. "That's the BBC. We'll have to go next door to watch the news."

"Cameron's not going to be on the telly as well, is he?"

"It's not every day someone finds a pearl that size. Are you still coming with me to help with the painting? Cameron said you can choose the colour."

"Don't feel like it."

She kept her eyes on them. Why didn't they all go away? If Frank hadn't got lost she'd have gone to Mrs Wallace's on Saturday morning and explained to Cameron that he'd picked up one of Dad's shells by mistake. She'd go and see Alice. That would make her

122

feel better. She tugged on her Wellingtons, shouted to Mum where she was going, and headed out.

"This is Cameron Wallace's house, isn't it?" called one of the reporters.

"He lives in the next road. Number 171."

She stopped outside the Cruickshanks'. When there was no reply, she pressed the bell again, leaving her finger on the buzzer. Mr Cruickshank snatched open the door, wearing a checked shirt and a pair of brown trousers up to his armpits.

"Sorry, Maggie. I thought you were one of that lot over the road."

"Is Frank here?"

"Frank?"

"He eats underpants. White ones."

Mr Cruickshank shifted his feet. "Frank the Underpants Nibbler is here?"

"A pair of yours might have blown off the line." They were the biggest in the world. Frank would have spotted them a mile off and he'd never be able to resist.

"Does your mother know you're here?" He bent forwards and looked down the street towards their house.

"She can't find Frank either. He ran off with a pair of Dad's. When we came back they'd disappeared from the fishing rod."

He turned towards the stairs. "Morag," he shouted. "It's Maggie, the wee girl from number 33. Says someone called Frank has run off with Brodie's underpants. His white ones. After they went fishing apparently. She's wondering whether he's here."

Hair wrapped up in a towel, Mrs Cruickshank appeared at the door clutching her hands. "What does this Frank look like?"

"Dark eyes. Moustache. A bit fat."

She frowned. "Sounds like Dewi."

"It can't be him, dear, she said his name was Frank." He shook his head. "I'm sorry, Maggie, we haven't seen him. We'll keep the doors locked. Please tell your father we hope he gets his undies back as soon as possible."

As she stepped into the General Store, three men and a woman wearing wellies were standing in a queue. Alice's mum shouldn't leave the shop empty like this. Anyone could steal the sweets.

"The lady's gone to make me a sandwich," said the man at the front. "You'd have thought they'd already be made up, but she said she didn't know anyone was coming. What did she expect? A letter two weeks in advance?"

"It mustn't get very busy round here," said the woman.

"The B&B's full, I can tell you that. Could only find somewhere ten miles away." He turned back to Maggie. "Do you live here, lassie, or have you come to try your luck too?"

"With what?"

"Finding a great big pearl like that bloke with the tan."

Three pearls tinkled in Brodie's aspirin bottle as he hoisted his boat onto the roof rack. Luck was on his

124

side again — he knew it would come back. He'd guessed that the huge pearl was in the Isla, and he'd been right. Now everything was telling him that it was the most likely place to find another one. Judging by the story in the *Chronicle* yesterday, Cameron and Mungo hadn't fished that much further ahead of them, which left the rest of the Isla for him this afternoon. Knots tied, he tugged at the rope to make sure it was secure. Lightning did strike the same place twice. He'd seen it.

Headed back towards Nether Isla, a warm gust scented with scabious skimmed his cheek as he wound down his window. The heather had turned the hills in front to amethyst. Why would you live anywhere else when you could have all this? No amount of money earned on a dusty island off Saudi Arabia could lift your heart as much as a view like that. It was ridiculous of Cameron to think that Elspeth would leave Scotland. She wouldn't, would she? He pressed down on the accelerator and fixed his gaze on the desperate grey of the road.

As he turned the final corner before the Isla, he thrust against the brake, jamming his back against the seat as he fought to come to a stop. There were cars everywhere. Some were parked in the road, others had been abandoned at reckless angles on the verge, crushing the start of the raspberry bushes. Who the hell were this lot?

There was a shriek, followed by hollow laughter like a magpie, as he headed for the river, stick and glass in hand. Once on the bridge, he looked down. People.

Dozens of them thrashing through the water, rucking up its silken surface. Others, wearing snorkels and masks, were face down in the river. White-legged women stood in the shallows, skirts tucked in their knickers, holding the hands of children carrying buckets and spades. It was hideous. Absolutely hideous.

Fury thumping inside him, he clambered down the bank. A short man with a bulldog neck was knee-high in the water throwing handfuls of young mussels, some of them still yellowish-brown, into a Co-op carrier. You'd only find those by digging into the gravel. Anyone with half a brain could tell they were too small to contain a pearl.

"Oi!"

Several people looked up. Not the moron, though.

"What do you think you're doing?"

The man glanced at the others in the water.

"You! The one who just put something in the bag. What are you doing?"

He squinted in the sun. "Looking for pearls. What does it look like?"

"You can't take those shells. They're too young."

The man shrugged. "Worth a go."

"There won't be anything inside them."

"You never know."

"I do know." He jabbed a finger at him. "Put them back."

"Think you'd better go back to the barber's, mate. They haven't finished."

Someone tittered.

"Put them back."

126

"Says who?"

That was it. He stalked into the water, grabbed the bag and turned it upside down. Water splashed his front as the shells hit the water. Still gripping the carrier he climbed back up the bank.

"I know you," said the man, his voice raised.

He didn't turn.

"Your picture was in the paper. You're the last pearl fisher in Scotland. The one who didn't find that huge pearl."

The car shook as he shut the door. He drove back up the lane, and once he was well away from them, he got out, slamming the door again behind him. He'd walk across the fields and meet the river higher up. As he passed through the wooden gate, he listened to the comforting silence. An unblemished sky stretched out before him. Along the dusty edge of the field he scuffed, picking a sun-warmed raspberry. He put it on his tongue. Summer.

Through the trees he followed a track that would bring him out opposite Elspeth's rowan. He'd put a wee sprig of it in a vase on her bedside table so she could see how far they'd come. Nineteen years and they still loved each other. He pressed on faster through the firs towards the bank. As he emerged he stopped still. A man in swimming trunks and goggles was ducking his head in the water. Another had a wetsuit on. What the hell was that woman holding? A rake. She was dragging it across the bottom of the river as if she were sweeping up dead leaves. And what was that ugly thing, hanging from Elspeth's tree? A black bin liner. Someone was tipping shells into it from a bucket. He slipped and tripped on the roots as he ran back through the trees. It was all ruined. Forever.

CHAPTER
EIGHT

"But I don't want to go," said Maggie, sitting on the bottom step in the hall. She clutched her knees. Mum couldn't make her. Outside the stupid car engine was still running.

"You've been moping around the house for days. Some fresh air will do you good."

"What if Frank comes back?"

Mum straightened after doing up her sandals, the high ones with the bronze straps she'd let her try on. "We've spoken about Frank."

"Why can't I just stay here?"

"Like I said, I'm back at work tomorrow. It's the last day I'll be able to take you out. There's that icecream parlour we could go to afterwards."

"Why can't Cameron go on his own?" She closed her eyes and lay back on the hard steps. Hadn't seen him since he found Dad's pearl a week ago. He was the last person she wanted to be with.

"Because he asked me to go with him. He's my new boss, so I've got to, unfortunately. I can think of much better things I'd rather be getting on with."

"But I don't like Mr McSweetie."

"You've always been perfectly happy to come with me before. What's wrong?"

A car horn tooted twice.

She sat up. "It's rude to do that. You always say so when Uncle Mungo does it."

"And it's even ruder to keep people waiting." Mum grabbed her handbag from the table and pointed to the front door. "Cameron's been out there for more than ten minutes, and he pays my wages. Where are your sandals?"

Her eyes fell to the floor. "Don't know."

Mum marched into the kitchen. There was a loud noise as she dropped them on the floor in front of her. Slowly, like caterpillars, she crawled her feet into them. The hall filled with the sound of a revving engine as Mum opened the door. Once she'd done up her Velcro straps, she looked at her toes. Sangria Shimmer. Ugly.

"Have you got your belt on?" called Cameron from the driver's seat.

Didn't see why she had to wear one anyway. Dad never crashed. "Yes."

As the car pulled out, his dark eyes appeared in the little mirror hanging from the roof. "What would you like to listen to, Maggie?"

"The Eagles."

"Haven't got any, I'm afraid." He opened a lid between his and Mum's seat. Inside was a neat row of CDs. "Got Robbie Williams here somewhere. My daughters love him."

"Hate him."

"Lovely car," said Mum quickly. "It's still got that new-car smell."

There was a loud beeping sound and Cameron's eyes appeared in the mirror again. "Someone hasn't got her seat belt on."

Mum turned all the way round with a look that meant she was about to get into trouble if she wasn't careful. She buckled up and stared out of the window. Dad's Fiesta was much better than this. His seats had blue checks and springs coming through the holes, whereas Cameron's were all slippery and cream. You definitely wouldn't get any pocket money if you got felt tip on them.

There was a black button on the door. She reached out a curious finger and pressed it. The window next to her started to slide down. She pressed it the other way and it closed. See if she could do it fifty times in a row. Up. Down. Up. Down. Up. Down. Up. Down.

"That's enough!" said Mum. "You'll break it."

"Look at the traffic," said Cameron. "I've never seen anything like it. It's worse than Manama."

They were stuck in the middle of the high street behind some big caravan. Loads of people were walking down the pavement in wellies.

"Are you sure Mr McSweetie's the best man for the job?" said Cameron.

Mum turned to him. "He's the only dealer in Scottish freshwater pearls in Perth. He makes beautiful jewellery out of them."

"I wouldn't want him to stuff it up, seeing as the pearl's worth so much."

"He won't. You *have* remembered to bring it with you, haven't you?"

It was Dad's pearl. Not his.

"It's wrapped in a handkerchief in my pocket. Stop me if I forget and blow my nose."

She tugged at a piece of white cotton sticking out the front of her dress, making the button move.

"Do you remember that maths teacher who was always blowing his nose at school?" said Mum. "What was his name?"

"Squeaker."

Why were those two laughing so much? She pulled again at the thread.

"What are you going to do with the pendant once it's made?" said Mum.

"I'm going to give it to someone."

She tugged much harder and the button flew off, disappearing under the seat.

"Finally I get to see it," said Mr McSweetie, his palms making a dry sound as he slid them together. On the wall behind him was a photograph of the Queen being presented with a pearl brooch. Dad had found all those pearls. He was the best pearl fisher in the world. Everyone knew that.

She reached for Mum's hand as they stood at the glass counter. It should have been Dad here with them, not Cameron. All three of them together, getting the pearl necklace strung. At least there weren't any other customers, which meant they'd be finished in a few minutes, and then she'd get her ice cream. The largest one possible, three scoops — strawberry, vanilla and chocolate.

With his hairy fingers, Mr McSweetie pushed his glasses up his nose, then held the pearl up to the light. "Quite remarkable." He looked as if he wanted to eat it. "I've never seen anything like it."

"I'd like it made into pendant, and get a nice chain for it," said Cameron.

"Excellent idea. I'd say white gold with this shade. You so rarely find it. I can't remember the last time Brodie found one this colour. Certainly not a round one."

Dad had a whole tinful at home, dummy.

He held it in his palm as if weighing it. "It said in the papers that you found it in the Isla, Mr Wallace."

"Beginner's luck. Brodie and Maggie were there, which made it even more special, seeing as though I'm a friend of the family."

He wasn't their friend. She looked up at Mum to see what she thought, but she was just staring at the pearl like it was the most beautiful thing she'd ever seen.

"So you saw it come out of the shell?" Mr McSweetie was peering down at her.

She studied the gold earrings in the glass counter.

"You had a ringside seat next to me, didn't you, Maggie? Saw history in the making. You'll be able to tell your grandchildren all about it."

Mr McSweetie was still staring at her, waiting for an answer.

She nodded.

Smiling, he slipped the pearl into a tiny red drawstring pouch. It was just like the grey one Mum had found in the washing machine. The one she'd denied knowing anything about, and thrown out when no one was looking.

"Just a moment while I put it in the safe," said Mr McSweetie, disappearing through a black curtain behind the counter.

Mum squeezed her hand. "What flavour ice cream do you fancy? How about chocolate, strawberry and vanilla?"

Why had Mr McSweetie asked her whether she'd seen the pearl come out of a shell? No one knew what she'd done, except Frank, and he wasn't going to tell anyone.

"Feel sick."

If one more person opened that door and asked her where the Isla was she'd clock them one. Elspeth breathed in and squeezed behind a chair to reach a customer who'd been waiting at least fifteen minutes. They'd only been open a couple of hours and look at it. The place was heaving. It was that lot who'd driven up in a minivan from Devon that had done it — sixteen of them taking up four tables.

"Sorry to keep you. What can I get you?"

"I would like to speak to . . ." The man took a newspaper cutting from his wallet. "Mr Cameron Wallace. They say I can find him here."

German, by the sounds of it. "He's at the cash and carry."

"Do you know where in the Isla he found that pearl?" He tapped at the article with a neatly cut nail. "It does not say the precise location. The river is seventy-four kilometres long."

"Couldn't tell you. What can I get you?"

He pointed to the plate on the next table. "What is that?"

"A teacake."

"A cake made with tea?"

"A sweet bun with dried fruit."

He frowned. "It is a little black. How do you say? Like ashes."

"Consider it good luck. Like black cats."

"I'll have two."

She felt a tap on the arm.

"Did you see the pearl? Was it really as big as it looked in the paper?"

She had to be Italian with that accent and hair.

"When will Mr Wallace be back?" The German grabbed her other arm. "I would like to hire him. He might help my chances."

"Does he have a wife?" said the Italian.

"You'll have to wait your turn, love," said Fiona from the next table. "Did you ever see that scene in *Jurassic Park* when hundreds of dinosaurs start herding across the field towards Sam Neill? It'll be like that with Cameron. And that'll be just the married women."

Elspeth picked up Fiona's dirty plate. "I'll put in a good word for you."

"I'm far too old for him. He'll want someone your age, Elspeth. Watch your back, Rev Maxwell's trying to come in."

What was Fiona trying to say? She'd only been with Cameron for five months during her first year of university. It was Brodie who'd suggested she go. When he'd first mentioned it, settling himself next to her on the deck of a boathouse, she'd looked at him like he was speaking another language. No one in her family had a degree. He'd believed in her when her father had given her every reason not to. And if she hadn't realised before how much she loved Brodie, sat there with his shirt off and feet in the loch, she knew it at that moment.

It was on one of the occasions when he retreated from her that she fell into Cameron's arms. Eventually, she began to understand why he did it. Things couldn't have been easy with his father dropping down dead when he was only nine and having to move to Nether Isla on his own, not that he ever talked about his family. She'd gone back to him as soon as she'd realised her mistake. Brodie wasn't like anyone else. He'd taught her things you could never learn from books — the calls of the birds, how to predict rain if clover and indigo folded their petals, and the best way of making tea from the red shoots of water mint. When she needed it most, he'd sit at the side of her bath and read her poetry, and never once did he miss out a verse of *The Rime of the Ancient Mariner*. The presents he gave her brought tears to her eyes, as no one else would know that she'd love such a curious thing as an old door

136

knocker in the shape of a woman's hand holding an orange. It wasn't until that awful moment last year that she'd begun to question it all. That sunlit morning when she'd come downstairs, assuming all was well in the world, and she'd had to sit down.

"You and Cameron have done a great job of this place, I must say, Elspeth," said Rev Maxwell, as he stepped in.

He was right about that. The hideous pine panelling was now a pretty shade of white. They'd pulled up the carpet, polished the floorboards, and replaced all the plastic furniture with small wooden tables and matching chairs. But just because she and Cameron had had a laugh while they were doing it, it didn't mean anything was going on.

"Hope you don't mind, Fiona," said Rev Maxwell, pulling out a chair next to her. "There's nowhere else to sit.

"I came in here hoping to escape everyone," said Fiona. "The phone's been ringing all morning. I'm booked up for the next three months. I've never known anything like it."

"Nor me. The pews are stuffed with people on their knees praying they'll find a pearl. We filled all four collection boxes yesterday, which we normally only bring out for midnight mass when everyone's so drunk they've forgotten their natural parsimony. No offence, Elspeth, but it's a good job it was Cameron who found that pearl and not Brodie. It gives the impression that any Tom, Dick or Harry can strike it lucky."

What in God's name was happening now? Brodie wound down his window and stuck out his head. It was locked solid in front of him all the way up the high street. He hadn't been to the shells for three days, not since he'd seen what they were doing to the Isla. Now that he'd finally got his head together, and decided to drive a hundred and fifty miles to the northern Highlands, he couldn't even get out of Nether Isla. Where was that motorhome in front of him from anyway? He leant forward and peered down at the sticker by the number plate. Now the French were here. That was all they needed.

Without bothering to look, he pulled out, the engine wailing bitterly as he put his foot down. He'd barely started to overtake, when there was a flash of lights ahead. He couldn't pull in, for Christ's sake, it was bumper to bumper. Another outraged blaze of headlights, much closer now. The car started to tremble as he accelerated further trying to find a gap in the idling traffic. A hysterical honking sounded ahead of him. There was no way he could stop in time. Elspeth and Maggie. He'd never told them they were the only things that mattered. How much he loved them. Just as he was about to close his eyes to his inevitable fate, a space emerged between the cars like an impossible parting sea. He swerved in as the still-honking car fled past. Heart pinched tight, he sat with his hands on the wheel, seeing what might have just happened.

Once he'd finally left them all behind he dared to lean back, lulled by the foxgloves rocking their mauve

138

mittens. Soon the reassuring granite slopes of the Cairngorms surrounded him. Things were going to get better. There wouldn't be a soul where he was going, just him and the Carron. That was the thing about being a professional, you knew which river to pick.

Hours later, the clenching in his stomach began as usual about a mile before the bridge over the Kyle. On the other side of that vast river was the place he'd once called home. He hadn't been back since Mum sent him away with the family teapot in a damp cardboard box that smelt of onions. He couldn't even say the village's name. All those hours he'd sat at his bedroom window watching the Kyle, a horizontal mirror stacked with sooty clouds shifting endlessly to the North Sea. All that time he'd spent imagining the thousands of ways he could have prevented what had happened upstream. Upstream, where the freshwater rivers feeding the Kyle were sweet enough to produce a pearl. He'd never fish one of them. The Oykel. Never. Not even if it had all the white pearls with a hint of pink in Scotland.

As usual, he turned off before he could even see the bridge. Soon, between the trees, he spotted the Carron, sleek as teak and just as silent. Further on, it would be bouncing down rocks in riotous white curls. He pulled over, and, back sore from the drive, he staggered to the water's edge in his waders. As he stepped in, the water clutched at his legs as if begging him not to go any further. Deeper into the current he stepped. Never give up hope. Dad had always said it was like a lantern lighting the way ahead. He'd find some decent pearls to sell to Mr McSweetie. Then, when he wasn't expecting it, he'd open a shell and there would be her final pearl. Even bigger than Cameron's. He lowered his head to the glass.

Eventually, his bag pleasingly heavy against his hip, he made for the bank. Eyes closed, he sat on a tufty patch listening to the endless blather of the water. What if the pearl was right next to him? He grabbed his tongs and a mussel.

Something jerked inside him as he peered between the open valves. Already? There was a tremble of his hands as he gently nudged his matchstick against the bulging beige flesh. Out dropped a gloriously round pearl with the kind of lustre that would make your heart sing. He'd always hated cream balls.

"Found one, you lucky sod."

He started, almost dropping the pearl. Standing next to him was a middle-aged man in camouflage trousers and a matching shirt, his sleeves rolled up to his red elbows. On his head was a blue cloth cap covered in enamel badges.

"Mind if I join you?" he said, sitting down.

He was from some city in northern England. Newcastle? Manchester? God only knew. Wherever it was, he should get the hell back there.

"That's a real beauty." There was a stench of stale beer as the man leant towards him. "Obviously not as big as the one in the papers, but you'll get good money for that. Mark my words. All I've found so far is a funny-shaped brown one. Apparently the brown ones aren't worth anything. Haven't even recouped the cost of my tent yet. Two hundred quid. I got one that

140

midges aren't supposed to be able to bite through. Not that it works." He pulled down the top of his trousers and revealed a ravaged, bony hip. "God knows how I'm going to get through the next two weeks."

"May as well go home."

"Not now I've seen what you've found, I won't. Where d'ya find it?"

He said nothing.

"You must be camped further downstream. Thought I'd met everyone already." He jerked his head. "Come and join us tonight for a drink. Show everyone that pearl. They're a canny lot."

"Everyone?"

"About a dozen of us. We get together at night and sit round a fire with a few cans."

He kept his eyes on the Carron.

"Want some advice?"

What he wanted was for him to go away. All of them. Now.

"Don't bother with the Isla." He adjusted his ridiculous hat. "It's rammed. You'll never find anything there now."

Silence.

"What's this?" He picked up his tongs. "Looks like a nutcracker."

"They're for opening the shells."

The numpty shook it, like it would do something.

"Use a knife, mate, like everyone else, otherwise you'll be here all day. This is the one I use." The sun caught the blade as he twisted it back and forth. "You can really get through them quickly."

Brodie flinched. "Put that thing away. You'll kill them, breaking the hinge with that. You have to use tongs like mine."

"Where do you get them from?"

"You make them."

"Seeing as though I'm six hours away from my toolbox, I'll use my knife, mate."

"You'll harm the mussels. It's illegal."

The man shrugged. "I won't tell anyone if you won't."

He had to get away from here. The shells clattered like broken china as he stuffed them back into his bag, and hurried with it to the water's edge.

"What are you doing?" shouted the man over the noise of the cascading mussels. "You haven't even opened them."

Brodie snatched up his things, and took off through the trees towards the road.

There was a cry. "Mate, you've dropped your pearl. It's a beauty. Come back. You might never find another one."

He hurtled even faster, gripping his stick and his glass.

The rattle of rain on the windscreen finally brought him back from the past, and he flicked on the wipers. Where was he now? He lowered his head. The Cairngorms were crowding round him, their gunmetal slopes darkening with the downpour. On one of the summits, skimming heaven, stood a row of skeletal trees, raven-black against a patch of bleached sky. He could walk for days over these mountains. Keep on walking and never come back.

Now he couldn't even get home. As he sat slumped in the stationary traffic in the high street, a whiff of fish and chips from a huddle of tourists on the pavement turned his empty stomach.

He stared at the dumb sign bearing the words "The Flaming Teacake" which Cameron must have put up above the cafe. There was Elspeth wiping a table, her hair tied back, revealing the gentle curve of her face. She was coming towards the window. He smiled and raised a hand, but she looked towards the hills as if searching for something.

A horn sounded behind him.

More customers were crowding round the door trying to get in. They were in the way. He couldn't see her. Was that Cameron coming up behind her?

Another toot.

What was happening now? He lifted himself off his seat. Still couldn't see her.

Two more honks of that sodding horn.

He flicked his eyes to the mirror. Dr Kerr was leaning out of his window trying to get his attention. Over the years he'd bumped into him on a number of occasions while the scientist was monitoring pearl mussel colonies for Scottish Natural Heritage. But he'd never seen him in Nether Isla before.

Back aching, Brodie approached his window.

"Thought it was you." There was a clicking sound from his mouth and a faint whiff of mint. "I've been following you for miles. You still haven't got your brake light fixed."

"The Isla. What are they going to do about it?"

Something stiffened on his jawline. "I thought people would try their luck, but I never imagined this."

"There are piles of shells on both sides of the bank. You must have seen them. People are raking up the juveniles, slaughtering them." He rested both hands on the door. "Who's going to stop them?"

"The police are sending their Wildlife Crime Officer along."

"Him? What the hell's he going to do? Arrest them all?"

Dr Kerr glanced ahead of him. "The traffic's moving."

"It's not just the Isla."

"Get a move on!" shouted someone from behind.

"Better get back to your car, Brodie. We're holding everyone up."

The smell of mint was even stronger as he leant into the window. "They're at the Carron. In tents. Expensive ones that don't leak after a day and make you go home."

"Which Carron?" He sounded like he didn't want to ask.

More horns blared as Brodie backed away towards his car. "In Sutherland. If they're up there, they'll be trying every river in Scotland. Tell that to the police."

A rumble from his stomach broke the silence. It seemed like he'd been sitting in his hut for hours. So

144

they were going to send PC Gibbons to sort it all out. What a joke that was. He got to his feet and picked up Dad's cap, reading the label though he knew it by heart. There was no other choice. Slowly he put it back on top of the pearling stick, closed the door behind him, and crossed the grass to the slumped fence.

"Shona," he called meekly, trying not to remember those sounds that kept coming through the bedroom wall. Dewi couldn't be that good, surely?

A head appeared and she stared at him as if trying to figure something out. "You should have come to me, Brodie," she said. "I told you I'd give you a discount."

"I was just wondering —"

"If I'd even it up? Someone's given you a right royal butchering. Did you go to that barber's in Blairgowrie?"

"I thought I'd ask if I could —"

"Don't worry, we'll fit you in. We'll probably have to take the whole lot off. Pretend it never happened. When you ring, just tell the girl you need an emergency appointment."

"It's not that."

She brightened. "Would you like access to our garden so you can get the fence mended?"

"No."

She looked down at it hanging perilously towards her, one gust away from total collapse. "It's nae bother. I'll give you the key to the back gate."

"It's not the fence."

She raised a hand to her mouth. "Oh, Brodie. You've not let the bath overflow again, have you?"

"Is Dewi there?"

"He's gone line dancing. Wanted me to go with him, but there's something about it that give me the creeps."

"I was just wondering —"

"Whether he'd invite you round for some fondue?"

There was no going back. "If there's a job going at the jammie."

CHAPTER
NINE

It felt like he was being lynched. Brodie tugged at the alien collar as he put a piece of bread into the toaster.

"Aren't you going to the shells?" came Elspeth's voice from somewhere behind him. A note of worry hung in it.

He could feel the current against his legs just thinking about it, and his heart pumping with the thrill of the chase. As he turned, her eyes dropped to his perfectly white shirt as if she'd never seen it. Which, of course, she hadn't. He'd had to go and buy the wretched thing. Thirty-five quid.

"Dewi might have a job for me. Meeting him at the factory at nine."

She blinked as though someone had switched on a bright light.

"Until the pearl hunters are gone." He squeezed a finger down his collar and gave it another yank. "Part-time. I thought I'd keep my options open."

"Options?" She tightened the belt of her dressing gown.

"So I can still go to the shells."

Her gaze drifted down him like a falling feather. "Which trousers are those?"

"My funeral ones." He pulled out the sides. "Thought I'd make a bit of an effort."

The chair scraped along the floor as she pulled it out. "You'll hate it," she said, sitting down with a thud.

"I'll get free jam. Loads of it."

"You don't even like jam. You know how Dewi is about it."

"I like blackcurrant. And I'm having Dundee marmalade for breakfast." He reached into the cupboard for the jar. "What more can the man want?"

There was a pause.

"Is that the tie you wear to weddings?"

He lifted up the end and inspected it. It had seemed nice and cheerful when he'd bought it all those years ago. Now it had an air of ludicrous optimism. "Only one I've got."

Looking at him now like she still didn't get it.

"Wouldn't you consider something else? Outdoors maybe."

That was the thing. What the hell could he do other than find pearls? "I'll love it."

"You said you found a good cream one up in Sutherland on Friday. Shall I take it to Mr McSweetie ?"

"Dropped it."

Silence.

"How was it up there?" she said eventually.

"Pearl hunters camped along the Carron like an advance guard."

"What about the other rivers?" She got up and flicked on the kettle. "The Shin or the Oykel. Did you try them?"

He tried to open the marmalade. "The Oykel's useless for pearls."

"Can't be. Your father found some lovely big cream ones there. Says in his ledger. Don't you remember when we were looking at it?"

The lid suddenly came off and fell to the floor where it spun loudly. "Got to go. I don't want to be late."

"But it's not even seven. What about breakfast?"

He peered into the jar. Grey velvet. "The marmalade's mouldy."

He could smell it before it came into view. The sticky stench seemed to be swelling up in his throat. Even the crested tits were refusing to open their beaks. It wasn't the glorious aroma of summer strawberries that shone like rubies in the fields, but more the whiff of strawberry bubble bath you'd give to a relative you didn't much like.

As he reached the end of the road through the pines, he stopped. All these years living in Nether Isla and he never imagined the factory looking like this. In a razed section of the forest, like a shaved patch of skin readied for a surgeon's scalpel, stood a huge grey metal box. Smoke was billowing out of the roof as if it were a crematorium trying to get through a backload.

Headed for a door marked "Reception", he traipsed across the car park. Inside, behind a desk, a woman looked up from a paperback that had that swollen look of having been read in the bath. She reached into her molehill of hair and, with purple fingernails, drew out a pen.

"I've come to see Dewi." He attempted a smile to hide what he was thinking: that he'd rather he soaking wet on a riverbank, with nothing in his aspirin bottle, than standing here in front of her.

"Take a seat." Her blackbird's gaze didn't leave him for an instant as she picked up the phone. "That man from the paper's here to see you . . . No, the other one."

She didn't have to sound so disappointed.

Silently she replaced the receiver and resumed reading.

As he sank down onto a grey plastic chair, he felt his trousers sticking to his legs. It must have been from sitting in the drizzle in the woods waiting for nine o'clock to arrive. He tried to pull them away, but they clung like chilly magnets.

"Like it, working here?" he asked doubtfully.

"Got a view," she said.

He glanced out of the window at the car park. For an awful moment he suddenly felt the urge to lift her up over his shoulder, and stagger towards freedom while they both had the chance.

Just as he was debating whether a fireman's lift would be in order, a set of double doors opened. Dewi appeared in a white coat that somehow failed to convey the air of authority that the garment instantly gave both the medical and scientific professions. His lack of height and whatever the hell was on his feet weren't exactly helping. What were they? Cowboy boots?

"Brodie!" he said, with a beam that moved both his ears. "Thrilled you've finally seen the light. How many

150

years have I been telling you that I've seen the future and the future looks like marmalade? Come this way."

He followed Dewi along a series of prefabricated corridors, which he couldn't resist flicking to test their flimsiness. As he trooped, he zoned in and out of the monologue on the company's history, which Dewi was valiantly trying to trace back to Queen Victoria's sole visit and a punnet of squashed raspberries.

"My office," said Dewi, as if opening the door to his fiefdom. He trotted behind a perfectly ordered desk, then installed himself in a large black leather chair and proceeded to swing contently. "Splendid shirt, Brodie."

Settled on a plastic seat, which had the same disregard for comfort as the one in the foyer, he eyed the metal blinds obscuring the coveted view of the car park. Even the anorexic spider plant didn't seem to want to be here. His gaze then settled on a furry red dragon with a green belly and horns sitting on top of the filing cabinet.

"Admiring Abertawe, I see," said Dewi. "Know what his name means?"

He shook his head.

"It's Welsh for Swansea." He smiled like he'd invented the place.

"I thought you left that ugly, lovely town even faster than Dylan Thomas did."

"Once you've moved away your affection for the place becomes a bit like malaria — very difficult to shake off. I remember you telling me over the fence that you've been to the motherland."

"I once looked for pearls in the Swansea Canal."

"Find anything?"

"A pram." He sat up. "The River Conwy now that was a different story. I'll never forget that day I found fourteen pearls in one shell. It was —"

Dewi held up a minuscule palm as if stopping traffic. "The Conwy's in the north. I never go to the tribal area." He leant forward with a frown. "Isn't that the tie you wore to our wedding?"

With his thumbnail he scratched off a crusty stain, which was probably beef Wellington.

"Recognised it from the photos." Dewi jabbed an accusing finger at it. "Some things you never forget, no matter how hard you try. You should both come round next Thursday. Have a drink to celebrate. It's our twelfth wedding anniversary."

"Congratulations."

Gently swaying, Dewi sat back. "Still being married doesn't mean anything. What matters is wanting to be. That your wife's not lying in bed wondering how to divorce you. That's the difficult part, still being the man she fell for, even if you have lost all your hair. Or one side of it, in your case."

Silence.

"How long have you and Elspeth been married?"

"Nineteen years." He'd married her as soon as he could once she'd finished her degree. It couldn't end now, not after all these years.

Dewi pointed at him with his stapler. "Rock solid, just like us. Come about seven thirty. We're having sausage rolls, the works. Going to invite Cameron too as a little thank-you for everything he's done."

There was no way he was going if that man would be there.

With a smile that spread his moustache, Dewi picked up the *Chronicle*, and showed him the front page. "See that?" He tapped loudly at it.

See it? The "PEARL FEVER!" headline was so large you'd spot it from space before the Great Wall of China. Below was a photograph of tourists packing the Isla like a beach in the Costa del Sol. It was horrific.

"They're all wanting something with 'Nether Isla' written on it as a souvenir," said Dewi, his hairless head shiny with pleasure. "And what's the only thing that Nether Isla produces? Exactly! Needless to say, we're tripling the font size on our labels. Both the Co-op and the General Store keep running out of product, and the factory shop's been heaving."

He stared at a slither of the car park.

"Jam waits for no man," announced Dewi, suddenly standing next to him. "I'll give you a quick tour, then we can get down to business. It'll be very nice having you on board, Brodie, I must say. I don't mind telling you that I run a very tight ship. I like to call it the SS *Preserve*."

From the back of the door Dewi took a white coat and held it open for him. "Think yourself lucky, only management and visitors are allowed to wear the white ones. It'll be another ten, fifteen years before you wear the likes of this again, so enjoy it. Good money when you get there. I've just ordered a hot tub."

Uncertain whether he'd heard right, Brodie shouldered on the coat and turned round. "A hot tub?"

"For Shona's wedding anniversary present. Paid extra for the disco lights. I'm going to put it next to your fence. It'll help keep it up. You'll never know it's there."

He almost didn't want to ask. "What's she getting you?"

In a feat revealing a hitherto hidden flair for gymnastics, Dewi hoisted a leg high above his desk before planting it next to the stapler with the dead thud of a joint of lamb hitting a butcher's block. Smiling coyly, he then inched up his trouser leg, exposing the full horror of his boot.

"Snakeskin," he said, as if no explanation were required for the purple bits, the alarming upward thrust of the toe, and why he was wearing them to work in the first place.

After a nimble dismount, he handed Brodie something from a small cardboard box on his desk. Blue and synthetic, it had the creepy feel of disposable underwear.

"What's this?"

"A hairnet. Hope it fits. Wouldn't want any of that ending up in the marmalade. Come to think of it, you'd better wear two." He passed him another.

Brodie fingered them silently.

"And you'll have to take off your wedding ring. No jewellery's allowed on the factory floor."

He could still remember the struggle Elspeth had had to get it on his finger. The feeling that they were going to start laughing any second right there at the altar and not be able to stop. "I've never taken it off."

154

"This isn't the time for sentimentality, Brodie. If a bit of metal gets into the machinery we've got a disaster on our hands. A jar might break. We'd have to stop production, dispose of six hundred jars of product, and search for every microgram of glass. I've got some WD40 if that'll help get the thing off. Shona used the last of the Vaseline."

The skin bunched against his knuckle as he gave it a reluctant tug.

"Quick as you like." Dewi was holding out that tiny hand of his. "Got a board meeting later this morning."

With a much firmer pull it was off, and he stood there feeling naked as Dewi dropped the ring into his desk drawer. Without a word Brodie trekked after him along more fake corridors, eventually passing through a pair of large, floppy, plastic doors. He found himself in a glacial room covered in mortuary-white tiles. From somewhere came the relentless drone of machinery. He lifted a foot. Sticky.

"See that?" Dewi pointed to a sealed plastic drum with his inexplicable silver toecap. "That's the Seville oranges for the marmalade. Glows like gold when you open it."

"I still don't understand how you can call yourself one of the last producers of Dundee marmalade." Brodie jerked his thumb towards the coast. "We're fifteen miles from Dundee."

"I like to describe us as having been blown off course. It's not like any of our export markets would have a clue anyway. Americans think Birmingham's in Alabama, Paris is in Texas and Cardiff's in New York."

Searching the walls for a window, a little corner of sky to cheer him, Brodie followed him round the corner. Beyond the puddles of water was a steel table that reminded him of the ones pathologists used on the telly. Stacked upon it was a mound of unearthly pink frozen strawberries. Scrabbling through the fruit with the ruthlessness of nit nurses were two women, well into their sixties.

"These two ladies are our sorters," said Dewi, in the same tone he'd used when showing him his new car. "Been with us since they left school. They check the fruit for any foreign bodies that might have been missed by our supplier."

"Like what?"

"Husks or insects."

"They stand there doing that all day?"

Dewi held up a finger. "Only the chosen few, Brodie. Only the chosen few."

Through an archway, they stopped in front of a row of vast copper pans filled with red liquid writhing like lava. Men with yellow earplugs were pressing buttons and jotting things down on clipboards. It was so hot, it felt like he'd just walked into another season.

"This is the heart of the factory. The boiler room," shouted Dewi over the racket. "Where we actually make the product. Steam-heated copper pans. Traditional. We use the rolling boil method."

"You can't even hear yourself think."

Dewi raised his eyebrows and shook his head merrily. "Don't need to."

156

An urgent rattling of glass took over from the roar of the boiler room as they passed a conveyor belt on which hundreds of jars trembled.

"Where are the windows?" he said.

Dewi seemed confused. "Why would you want to look outside?" He opened his arms. "It's all happening in here. You'll never have to stand in one of those miserable rivers all on your own again. See Derek there?"

The white-haired man didn't turn, as if he no longer knew his own name.

"Been with us for forty-four years. That's the beauty of this place. Nobody ever leaves."

The tour over, Brodie was back on his plastic perch as Dewi studied him from behind his desk.

"Now, Brodie. What can you do? Apart from fish for pearls, that is."

There was a pause.

"I could drive one of the forklift trucks in the warehouse, like Stugly does."

He raised both palms. "Let's not forget what happened when you tried to park in front of my new Peugeot."

"I said I'd pay you back. You wouldn't let me."

"Friends forgive, but we don't forget."

"What about a taster? I could taste the jam like those women in that little room you pointed out."

"Taster? That position requires the palate of a master sommelier." He frowned. "I know your position on Blue Nun, Brodie. You bring it round often enough."

"I could stir the jam. I've got good upper-body strength."

Dewi looked as though he hadn't quite heard him correctly. "Have you seen the hands of our good lady the stirrer? She has the touch of a classically trained concert pianist."

"What about the development kitchen? That room you need special security clearance to enter. I could invent a new flavour."

"You'd find it easier getting a job with MI5."

"I could serve in the shop," he said on the edge of his seat. "I'd shift all the blackcurrant jam by lunchtime."

A shake of the head. "We don't make it. Blackcurrants make me shudder." He stood up. "A sorter, Brodie, that's what we'll make of you. As I see it, if you can find a pearl, you can spot a weevil. Hours are 7.30 a.m. to 5 p.m. Monday to Friday."

He couldn't do that. The shells. "I was thinking part-time."

"Part-time? No one works here part-time. We're all in it together. A nest of singing birds." He paused. "Apart from the labellers and the sorters. They've never got on. Goes back generations. It started with a well-aimed blackberry, apparently. The Christmas party is always a nightmare."

Dewi rounded the desk and held out his hand. "Welcome aboard, Able Seaman McBride. Don't forget there's a free jar of product after every year of service. Any flavour you like as long as it's not Dundee marmalade. Those oranges have come a long way. It'll be in your contract to avoid any misunderstanding. See

158

you next Monday seven thirty sharp. Fortunately for the rest of us you won't need to wear that tie."

"My wedding ring."

"Oh yes. Almost forgot with the excitement of it all." He opened his drawer and handed it to him.

The band wouldn't go back over his knuckle. It was his all right — he could tell by the scuffs marks from years of opening shells. He kept pushing until it slid over the vulnerable white patch again. But no matter how much he twisted the ring, it didn't feel right. Like something had broken.

His foot wagged as he sat in the *Chronicle*'s reception next to a large plastic plant furry with dust. If Ailsa wrote a story about it being illegal to kill or injure a pearl mussel, then all the tourists would go home, and there'd be a chance that the tradition would last another two thousand years. He'd have the mussels all to himself again, and wouldn't have to work in the jammie. He could still smell the wretched place even though he was thirteen miles away in Perth.

He leant across the front desk again. "She does know I'm waiting, doesn't she?"

The receptionist gave him a smile that was as phoney as the plant. "As I explained, she's on the telephone," he said. "Interviewing someone, I expect."

"They shouldn't be opening the shells with knives. It's illegal to kill or injure a pearl mussel."

"So you said. Twice."

"If it carries on like this, the mussel colonies will never recover. Not in my lifetime. It takes thirty years to produce a harvestable pearl. Thirty."

"Why don't you sit down again, sir?" The young man gestured to the chair. "She'll be down in a jiffy."

"Yet another Scottish tradition would be lost."

The receptionist didn't look up.

Back in his seat, he took off his wedding tie, and wiped the sleek satin across his forehead, still damp after his run from the multi-storey car park.

"See these tongs?" he said, the moment Ailsa emerged through a door wearing a powder-blue jacket and matching skirt. "I made them. They don't kill the mussel when you open the shell." He pointed through the window at the rest of the world. "All those tourists, they're using knives to butcher them. Seven years ago the freshwater mussel became a protected species. Which means it's against the law to kill or injure one." He looked at her hands. "Where's your pad? You should be writing this down."

She didn't move.

"Speak to that Wildlife Crime Officer they're sending down to the Isla. PC Gibbons. Red hair. Looks like one."

Reaching a pale finger into the opening of her pink blouse, she gently scratched at her collarbone. "I'm going for a drink. Want one?"

"But you've got to get it in the paper tomorrow."

"It's gone six. It's too late."

He swallowed. He should have come earlier instead of spending all those hours walking the woods wondering what to do about it all after he left the jammie.

"Like I said, I'm going for a drink."

Across the small, scuffed table in the Desperate Duck, she dragged a strand of hair from her eyes. Even in this cheap flat lighting it was the colour of wild honeysuckle.

"What does your dad make of it all?" she said, putting down her glass. "Bet he's furious too."

A song too loud and unfamiliar started up from the jukebox. "Died when I was nine. A stroke." He'd said it so often he almost believed it himself.

"I'm sorry. What about your mum? I can't imagine she's ever seen a pearl rush."

"She died a couple of years after Dad." At least that wasn't a lie. "By then I was living with my aunt in Nether Isla as Mum hadn't been well."

"Nice of your aunt to take you in."

"Nice" wasn't exactly a word he'd use to describe Aunt Agnes. "She had a lot of books. I read them."

"You must have lovely memories of pearling with your dad."

"He took me to every pearl river in Scotland and showed me where the shells were." The awful truth was that he'd had to find out where they all were from the ledgers.

She raised her glass to her lips. "I expect you still miss him."

"Who?"

"Your dad."

Miss him? There were times when he could punch him in the face. "You're not from round here."

"Mother's Norwegian. Father's English. Grew up in Oxford."

"What brought you up here?"

She drained her glass, beating him to it. "Job. Just started. Bigger paper. Was on a weekly before."

He could hear the full stops in her replies, signalling that she didn't want to elaborate. "You're not up here all on your own, are you?"

"My husband buggered off with someone from work. I decided to come here and freeze myself to death. Trouble is, turns out I quite like it."

Silence.

"The strange thing was," she said, her voice beginning to thicken, "I was divorcing him, yet when the court clerk asked me for our marriage certificate, and said I wouldn't be getting it back, I didn't want to hand it over. Right after we'd got married my dad drew a love heart with our initials on the back of the envelope I'd kept the certificate in. Everyone loved him as much as I did."

More silence as they held each other's gaze.

"Sorry, I don't know why I told you all that." She looked down.

She wasn't going to cry, was she?

Before he knew what he was doing, he'd rested his hand upon hers, delicate and white on the table. The raucous sound of cascading coins from the nearby slot machine startled him and he then hid his hand underneath the table, the ghost of her skin still warming his fingers.

CHAPTER
TEN

Elspeth turned the key in the cafe door. She was almost an hour early — Stugly would have keeled over backwards if that had happened on his watch — but she was hoping to catch Cameron before the customers started flooding in. All she had to do was ask him, but would he say yes?

Carefully she stepped in so as not to knock the cake tin she was carrying. Cameron was sitting at a table, his head bent over scattered paperwork. As he looked up something flittered inside. How could he still do that to her after all these years? There was something about the first person you made love with. You were bonded for life. But she shouldn't be thinking about things like that. It wasn't right. She'd made her choice years ago, and was sticking to it.

"It's not even eight," he said with that smile of his.

"Thought I'd get on with things before the rush." She placed the tin on the table.

"Mr McSweetie rang to say the pendant's ready. Would you mind coming with me to collect it tomorrow morning? We'll open a bit later."

"Have you decided who you're giving it to?" She shouldn't have asked. It was none of her business if he were seeing someone. She loved Brodie and that was that.

"Thought I'd auction it for charity. Not sure which one yet."

She took off the lid. "I was wondering if we could sell these."

He leant over. "Monk biscuits? I haven't seen any for years."

"I thought the tourists might like them as they've been made in Nether Isla for centuries."

"I didn't realise people were still making them."

"There's only me left. When the bakery closed I dug out my great-grandmother's recipe. I didn't want the tradition dying out. People just buy those American cookies in the Co-op these days."

"I can smell the cinnamon and nutmeg from here." His familiar fingers were hovering over the tin. "Can I try one?"

She pushed it closer to him. Waiting for the right moment, she watched him eating. It was now or never. "I'm trying to save some money. For Maggie."

"You want to sell them here, and give the money to Maggie?"

She could feel in her cheeks the humiliation of having to ask. "Not give it to her, save it for her." It would take years, a few pennies here, a few pennies there, but it was only natural, wanting the best for your child, particularly if it was your fault. "I'm going to buy her a new prosthesis. The most advanced you can get." She raised her chin. "From America."

With the back of his hand, he brushed the crumbs off his lips. "Lovely as they are, you're going to have to sell a hell of a lot of them to buy a new prosthesis, Elspeth."

He thought she was mad, she knew it. But he didn't have a kid who came home crying because she couldn't play the recorder like everyone else at school.

"Do you really think she needs it? She's great as she is. I've seen her on her bike."

"She can't put the back brake on." She nudged the tin towards him. "I could make them here in the evenings. In a big batch fresh for the next day."

"I thought you cleaned people's houses in the evenings."

"Who told you that?" She could feel herself going red again.

He shrugged. "Nothing's a secret round here for long."

Unable to look at him, she drew out a chair at the next table and sat down. He knew what she'd become: a skivvy. All that scrimping her mother had done to help top up her grant while she was at university. All those years of studying to make a success of herself. Getting first-class honours. And now look at her.

"So can I sell them or not?" she said, her back to him. All she could hear was the tapping of his pen.

"The money from auctioning the pendant," he said. "It'll cover the prosthesis."

Heart tight, she turned. "But what about the charity?"

"It's all in the same spirit. And anyway, there might be something left over. I've no idea how much these things cost. We'll still sell the monk biscuits. The tourists will love them."

It was too much to take in. "You'd do that for Maggie?"

"I'm doing it for —"

The door opened.

"Can't believe it," said Alpina, squeezing her way through the tables. "I've just been interviewed by a Japanese TV crew. They wanted to know how things have changed in Nether Isla since the pearl rush. I told them to speak to Alan. He's renting out his coffins to tourists who can't find a bed anywhere. Fifteen quid a night."

Eyes on the mantelpiece clock, he fiddled with the loose threads hanging from his armchair. The story would definitely be in today. Ailsa had said the day after tomorrow. Unable to bear it any longer, he stood up. He'd go and see Mungo at the chippy while waiting for the *Chronicle* to be delivered. They'd sit in the back with a cup of tea before opening time, and he'd tell him all about the jammie. How there wasn't a single window on the factory floor in case someone tried to escape. How, just like a casino, there were no clocks on the walls so you wouldn't realise how much of your life you were wasting. But most of all he'd tell him, in the most glorious of details, about Dewi's boots.

As he pushed against the door to the chip shop, he couldn't even see the man for the rabble cluttering up the place. What the hell was this lot doing here anyway? It wasn't even time for elevenses yet. When he finally reached the front of the queue, he saw that Mungo was wearing a T-shirt emblazoned with the words: *I went to Nether Isla and all I found was the Frying Scotsman.*

"I waited for you in the Victoria last night."

"Couldn't make it." Mungo wiped his forehead with the end of his grimy apron. Even his ears looked tired. "I was here until midnight."

He rested an elbow on the counter. "In 1960 which country had the first ever woman prime minster?"

Mungo looked towards the back of the queue. "Half-price T-shirt with orders over a tenner," he called. "What are you after, Brodie? We've run out of haddock."

"While you're deciding, gimme some cod and fries — I mean chips," came an American woman's voice from behind.

"Want a clue?" Brodie said encouragingly.

Mungo's gaze drifted somewhere behind him.

"And one of those pickled eggs while you're at it," came the same voice. "I wanna see if they taste as bad as they look."

"What do you want, Brodie? Spam fritter? I've got to get on."

"Just wanted to say that I'll see you in the Victoria tonight. We'll have a game of Cluedo."

Mungo dumped a shovelful of chips onto a piece of paper, then balanced a piece of battered fish on top, its back arched as if in a death spasm.

"Salt and vinegar?"

"Just on the fries," said the woman.

168

He grabbed the maroon bottle and started shaking it. "Not tonight. I'm too busy here."

Brodie leant over and raised his eyebrows. "Ceylon. Otherwise known as?"

Mungo didn't even look up.

He fiddled with a pink plastic chip fork from the dispenser. "You'll never guess what Dewi was wearing yesterday."

"He was wearing them when he came in for his tea after work last night," said Mungo, stretching past him with the paper bundle. "It must have been about eleven. I tell you, we're both going to be retiring early at this rate."

The *Chronicle* caught underneath the door as he stepped in. He strode with it to the living room, where he settled himself into his comfy armchair, already feeling the relief of it all being over. It would be on the front page and everyone would finally go home. Sitting back, he turned over the paper. COUNCIL IN CORRUPTION SCANDAL said the headline. It was something to do with a building contract having gone to the leader's brother. Who cared about that? He snatched it open. They were still going on about it on the inside page, with more photographs of men in suits. Taking up the whole of page 3 was Horatio the tortoise, who'd been given a set of wheels after his back legs were gnawed off by rats while he was hibernating. Over the page was Dewi, standing in front of the jammie with both thumbs up wearing those ludicrous boots. He'd just received a huge order from America, according to the story, and was about to take on more staff. Frantically he flicked through the paper until he reached the stagnant backwaters of the obituaries, then tossed it on the floor. Not a single word.

Maggie poked her head out of her bedroom, and listened. She had to find somewhere to hide, otherwise she'd be forced to go with them to pick up Cameron's stupid pendant. From behind Mum and Dad's closed door came the sound of drawers opening and closing. It was now or never. The carpet felt all mushy as she stole down the landing. Suddenly the banging stopped, and she froze. There was no way Mum could catch her. As the wardrobe doors squeaked, she reached with her toes for the first step. Then the next. And the next. Silence again. She stopped, hand gripping the rail. What was Mum doing now? Holding her breath, she ran down the rest of the stairs and, careful of where she was stepping, opened the door of the cupboard under the stairs.

"What are you after in there?" said Mum, looking over the banister.

"My anorak."

"But it's sunny." She was coming down the stairs.

"My sandals, I meant."

In a pair of white jeans and a strappy top that showed her shoulders, Mum was now standing in the hall staring at the carpet.

"What are all these crisps doing on the floor?"

"Pickled onion. I'm trying to lure Frank out from wherever he is." She was about to get told off, she could tell by the way Mum was looking at the carpet.

A car horn sounded outside.

"He's here. Where are your shoes?"

"I can't come. Feel sick."

"Again?"

There was a warm pressing feeling as Mum clamped a hand against her forehead.

"You haven't got a temperature."

"It's just starting."

Mum felt the glands in her neck. "I'd better get you an appointment at the doctor's."

"I'll go back to bed. If it's not gone by this afternoon, then you can call the doctor."

Why was Mum smiling all of a sudden? She was meant to be feeling sorry for her. Telling her she'd stay at home and bring her up a dippy egg and toast soldiers like she always did when she was poorly. Not standing there with her hand over her mouth laughing like she did at one of Dad's rubbish jokes.

"Look, Maggie," she said, pointing to something inside the cupboard. "On top of the Hoover."

Her sandals? She turned to see what Mum was on about.

"Frank!"

It was the excitement that had done it. Everything had gone out of her head as she grabbed Frank and hugged him so tightly he tried to wriggle over her shoulder. Which was why she was now sitting in the back of Cameron's car on her way to Mr McSweetie's when she never wanted to go anywhere with him again.

"Are you sure it's all right for Frank to be in the car?" said Mum to Cameron.

"He already said it was." She sniffed Frank's velvety head. It was all warm and rabbity.

Cameron's eyes appeared in the little mirror. "So where's he been hiding all this time?"

She frowned. "Wasn't hiding. He went on holiday."

"Anywhere nice?"

"The cupboard under the stairs. Activity holiday."

Frank's heart was beating really fast against her lap. She wasn't getting out and they couldn't make her.

"You can't bring him into the jeweller's," said Mum. Her voice was all echoey as she stood next to Maggie's open door in the multi-storey car park. "I've already explained."

"Your mother's got a point," said Cameron next to her, his hands on his hips. "Mr McSweetie doesn't exactly strike me as a bunny-hugger."

"If Frank stays, I stay."

Mum hoisted her handbag higher into her armpit. "I'm not leaving you here on your own."

She pointed to the gearstick, up to its neck in cream leather. "Frank'll chew that thing if we leave him in the car. He hasn't had his lunch."

Cameron dropped his arms. "We'll bring the rabbit."

"What's with the moustache?" Mr McSweetie fingered his throat as he peered. "Is it the result of some sort of in-breeding?"

172

She clutched Frank even tighter, his fur warm between her fingers. Her arms were really aching after carrying him all the way from the car park. Why couldn't they just go home?

"We don't allow animals in the shop, I'm afraid," said Mr McSweetie, a red handkerchief, the same colour as his tie, sprouting out of his jacket pocket. "There's the carpet to consider, as well as the comfort of the other customers."

"He's not touching the carpet," she said.

"We couldn't leave the thing in the BMW," said Cameron. "There's a gnawing issue."

Mum's handbag landed on the counter with a small thud. "We've come to pick up the pendant. I understand it's ready."

"Certainly. I'll just get it out of the safe." His hairy fingers slid down the front of his tie. "How's Brodie, by the way? I haven't seen him for a while."

"About to start work at the jammie, poor sod," said Cameron.

Mum smiled the way she did when she didn't want her photo taken. "Just until things calm down again."

Palms on the glass counter, Mr McSweetie looked down at her. "And both you and your dad saw the big pearl dropping out of its shell? It must have been quite something." He paused. "To see it."

One of Frank's paws slipped from her arms. Why was he going on about seeing the pearl fall out? He'd asked her that the last time.

"Mum, can me and Frank wait outside? I've got a headache."

"You couldn't believe the size of it, could you, Maggie?" said Cameron. "Neither of them could. Did I tell you how it happened? About the storm? We'd just filled our bags and —"

"When does the ticket for the car park run out?" said Mum. "I think we only paid for half an hour."

"You weren't there, were you, Mrs McBride? When Cameron found his pearl."

"Missed all the excitement, I'm afraid."

"Thought not." He took off his glasses and started wiping them on a little yellow cloth. His eyes were so small it was like he hadn't slept all year.

"Mum, can I take Frank outside?" She was going to drop him any minute.

"Not on your own. We won't be long."

"Can't wait to see it." Cameron patted the back of Mum's hand. "You could try it on, Elspeth. See what it looks like."

"I'll just fetch it," said Mr McSweetie, his eyes twice the size again. He reached for the black curtain behind him. "Do take a seat."

Settled in the red leather chairs next to the counter, Mum and Cameron started talking about school again. When she was a grown-up she'd never talk about school. It was really, really boring. She carried Frank to the window display and lifted up one of his ears. "I'll show you the pearls Dad found."

Standing on her toes, she pointed his nose at the necklaces, earrings and brooches arranged to face the street, and then at the label above them saying "Scottish River Pearls".

"Did Brodie really find all those pearls?" said Cameron, standing next to her. "Surely the part-timers must have found some of them."

"The lady from the paper said Scotland should be proud of him because he hasn't given up."

"What lady from the paper?" said Mum, joining them.

"The one he invited into his hut."

"He invited a woman into his hut?"

"Come and look at these diamonds, Elspeth. The size of them."

Frank started to scrabble, digging his nails into her. Unable to hold him any longer, she lowered him to the ground, where he started to sniff the carpet like it was a TV aerial cable. Just as she was about to pick him up again there was a flash of white tail as he leapt across the floor, and disappeared underneath the curtain.

What had he done that for? He wasn't allowed behind there. Mum and Cameron hadn't noticed, so she crawled after him, lay down on her tummy, and slowly lifted the black edge. Those were Mr McSweetie's feet walking around in his hard, shiny shoes. The trainers belonged to Freddie, the boy with the spots who helped him. Much older than she was, he was sitting on a stool at the work table, putting something into a tiny plastic bag. And there was Frank washing his face underneath the table as if he wasn't trespassing.

"I must say, we're doing quite well out of it. All these people suddenly bringing in pearls," said Mr McSweetie. "Though unfortunately the quality's not always there."

If Freddie didn't stop swinging his massive red trainer back and forth he'd kick Frank any minute.

"The gold one the Irish woman brought in yesterday wasn't bad," he said.

Flat on her belly, Maggie could hear a clicking sound as Mr McSweetie started turning the dial on the safe. "This whole business with Cameron Wallace puts me in a very awkward position. A very awkward position indeed."

"Are you sure about it?"

"Of course I'm sure," he said crossly. "I saw the white bead through the hole after I'd drilled it. It's an Akoya pearl. All the way from Japan."

Her heart started banging against the carpet.

The safe door opened. "Brodie was quoted in the paper saying he'd seen it come out of the shell. I've known him thirty years, and never had a reason not to trust him. And his daughter said she saw it drop out of the shell too."

"Do you think they're all in on it, then?" said Freddie, taking a swig from his mug.

"I've no idea, but I'm not getting involved. They came in to get it made into a pendant, not for me to authenticate it. Like I said before, don't mention it to anyone or the pearl hunters will leave. God help whoever's behind it if folk ever find out it's a cultured oyster pearl."

She felt sick. He was talking about her. Everyone was going to find out what she'd done, including taking the money. She was exactly that horrible word that Samantha Grey always called her.

CHAPTER
ELEVEN

"Wrong entrance," said the receptionist. She stabbed a bitten pen in the direction of the other end of the building. "Staff use the door round the back."

"But I came in this way last week," said Brodie, trying a smile.

"This one's for management and visitors only."

But it was different for him, didn't she see? On countless bowel-cementing occasions he'd endured Dewi's fondue. He'd seen him pottering around the garden in nothing but his flapping dressing gown. He even knew what the man cried out when he made love to his wife, for goodness' sake. You couldn't exactly call him staff, more a friend of the family.

"Thought I'd say hello to Dewi before starting," he said chummily. "Have a cup of tea with him."

She sat back and folded her fleshy arms, her blackbird eyes on him. "He's in a breakfast meeting with the chairman. Report to Doreen, round there. The door with all the fag ends on the ground."

Through the trampled butts he trudged, and yanked at the handle. Inside, it was just like the cloakroom at school, that other prison. Along the rows of pegs and benches was that undeniable whiff of fetid socks

177

withering at the bottom of a laundry basket. Several blank-faced workers were feeding their hair into nets.

Brodie slipped off his jacket and hung it on the nearest peg.

"You can't put it there, that's Angus's," said a man with a greasy ponytail.

He moved it down one.

"That's Sheila's," piped up a woman.

For God's sake. He chose another.

"Not that one, it's mine."

It was Andy Brady. One of the numpties who'd blown up the frogs in biology. He'd lost his hair and gained several stone, but it was him all right.

Brodie shrugged. "Does it matter?"

"I've had it for eighteen years. Which section are you working in?"

"Sorting."

He pointed to a peg. "That one's free. In the corner." From a locker he took out a navy coat and passed it to him. "Should fit. You'll need a pair of Wellingtons. Take the pair on the rack underneath the peg. They were Christine's. Feet the size of Atlantic tuna."

Brodie picked them up, and studied the sweat-stained soles. "Won't she need them?" he said hopefully.

"No longer with us."

"I thought no one ever left this place."

"Died on the job. Face down in a pile of blackberries."

He'd already caught athlete's foot, he could tell. As he slapped his way through the puddles to the sorting table, the two women he'd seen last week looked up, pale as undertakers in the brutal glare of the strip lighting.

"I'm Moira," said the really short one. "You're lucky you didn't end up in labelling."

With her prominent teeth, and tiny gloved hands clutched in front of her, he couldn't help thinking of a water vole.

"Doreen," said the one with the moles and no eyebrows. "You're better off with us."

Like terriers at a rabbit hole, the women started scrabbling through a mound of frozen strawberries. From a dispenser on the wall, he helped himself to a pair of latex gloves, and started poking through the cold pile.

"You'll soon pick it up," said Doreen. "Just watch Moira. She's a natural. Found the big five within her first year, didn't you, Moira?"

"Big five?" he said. "Like on safari?"

Doreen counted them on her fingers. "Whitefly, weevil, caterpillar, aphid and beetle."

Moira blinked rapidly, and for one awful moment he thought she was about to burst into tears.

"Very kind of you to say so, Doreen, but Christine was always the best."

"God rest that woman's soul. She could detect the presence of a weevil at fifty yards. Nothing with a set of teeth dared enter her garden."

"Except poor Tom."

"Poor Tom."

"Mind you, I think his are false. Did they bury her in her boots after all? She always said she wanted to be."

"Couldn't have," said Doreen, indignant. "This one's got them on."

Moira's eyes fell to Brodie's feet, then studied him as if he'd torn open Christine's coffin and yanked the boots off her corpse's feet.

"At least it was blackberries," said Doreen. "It's my only comfort."

"Her favourite. Never minded the bits in her teeth."

There was a pause.

"Don't worry, Brodie," said Doreen. "One day, you too could be as good as Christine. Might take you thirty years, but you'll get there."

"No offence, but no one will ever be as good as Christine. She could find a strawberry husk blindfolded."

"Like this?" He held one up.

There was a horrible pause as both women looked at it incredulously.

"Beginner's luck," said Doreen. "Like Cameron Wallace and that pearl."

Moira nodded. "The one you missed."

After what seemed like hours a siren began to wail, so invasive and persistent Brodie wondered whether a bomb was about to drop.

"Morning tea break." Doreen snapped off her gloves. "You've got to be fast. We only get fifteen minutes."

A cup of tea. He couldn't think of anything he wanted more. Gloves pulled off, he raced after her, his hair lunging back and forth in its net. He soon found himself in a large room, which, with its "No Smoking" sign and rows of plastic tables and chairs, had the desolate air of a railway waiting room. A queue of workers, all in navy coats, lingered at a hole in the wall where a short, stout woman with a phenomenally large chest was pouring tea from an equally outsized kettle.

"You'd better bring in your own tea tomorrow," said Doreen, sitting down. "By the time you get served it'll be time to get back to work. Labelling always gets to the front of the queue first. We've been complaining about it for almost forty years, but no one listens."

He swallowed, drily. He had to get some air. See the sky. Even a tree would do. "I think I'll go for a walk outside."

"Not allowed."

Moira appeared with a Thermos flask and he watched silently as she poured out two cups of strong, hot tea. The kind you'd kill for. Just as he was wondering if they locked the doors so that no one could walk out, he spotted a copy of the *Chronicle* on the next table. The story was supposed to have been in last Wednesday. Today was Monday. In a second he was on his feet, grabbing the paper. He couldn't believe it. It was on the front page. There was even a quote from PC Gibbons saying that measures were being put in place to monitor all the pearl rivers in Scotland. Finally, it was going to end. Next week, once everyone had left, he'd tell Dewi he was jumping ship. He could see himself standing in a pretty burn, the sun on his face, listening to the scramble of the water. Just the thought of it made him feel as if someone had opened a window.

A freckled hand grabbed his arm. "There's something you ought to know."

It was Stugly in the same uniform as everyone else, those teeth of his too close to his ear for his liking.

"If it's about Christine's athlete's foot, I know." He tossed the paper onto the table.

"It's got nothing to do with fungus." He was looking around like he was a double agent or something. "Can't tell you in here. Some of these women have got better hearing than bats." He jerked his head. "Come with me."

Brodie followed him as he walked along a corridor in that hunched way of his, as if it were always raining. Eventually he came to a halt outside the development kitchen, and, with a glance over his shoulder, started tapping at the keypad on the wall.

"I thought that number was more closely guarded than a nuclear launch code," said Brodie.

"Everything has its price."

As the door closed behind them, he found himself in a small, clinical kitchen with a stove covered in copper pans. On the table were several open notebooks, and a stack of coloured files. Stugly walked over and started inspecting them.

"You're not selling information to the competition, are you?" He'd been joking, but there was something about the look on Stugly's face that made him think he'd hit the nail on the head. "I'd watch it, if I were you. You could start a jam war if you're not careful. Things could get very . . . sticky."

"How else are you meant to earn a living in this place? I presume you know how much we get paid? And there's Dewi swanning around in that great big Peugeot of his."

"If it's any consolation, I reversed into it last month."

"He's another one, Cameron."

Brodie put his hands on his hips. "Whoever works in here will be coming back from their break any minute now."

"Can't believe how much I sold that cafe for. It only covered my debts. Look at it now. Heaving."

"What is it you wanted to tell me?"

Stugly was smiling in that treacly way of his that didn't do him any favours.

"Make it quick, for God's sake."

"You know the pearl Cameron found . . ."

That. It was the last thing he wanted to talk about. He opened the door, but Stugly slammed it closed again.

"It didn't come from a river."

He'd dragged him all the way here just to come up with that? "I've got to go, it's my first day."

"It's cultured."

The man was being ridiculous. He reached again for the handle.

"Apparently they put a bead inside an oyster and leave it in the sea until the oyster's covered it with nacre so that it looks like a pearl. The jeweller saw the bead through the drill hole when he was making it into a necklace."

He smiled. "I know how cultured oyster pearls are made, thanks, Stugly."

"I'm being serious. Freddie told me. We're in the same cricket team. He got hammered in the pub last night and rang me this morning to say he wasn't meant to tell anyone, and that I should keep it to myself or he might lose his job. Thought you ought to know, considering."

"I know Freddie. He was pulling your leg."

"Ask that jeweller, Mr McSweetie, if you don't believe me."

"I saw Cameron open the shell, for God's sake."

"Bet he thought no one would notice. Thinks he's such a hotshot swanning around in his Ralph Lauren T-shirts and BMW. I remember when he didn't even have a bike."

Brodie snatched open the door. "Like I said, I saw it drop out of the shell. We all did." As he stood in the corridor, he suddenly realised he was lost. It *was* impossible, wasn't it?

Her fingers were really hurting, she was holding on so tightly. Why did the cars have to pass so close to her? They kept making her wobble. She wasn't allowed to go this far on her bike, but if she stayed at home Mr McSweetie might knock on the door and ask her what she'd done. Just the thought of it made her want to cry. She'd chosen the only big pearl in the shop that was the same colour as the ones in Dad's tin. The lustre was lovely. Everyone was supposed to believe it was a river pearl as it had come out of a mussel. How was she to know that you could tell it was cultured when you drilled it?

Crouched over the handlebars, she pedalled faster, the tyres skimming the grass verge as she tried to keep in. Frank, huddled in the basket at the front, raised his head, ears fluttering behind him like a magic carpet. Her legs started to feel hot inside as she pressed down even harder on the pedals, her prosthesis resting on the left handle. She knew what she'd do — she'd take the pearl pendant and hide it. That way no one else would find out that it was cultured and then everything would go away. It was wrong to steal, but she'd already taken Mrs Campbell's money, and one more thing wouldn't count as it was connected. God would know it was. And anyway, the pearl was Dad's, not Cameron's.

Her cheeks started to judder as she dragged both heels on the ground. Eventually she came to a stop, and, buffeted by the passing cars, she waited for a gap in the traffic. In a long, slow, shaky circle she turned round and headed back the way she came. Dad had bought her this bike. It was second-hand, but it was still beautiful. It had taken him ages to get it. Mum said it was too dangerous for her to ride one, but Dad told her it would be all right as long as she stayed in their road. You were meant to do what your mum and dad said, but it wasn't your fault if sometimes your legs pedalled really fast because you were brilliant at running and the road come to an end so you had to turn into another one.

She managed to keep her balance as she turned into the narrow alley that ran down the backs of the houses. Moments from home, she began to speed up again. There was someone ahead of her. Samantha Grey with that horrid dog. She was just standing there in a blue dress, her dark hair tied in a ponytail, not getting out of the way. If they didn't move she'd crash into them. Any second now. They were still blocking the way. She squeezed the brake and instantly rose with the back end of the bike, plunging over the handlebars.

All she could hear was the whirring of a wheel as it spun round and round. Everything seemed to hurt. She opened her eyes. A pair of white legs with no socks. The bike was lying on top of her, and her prosthesis had come off. She could tell Samantha Grey was staring at her stump with its tiny fingers at the end, as small as baby's toes. When she lifted her head, it felt like someone had kicked it. Her prosthesis had landed in a clump of stinging nettles next to the fence. What about Frank?

"Serves you right for cycling along here. You're not allowed. The sign says."

The dog lurched towards her, pulling on its lead as it barked, its rubbery black mouth so close she could smell its horrible breath. It was going to bite her. A movement caught her eye. Frank was running down the alley, his white tail flashing up and down. Where was he going?

"Is that what your mum and dad bought you? A giant hairy rat?"

186

From underneath the bike she pulled out her legs, staggering as she stood. She hauled it up by the twisted handlebars, and listened to the feeble clanking as she began to push it home.

"That animal's disgusting. Just like you. No wonder it ran away from you."

Her head thumped even more as she bent down, picked up her prosthesis and dropped it into the empty basket. As she limped towards the back gate, her sandal with its broken strap flopped against the ground. The witch had better not say it, not after Dad told her not to. Then it came, loud enough for the whole world to hear.

"Spazza!"

"But I don't want to go to Mrs Wallace's house," said Alice, lying back on her purple duvet. Above her was the poster of the Spice Girls Maggie had given her for Christmas. "I thought we were going to do our hair and make-up."

Her knee still aching from earlier, Maggie sat down on the edge of the bed. "She's got a brand-new stairlift. We'll be able to have a ride on it."

Alice propped herself up on her elbows. "How fast does it go?"

"Dunno, haven't seen it yet. We might have to wear a helmet."

"But the rollers are ready." Alice nodded to the dressing table with its three-sided mirror where she hung all her necklaces. "Look, the red light's on."

"We'll get a Wagon Wheel. Sometimes Mrs Wallace forgets she's already given me one, so I get two."

"Don't like them." There was a thump as Alice fell on her back again.

"You used to."

"Don't any more."

Alice had to come with her and keep Mrs Wallace busy while she searched for the pendant.

"She's got this old cabinet with special things inside."

"Like what?"

"A witch's tears."

Alice lifted her head. "Real ones?"

"Says on the label."

She was up on her elbows again. "What colour?"

"Bit silvery."

She frowned. "Everyone says she's weird. And anyway, we're not going to have time to do both. I've got to be at my dad's later and the rollers have to stay in for at least twenty minutes, otherwise they don't work."

"We'll go and see Mrs Wallace while they're working." She shrugged, like nothing could be simpler. "Then we'll take them out when we get back and you'll look lovely for your dad."

Alice's forehead creased. "My dad told me I look too much like my mum to be pretty."

Dad never said that to her. He always said she was as beautiful as Mum, and Mum was the most beautiful person in Scotland. She could feel the heat of the curlers as she lifted the lid. "I'm going to make you look like Princess Diana."

"Mum says the shop's doing so well we can go to Spain on holiday," said Alice, a roller swinging by her ear as they walked down the high street. She looked really lovely already. She'd given Alice lots and lots of black eyeliner and blue eyeshadow.

"Spain." Just saying it made her feel special.

"You don't have to eat their food. They have proper cooked breakfasts with bacon and eggs and everything. Mum said."

"Will there be a pool?"

She nodded. "And a beach."

The curlers rattling against her head was making it even sorer. "How long for?"

"Two weeks."

Without her for two weeks.

"What have you done to your knee?"

She looked down at the red graze, still full of dirt, that she'd tried to cover with blue plasters. "Fell off my bike."

"Must have really hurt."

Silence.

"How's Frank?"

She should have waited for a goldfish. They couldn't run away from you no matter how much you loved them. "Dunno."

"No one's in," said Alice. "Let's go."

"It always takes her ages to open it."

Eventually there was the sound of shuffling, and Mrs Wallace's face appeared at the door. The skin on her neck was too big for her, like she'd borrowed someone else's. Her eyes moved between her and Alice.

"I was wondering if I could show Alice the witch's tears."

"Do I know you?" Mrs Wallace peered at her.

"It's me, Maggie. This is Alice. My best friend." Her only friend, but she didn't like to say.

"Sorry, I didn't recognise you, Maggie, with all that make-up. Come in, come in."

She waited underneath the buffalo head in the hall while Mrs Wallace shut the door. It always smelt funny in here, like the blankets Mum put on her bed when it snowed. Once told to go through, she took her usual place at the end of the green sofa next to the fire. Alice sat down so close to her they were touching.

"Orange squash, girls?"

They nodded.

As soon as Mrs Wallace had left the room, she jumped up. The walls were covered in glass cases filled with stiff birds standing by nests, dressed kittens playing musical instruments and brightly coloured butterflies resting on branches. No matter how long you looked at them they never moved because they were all dead. Cameron could have hidden the pendant anywhere. She could be here a whole week and never find it. What had she been thinking?

From a side table she grabbed a tiny silver box, wedged it between her elbow and body, and tried to open it.

"What are you doing?" hissed Alice. "She's coming back."

"Just wondered what's inside."

The sound of slippers sliding down the hall was getting louder. If she could just get this stupid lid open! She tried again and a gold coin dropped to the floor. Just as Mrs Wallace appeared, she sat down and hid the box underneath the green velvet cushion next to her.

Mrs Wallace put the drinks on the coffee table, then reached into the pocket of her flowery pinny. "Wagon Wheel, girls?"

"No, thanks," said Alice, her hands tucked between her thighs.

As she began to nibble the huge biscuit, Maggie reached out a foot and started dragging the coin towards her.

There was a thump as Mrs Wallace sat down. "How's that new dog of yours, lassie? I saw you taking it for a bicycle ride earlier."

Her foot stopped. "It's not a dog, it's a rabbit."

Mrs Wallace blinked. "I thought it was some sort of basset hound."

There was a knock on the door.

"More journalists, I expect," said Mrs Wallace, not moving. "There was a pair round this morning from some magazine in Canada. Apparently they have lots of pearl mussels over there too."

"Did you show them the pendant?" She'd said it too quickly.

"They wanted to take a photograph of it, but I told them they'd have to speak to Cameron. I've no idea where it is. I offered to show them the garden instead. Didn't like the idea of them coming all this way for nothing."

The doorbell sounded this time.

"I'll just get rid of them." Mrs Wallace pushed hard against the armrests as she got to her feet.

"Come on," said Alice, once they were alone. "I'll be late for my dad and get into trouble."

Maggie fumbled the coin back into the box, and returned it to the side table. Maybe the pendant was in Cameron's knicker drawer. Mum kept all her jewellery in hers because it was rude for burglars to look inside.

"Is it all right if Alice sees the little bottle with the witch's tears inside?" she said as Mrs Wallace shuffled back in. "In the cabinet. The curious one."

"My cabinet of curiosities? Come with me, Alice." She headed out again. "It's in my bedroom. Unfortunately the stairlift's out of action. I broke it yesterday afternoon while I was trying it out. Cameron said it was to get me up the stairs, not a fairground ride."

A hand on each banister, Mrs Wallace started to climb, one furry slipper at a time.

"It's going to take ages," hissed Alice.

"She always speeds up nearer the top."

Once they were all finally upstairs, Maggie hesitated on the landing. "I'm just going to the loo."

"Right you are, lassie. You know where it is. I've just put out a new roll."

She slipped into the spare room where a pile of folded clothes was stacked on the neatly made single bed. A can of deodorant stood on the dressing table next to a spill of loose change and a hairbrush. Her heart was beating so fast that even Mrs Wallace might hear it. Where did he keep his knickers? A white mothball rolled from side to side as she pulled open the dressing-table drawer.

Where? Where? The chest of drawers. She grabbed one of the top rings and tugged. Pants. Loads of them. They were nothing like Dad's. Cameron's had other people's names on them like Hugo Boss. She reached in and groped around the back. Nothing. As she tried the other corner, her thumb brushed against something hard, a box maybe. She grabbed it.

"What's that you've found, lassie?"

She jumped. Mrs Wallace was standing next to her. One by one she opened her fingers.

"Condoms," said Mrs Wallace. "What on earth does Cameron need them for?"

CHAPTER
TWELVE

"Where are you going?"

One foot halfway into his jeans, Brodie staggered at the sound of her voice, still soft with sleep. He'd been woken at dawn by a jolt to the heart as if someone had fired a gun next to his head. For hours he'd just lain there turning over what Stugly had told him, like a cat worrying a dead mouse. He couldn't stand it any longer. He had to know.

"Won't be long." He climbed into his trousers.

Head raised, Elspeth was trying to get a better look at him in the needle pricks of light piercing the curtains. "I thought we might have a cooked breakfast," she said in that disappointed way that always made him feel guilty. "All three of us. Like we used to."

The zip on his trousers finally moved, and he felt his pockets for his keys.

"Cameron's got a Saturday girl," she said. "I'm not going in today. Thought I told you."

Silence.

"Where are you going?"

It was louder this time, more insistent.

"Perth."

"Maybe we can all go," she said, brightening. "Cheer up Maggie. I still don't understand how she could fall over in the garden and graze her knee so badly."

He groped for some socks in his drawer. "Not today."

"We could have breakfast there in that nice cafe with the scrubbed tables." She was sitting up now, one of her nightie straps hanging off her shoulder, seeing how the morning was going to pan out. "It would be nice to be waited on for a change."

The hangers screeched as he chose a shirt. "I'll bring you a cup of tea in bed. Before I go."

"But you still haven't told me where you're going."

"Got to see Mr McSweetie," he said, chin to chest as he did up his shirt buttons.

She smiled. "Have you got some pearls to sell?"

He reached for the door.

The bairn was lying facing the wall, tangled blonde hair scattered over her pillow. He could tell she was awake by her twitching toes. She'd taken off the nail polish, leaving a faint red residue.

"Maggie?"

Silence.

"I'll help you look for Frank again when I get back."

The small lump under the duvet covered with flying hippos didn't move.

"I'm just going to see Mr McSweetie."

She turned round, startled. "What for?"

"Nothing important. We'll ask some of the neighbours when I get back. The Greys might have seen him. They're always walking that hideous dog of theirs along the back."

"Frank's dead," she said to the wall.

There was nothing he could do when she was like this. He headed for the door.

"Dad?"

"Yes."

"What's condoms?"

He stopped. "Condoms?"

She lifted her head. Her face was spongy, like she'd been crying. "They were in Mrs Wallace's house."

He frowned. "Mrs Wallace has condoms?"

"They're Cameron's. She said I had to ask you what they're for if I didn't know."

"I need a doppelgänger," he said as the lunatic budgies started to shriek.

The assistant continued feeding a piece of apple to a silent reptile clutching her shoulder. He glanced at his watch. Once he'd sorted out Maggie, he'd go to the jeweller's. Be there the moment it opened. Get Mr McSweetie on his own and find out once and for all whether it was true.

"We don't stock doppelgängers, I'm afraid," she said, still gazing at the scaly thing with the tail. "I could try calling head office if you like, to see whether we can order one, but they probably wouldn't answer the phone."

"That rabbit you sold me. I need another one. Exactly the same."

196

There was a creepy tap of claws as she set the creature down on the counter where it remained suspiciously still. She then pointed to one of the cages behind her. "What about that one?"

Brodie peered. "Fur's too neat. It's got to give the impression that it's just stuck its front paws in a toaster."

"That one?"

"Looks too much like a rabbit. Wrong colour anyway."

"The one to the left?"

"Too cute. Should have a sanctimonious air. Like it would rather be reading Proust."

"How's about the one in the top hutch?"

He shook his head. "The ears aren't right. They need to hang down like two deflated barrage balloons. And a moustache. It definitely needs to have a moustache."

"What sort?"

"Tom Selleck."

The monster on the counter was now looking at him.

The assistant shrugged. "Nothing with a moustache. Could possibly get you a bearded collie. Again, that would be a head office situation. I wouldn't recommend it."

He blinked.

"What about a bearded dragon?" She pointed to the reptile still staring at him. "Ever so affectionate."

He hadn't got time for this. He needed to see Mr McSweetie and get what Stugly had said out of his head. Finally be able to sleep at night. "What about that one directly behind you? It's the right colour."

197

"Short-haired version of the last one you bought. No moustache."

"What's it doing to that other rabbit?"

She tilted her head to one side. "Looks like it's been reading *Lady Chatterley's Lover*."

"I'll take it." He flapped his hand in its direction. "The one doing that thing."

This wasn't happening. A woman with bare shoulders and a pair of sunglasses on top of her head was talking to Mr McSweetie. It had only just gone half past nine. He'd run all the way from the car. Eyeing him for a sign, he sank down onto one of the red leather armchairs while Mr McSweetie continued talking to her in that ingratiating way of his. The same one he used for Elspeth so she wouldn't go to one of the dealers in Edinburgh.

His fingers traced the brass studs on the armrests. Why was she taking so long to choose a pair of earrings? Of course her niece would like them. Just buy the sodding things and get out.

Brodie got to his feet. "They're beautiful," he said, hoping that it would put an end to the matter.

Her eyes travelled up to his hair. "Do you really think so? I was wondering whether silver would suit her better."

He shook his head. "Gold. Classical."

"Not too cheap-looking?" She held one against her ear.

"She'll know they weren't cheap by the name on the box. There's a reason why Mr McSweetie drives a Mercedes with a personalised number plate."

198

Once she'd left, he stood at the counter while Mr McSweetie cleared it of everything she'd rejected.

"You've got some pearls for me, I hope," he said with a smile.

"I've heard a rumour."

His hands stopped. "If it's about the woman from the golf club, we're just friends."

"It's about that pearl."

He cocked his head. "Which pearl?"

"Cameron Wallace's."

Something moved in his neck as he looked down and continued placing the earrings back inside the counter. "What about it?"

"Apparently it's cultured."

The door opened and a white-haired man in a striped shirt came in. He hesitated, then turned his back and started looking at the window display.

"Forgive me, Brodie, but I need to attend to my customer. It's been very nice to see you, I must say. Bring some pearls with you next time."

"Is that pearl cultured?" It came out as a low hiss.

Silence.

"I asked you a question."

Still he didn't say anything.

"There are other dealers I can take my pearls to, you know."

Mr McSweetie glanced at the customer, then leant forward. "Mr Wallace brought in a pearl to be made into a pendant," he said in a short, sharp whisper. "I carried out his request. He didn't enquire as to its provenance."

"Well, I am."

He fiddled with his glasses. "I only realised when I drilled it."

"Why the hell didn't you say anything? People have been tearing up mussel colonies all over Scotland for the last two weeks." His voice was getting louder. "You could have said something over a week ago when they came to collect the pendant. You didn't want anyone to know, that's why. Wanted everyone to keep bringing you more pearls."

"As I said," he whispered, "I just did what Mr Wallace asked me to do and I made it into a pendant. He didn't ask me for authentication."

There was a nasty silence.

"I'll be with you in a moment, sir."

"Don't mind me," came the reply.

"You ought to take a long hard look at yourself," said Brodie.

"Forget about me. The question is who would be idiotic enough to put a cultured oyster pearl into the shell of a river mussel?"

"How the hell should I know?"

"I'd find out, if I were you, before everyone thinks it was you. Something tells me this isn't going to end well."

In the savage glare of the sun, he pushed through the shoppers on his way back to the car park. He had to speak to Cameron. It was grotesque what that man had done. Thousands of people were destroying the mussel beds for nothing. It was the biggest pearl rush in living memory. Reporters had come from all over the world to cover it. It wasn't even as if Cameron needed the money. It must have been some sort of ploy to get Elspeth back. Prove to her that he was better than him. That she'd married the wrong one.

"Brodie!"

Disorientated, he turned.

"Did you see the story in the paper finally?"

He shielded his eyes. It was Ailsa. Smiling.

"It got held up by all that council stuff. The editor wanted it on the front page."

He said nothing.

"Are you all right?" She placed a hand on his arm.

A thin woman was pulling a tartan shopping trolley with a white sliced loaf on top. Across the street a man in a pair of trousers that were too short for him was hurrying to the post office with a parcel. Both of them going about their business as if nothing had happened. No one had a clue what that man had done. No one. He'd duped the whole world. "I've got to go and speak to someone."

"If it's Cameron Wallace, he's just been in."

His eyes found her then.

"He wanted some publicity for the auction."

"What auction?"

"For the pearl pendant. Thought it was really nice of him to buy Maggie a new prosthesis with the money he raises. You must be thrilled."

"He's dead." With her stone she scratched more white scars onto the back step. "I'm not looking for him."

"We've been keeping the gate open, just in case he comes back," said Mum, sitting down next to her. "He might be behind the hut where all the dandelion leaves are."

"Doesn't like them."

"We could go for a walk when Dad comes back from Perth and see if we can find something for your flower press. It's a lovely day. We'll take a picnic."

"Don't feel like it."

"Then why don't you go and see Alice? You could do each other's hair again. It looked lovely the last time she did it."

She scratched even harder. "No, it didn't. Samantha Grey shouted 'Bog-brush head' through the letter-box when I walked past."

Mum put her arm round her. "I've got some good news for you. Cameron's going to sell the pearl pendant in an auction. Lots of people will try and buy it, so the price will go up and he'll make a lot of money. He said he'd like to buy you a new prosthesis with it, the best we can get — from America. We could go over there and have it fitted. Have a little holiday. You'll get to fly in a plane!"

The stone rattled on the paving as she dropped it.

"Isn't that nice of him?"

Nice? It was terrible. Loads of people would see the pearl and someone else might realise it hadn't come from the Isla. Then everyone would guess that it was her. The whole world would know what she'd done, how bad she was. That she was a complete and utter spazza.

202

Brodie switched off the engine outside the house and stared through the windscreen. He could see it all. Cameron opening the shell with a knife while Mungo was distracted. Taking the cultured pearl out of his pocket and slipping it inside. Meeting him and Maggie on the bank. Agreeing to open his shells under the bridge, then the satisfaction of finding the pearl in front of *him*. That sick way he pretended to be surprised when it dropped into his palm.

Hands still on the steering wheel, he played it back, watching it again and again, each time the scenes more vivid, more abhorrent. Eventually he could stand it no longer, and he got out. For a moment he stood gazing at Mrs Wallace's house. Some things you just couldn't forgive.

Standing in the hall, claws as sharp as fish hooks piercing his shirtsleeves, he listened for the sound of Maggie running towards him. Nothing. With his foot he slowly pushed open the living-room door. Slumped on the sofa, chin to her chest, she was staring at the still-dead television.

"Look who I found!" he said, holding the impostor aloft in his arms.

"Frank!" She got to her feet.

The cry must have roused Elspeth, as she was now standing next to him, fingers grey with modelling clay.

As Maggie took a step towards him, the corners of her mouth fell. "Where's his moustache? And all his fur?"

"Wasn't very clean when I found him," he said gravely. "His fur was all matted. I took him to the dog parlour for a spruce-up, but they couldn't fit him in, so I went to the barber in Blairgowrie instead. The apprentice went a bit mad with the electric razor. Don't worry, the moustache will grow back. He'll be looking like Fu Manchu by the end of the month."

She seemed doubtful.

"I'll grow one too. We'll do it together. Shoulder to shoulder."

"But his ears look all funny."

"So would yours if you'd been given a buzz cut."

She hesitated, then took the rabbit in her arms and buried her nose in its neck. A frown. "Doesn't smell like Frank."

"That's because they had to give him a good wash in the basin with loads of shampoo," he said, resting a casual hand against the door frame. "They even got the conditioner out. Like I said, he was really grubby when I found him. He must have been trying to tunnel his way back to you."

With a smile, she carried him back to the sofa and started stroking his head. He turned to Elspeth, ready for a kiss of gratitude, but she jerked her head towards the kitchen in an *I need a word in private* sort of way. He trailed in after her, not liking the way she closed the door behind them.

"Fu Manchu?" she said, hands on her hips.

He bent down towards whatever the hell it was she was sculpting on the table. "Looks like the Parthenon," he said hopefully. "That must be the temple of Athena Nike."

"What are you planning to do? Buy a fake moustache from the joke shop and stick it on that poor animal?"

"There's magic in the world, Elspeth. You just have to be willing to see it."

Silence, apart from the muttering of the fridge.

He shrugged. "I was just trying to make her feel better. Isn't that what fathers are supposed to do?"

"By lying to her?"

"She's only a kid. They're meant to be happy."

"Children need to learn that sometimes there just isn't a happy ending."

He knew all about that.

She started wiping her hands on some kitchen roll. "You're going to have to tell her it's not Frank. Before it goes any further."

"But look how pleased she is. I haven't seen her smile for ages."

"How do you think she's going to feel when that moustache doesn't grow back?"

"I'll just say it was the shock of it all. That he's got alopecia."

She blinked.

"Anyway," he said dismissively. "You'd better sit down. There's something you need to know, and you're not going to like it."

She stayed where she was.

"Cameron. He's auctioning that pearl pendant of his, and went and told the *Chronicle* he's going to buy Maggie a new prosthesis with the money. I can't believe the cheek of the man. What makes him think he can interfere in other people's lives? He didn't even have the courtesy to ask us."

She sat down. "He asked me."

"He asked *you*?"

"About a week ago. I was going to tell you, but I wasn't certain whether it was the right thing to accept it. I only told Maggie this morning to cheer her up. I wasn't expecting him to go the paper."

"He asked you?"

"She'll be able to pick things up."

He couldn't even tell her the worst of it. Not yet. He'd take it up with Cameron first, make him confess. She'd believe it then. "I don't want you working in that cafe any more."

"Why not?"

"Trust me."

"But we need the money."

"You'll see." He started pacing the room.

"I've only just paid the phone bill."

Fists deep in his pockets, he shook his head. "It'll all come out."

"Do you know how much the weekly food shop is? And that's with macaroni cheese three times a week."

"And then all hell will break loose."

Still no reply. He pressed longer this time, then stepped back and looked up at Mrs Wallace's spare bedroom. No sign of life. Cameron must have guessed he was on to him and was lying low. Eyes fixed on the pavement, he headed to the quiz. How the hell the man thought he'd get away with it was beyond him.

Through the noisy crowd he shouldered his way to the bar, where he stood waiting to be served. All these people were here under false pretences, hoping to pay off their mortgages. You could almost feel sorry for them.

"Liking it at the jammie?" said Alan, a spec of sawdust on his eyelashes.

"Won't be there long."

"That's what they all say." He held a glass underneath the tap. "Next thing you know thirty years will have gone by, and you'll be needing that coffin."

When he finally reached their table by the fire, he found that it was already taken. They were either pearl hunters or reporters, he couldn't tell. He settled himself at the only table left, and raised his glass to his lips. The sooner they were all gone the better and he'd have the pub and the rivers back to himself.

"There you are. Someone's sitting at our table," said Rev Maxwell, setting down what was no doubt a double gin and tonic. He was wearing some kind of Hawaiian shirt bearing a surfer riding the crest of his stomach. "I still can't believe how busy everywhere is. The only sign of life three weeks ago was the deathwatch beetle dining on the church roof."

"You missed the training session. Only Mungo bothered turning up."

"That man needs all the help he can get."

"I seem to remember that you thought an orchestra tunes to the first violin."

He swilled round his drink. "They must have only just started tuning to the oboe and no one thought to tell me."

"Why are those people sitting at our table?" said Fiona, clutching a large glass of white wine with an apricot lipstick mark. "I'd ask them to move, but one's a guest of mine and he's booked in for the next month."

Brodie pointed at her. "You also missed training."

"Thought it was just for Mungo."

"What was just for me?" said Mungo, sitting down.

Standing smiling behind him, a pint in each hand, was Cameron.

For God's sake.

"Thought I'd come and help you out."

His back stiffened. "Don't need any help. Anyway, the team's full."

"I told him," said Mungo. "But he wouldn't listen."

Cameron shrugged. "I'll just watch. Fetch the drinks. I can't tell you how nice it is to be in a proper pub after all those dreadful Irish bars in Bahrain."

"There's nowhere to sit," said Brodie.

There was a dragging sound as he brought a chair over from the next table. "Sorted."

"Glad to have you with us, Cameron," said Rev Maxwell. "You can take Mungo's place."

Mungo scowled. "No, he can't."

Cameron was smiling at Brodie in a way he didn't like. "Are you going to tell everyone what you did?"

Something leapt inside him. "You're not trying to blame me, are you?"

A pint glass filled with change appeared on the table.

"Fifty pence each please, ladies and gents," said Alan, offering him an answer sheet. "Winners take all as usual. Let's hope it's you lot for once. You can buy Brodie a pair of new underpants. Apparently someone called Frank took his white ones."

"You have got some on now, haven't you?" said Fiona, looking him up and down.

Cameron was leaning back, fishing inside his trouser pocket.

"You're not on the team," he said, much louder than he'd intended. "No need for you to pay."

"Tell them what you did, Brodie."

"Tell us what?" said Mungo.

"Couldn't find you," said Stugly, pulling a stool behind him. "Someone's sitting at our table."

From somewhere above came a tapping sound, followed by Alan's strangely intimate voice through the microphone. "Question one. From which country does the Rhine empty into the sea?"

"Germany," said Stugly, sitting down.

Brodie shook his head. "Too obvious. It would be like asking from which country does the Seine empty into the sea."

"The Seine doesn't empty into a sea," said Cameron, an arm draped over the back of Mungo's chair as if he owned the place.

"Does. The English Channel."

Cameron studied him. "Which is an arm of the Atlantic Ocean. Not strictly speaking a sea."

"I know, I know," said Mungo. "Switzerland!"

Fiona gave him one of her looks. "Switzerland's landlocked. Even Stugly knows that . . . Though judging by his expression, it might be news to him too."

"Belgium," said Cameron, sitting forward.

"You're not on the team," said Brodie. "It's the Netherlands. Fiona, put down the Netherlands."

She picked up the pen and started to write.

Incredulous, Brodie tapped on the answer sheet. "You've put Belgium down. Why have you done that? He's not on the team."

"No offence, Brodie, but you don't even know where your underpants are."

"Number two," said Alan. "What does UNESCO stand for?"

"Brodie, tell them what you did," said Cameron. That smile again.

"What did he do?" said Mungo.

"He found a husk in a batch of frozen strawberries at the jammie. They were talking about it at the post office counter. Sounds like you've found your calling."

Stugly grabbed Brodie's arm. "Did you see the jeweller?" he hissed, pushing his hot breath into his ear.

"This morning."

"What did he say?"

"Same as you."

"Have you said anything to Cameron?"

"Not yet."

"If you don't, I will." His voice was low and urgent. "That man made you look an idiot finding such a huge pearl as that. And he still is. Look at the way he talks to you. He's not even on the team."

"United Nations Emergency . . ." said Mungo.

Cameron shook his head. "It's not emergency."

Stugly slammed his empty glass on the table. "I'd call it a fucking emergency."

"It's the United Nations Educational . . ." said Cameron, looking into the distance, eyes narrowed.

"I've got a mortgage to pay." Stugly pushed away his glass.

"Scientific . . ."

"To say nothing of my family to support."

"And Cultural . . ."

"I had my own business. Now look at me. That forklift truck doesn't even go faster than ten miles per hour. You can forget any wheelies."

"Organization," Cameron concluded triumphantly. "Unfortunately, it's spelt with a 'z' instead of an 's', which is cultural sacrilege if you ask me."

Stugly leant towards him. "You planned it from the start, didn't you?"

Cameron looked over at Alan. "They should give us an extra point for spelling it correctly. Bet we're the only ones who do."

"You came to me all friendly wanting to buy the cafe. And then all this kicks off and you make a fortune. Funny that, isn't it?"

"Can I buy you a drink, Stugly?" said Cameron.

"You should never have come back."

He was right about that.

"Number three," said Alan, in that bingo caller's voice of his. "Who were Germany's allies during the First World War?"

Stugly poked Cameron in the chest. "Did you think nobody would find out?"

"For God's sake," said Fiona. "No one knows what the hell you're on about, Stugly. Just shut the fuck up. We're trying to think. One of them was somewhere weird like Bulgaria."

Then came his greasy smile. "Cameron knows what I'm talking about. Knows all about that huge pearl of his being cultured."

It was as if someone had smashed a glass.

"Rubbish," said Cameron.

"The jeweller said it was. That Mr McSweetie who made it into a pendant. He should know, he's a pearl dealer for God's sake."

"Nonsense." Cameron sat back with a grin that failed to reach his eyes.

Just sitting there denying it.

"How the hell would a cultured pearl get inside a mussel in the Isla?" said Fiona.

Stugly nodded towards Cameron. "Ask him."

"Me? I haven't got the foggiest what you're on about."

Wasn't even man enough to admit it.

"Tell them, Brodie," said Stugly.

Mungo turned to him, looking confused. "Is it really cultured?"

He nodded.

"I know nothing about it either, if that's what anyone's thinking," said Mungo.

Everyone turned to look at Brodie. Even Mungo. "You can't think *I* did it?" he said, holding up both hands.

"Come clean, Cameron," said Stugly. "It's not fair on Mungo and Brodie."

Swinging back on his chair, trying to look like he was innocent.

"Number four," announced Alan cheerfully. "What is an otter's home called?"

"He charmed Elspeth so much she's not even late to work any more, by all accounts." Stugly raised his eyebrows. "You'd wonder what that's all about."

Brodie got to his feet. The next thing he heard was an awful crunching sound as his fist met Cameron's face. The chair lurched backwards, taking the man to the floor with it. And he watched, appalled, as a crimson streak began to make its hesitant way from his nose to the carpet.

CHAPTER
THIRTEEN

Something was wrong with Brodie, she could tell, ever since that pub quiz on Saturday night. He'd come home early with a carrier from the off-licence, then retreated into his hut without a word. When he still hadn't emerged, she went to bed alone, and lay there wondering why that place was a better option than being with her. That was the problem with marriage. You gave your husband your heart, your most tender thing, convinced he'd keep it safe. And he had. For years. Then the squeezing started. But she wasn't going to cry. It wasn't even eleven o'clock on a Monday morning.

Holding three plates smeared with the lurid remains of breakfast, she turned at the sound of the door. "What on earth happened to you?"

"Nothing," said Cameron, a folded copy of the *Chronicle* tucked under his arm.

Nothing? There was white tape stuck across the bridge of his nose and he had two black eyes, for God's sake.

As she stacked the plates on top of the dishwasher, Alpina continued to ignore her, the bulges either side of her bra strap shaking furiously as she scrubbed a cake tin. All morning she'd been funny with her. She hadn't even put on the radio. Why didn't she just say it, whatever it was, and put the world out of its misery? "Cameron's just arrived. Looks like he's been in a fight."

"Thank God that pub's got carpeting. He could have broken his skull."

"What pub?"

Alpina looked at her for the first time that morning, an ominous hot coal in each cheek. "Brodie didn't tell you about Saturday night?"

She shrugged. "All he said was that they'd lost, which wasn't exactly news, if you know what I mean."

Alpina cast the cake tin onto the drainer and started on a frying pan. "Never even apologised. He just left Cameron on the floor and walked out of the Victoria. We had to wait four hours in A&E for him to be seen. Couldn't get a cup of tea as the machine was broken. Then Mungo didn't sleep when we finally got home. You know how much he worries."

"Someone hit Cameron?"

Her head snapped round. "Your husband."

She couldn't help smiling. "Brodie would never do that, hit someone."

"He's obviously not the man you thought he was. Specially considering what he did with that pearl."

The door flapped wildly behind her as she strode out. She had no idea what Alpina was on about.

"What can I get you both?"

Lying on Rev Maxwell and Fiona's table was a copy of the *Chronicle*. Idly, she tugged it towards her.

WORLD'S LARGEST RIVER PEARL FOR SALE said the headline. She pulled it even closer. Underneath was a photograph of Maggie. It was the one the paper had taken of her at the school sports day, after which she'd cried all evening because she hadn't won any of her races. The caption said that the money raised from auctioning the pendant would be used to buy her a new prosthesis. Why hadn't she known this was going in?

"Blimey, was that Brodie's handiwork?" said Fiona, looking past her.

"You could call it that." Cameron sat down at the table.

She didn't believe it. Brodie would never have done that to anyone.

"You're not going to press charges, are you?" said Rev Maxwell.

He shook his head. "Must have thought he was back in the playground."

She still didn't get it. "Why did he hit you?"

"Have you seen this, Cameron?" said Rev Maxwell, tapping at the paper. "You can hardly auction it now."

"I called them earlier this morning. Told them I'm cancelling it."

"Cancelling it?" said Elspeth. "Why?"

Fiona clutched Cameron's arm. "You didn't tell them why, did you?"

"I said it was for personal reasons. They'll put something about it in the paper tomorrow."

"What's happened?" said Elspeth. Why wasn't anyone answering her questions?

216

"Listen," said Fiona, both hands on the table. "I've been thinking. I still don't reckon we should say anything to anyone. I'm booked solid for the next three months." She looked at her. "Brodie won't say anything, will he?"

"About what?"

Fiona glanced around, then leant forward again. "It's in everybody's interests to keep quiet. Mungo's got people queuing out of the door, and Alan's so busy he's had to hire someone to help behind the bar."

"And the jammie," said Rev Maxwell. "They've all been offered overtime."

Fiona pointed at him. "You're not doing too badly either."

"Never known collections like it."

"And don't forget Nessa," said Fiona. "She's had to turn off that country music so as not to upset the customers now that she's finally got some."

Elspeth tossed her pad onto the table. "What in God's name is going on?"

"Hasn't Brodie told you?" said Cameron, looking at her for the first time. "The pearl. It's cultured."

She laughed it was so ridiculous. "It came out the Isla. Brodie and Maggie both saw it!"

"Mr McSweetie realised when he was drilling it but somehow forgot to mention it when we came to collect it."

It was all too much to take in. "Who would do something like that?"

"That's what we're all wondering," said Rev Maxwell.

Cameron fiddled with the sugar bowl. "I know who my money's on. The man's unstable."

He couldn't mean Brodie — he's always hated cultured pearls. She shifted her weight. "Of course you have to say something. They're destroying the mussels thinking they'll hit the jackpot too."

"Keep your voice down," said Fiona, pointing at her. "People will hear. And tell Brodie not to say anything either. It's in his interests too. Half the people out there will assume *he* did it."

The door opened and a young woman stepped in. She looked around, and then just stood there staring at Cameron. "What happened to you?"

She wasn't a pearl hunter. Not in that dress, just low enough to hint at what was beneath it. Perhaps it was his girlfriend. He always went for the good-looking ones.

Cameron didn't get up. "A fit of pique."

"I was wondering if I could ask you some questions."

"We're a bit busy."

"It's about the pearl."

"I called you this morning." He sounded irritated.

The woman adjusted the strap of her handbag. "It's not about the auction."

"What is it, then?"

"I've just been speaking to Mr McSweetie."

Palms flat against the cold white tiles, she stood with her back to the kitchen wall. There were customers waiting to be served, but she had to know what was going on.

"Who told you?" said Cameron, leaning against the fridge, arms folded.

"Someone called the paper after I spoke to you," said the woman.

Her name was Ailsa, now she remembered. Her byline had been on all the stories.

"Was it Brodie? I bet it was," said Alpina.

What was she implying? That Brodie was trying to shift the blame? Alpina had a talent for poking her where it hurt. She always had. After all these years she still held it against her that Mum had supported her through university, typing for that awful man with the wandering hands, when it had never been suggested that she, the elder one, went. She wouldn't have got in, anyway, not with those crummy exam results.

"That's not for me to say." Ailsa drew out a notepad and pen from her bag then turned to Cameron. "You told me you found the pearl in the Isla."

"I *did* find it in the Isla," he said emphatically.

"Then how do you account for it not being a natural freshwater pearl?"

She bit the side of her little finger. The rusty taste of blood.

"All I know is that I went pearl-fishing, opened a shell and there it was."

Ailsa looked up from her pad. "When did you find out it was cultured?"

"Brodie told me on Saturday night. He said Mr McSweetie realised when he was drilling it."

Why hadn't Brodie told her when he got home?

"How do you think it got into the shell?" said Ailsa.

"Put it this way. It wasn't me."

"Nor Mungo," said Alpina, pointing at the woman with a bread knife. "Make sure you write that down."

"Who do you think it was?"

Jiggling her pen, still waiting for him to answer.

Cameron was looking at her now, as if weighing up what to say. Hands still on the cold tiles, she returned his gaze.

"It wasn't me or my brother. That's all I know."

Ailsa reached down and picked up her pen top from the floor. "Do you know where I'll find Brodie McBride?"

All that white cleavage. She'd been in Brodie's hut. "It wasn't my husband."

"Will he be at the jam factory?"

She took a step towards her. "It wasn't Brodie."

"What time will he be home from work?"

Why wasn't the woman listening to her? How could it be Brodie? "Like I said, it wasn't him."

"They finish at five," said Alpina, tapping her watch. "You can catch him then. As soon as he comes out."

He winced as he groped inside his jeans pocket for the front-door key. Having to riffle through buckets of frozen raspberries all day hadn't exactly helped the pain in his hand. Whatever that man was involved in, he shouldn't have hit him. How would he explain it if Elspeth and Maggie ever found out?

His stomach shifted again. He hadn't eaten anything all day, having spent his breaks in the men's toilets, head in his hands, still trying to figure out what to do. If

Cameron didn't confess, the pearl hunters would continue ripping up the last of the mussel colonies and wipe out the entire species in Scotland. It would be a disaster.

Opening the fridge, he batted aside the useless bunch of radishes. He couldn't believe it. No cheese. What was wrong with this place? Was someone feeding a secret squadron of mice? As he shut the door, he jumped. Maggie. Standing right next to him, even paler than usual.

"What's wrong?"

"Nothing."

She was still standing there, eyes like her mother's.

"Fancy something to eat? We seem to have a surfeit of radishes."

"Will I be able to visit you?"

He pulled out a chair. "The jammie's not really a place for children."

She hesitated. "In prison, I mean."

"Prison?" He sat down.

"Fatty McEwan said you tried to murder Cameron Wallace in the pub."

"I could murder some cheese on toast, that's for sure." He brushed some crumbs off the plastic tablecloth.

Loud and intrusive, the doorbell rang.

Maggie took a step backwards, stumbling into the bin. "Is that the police?"

"Police? It'll be a Boy Scout after some money to feed his drug habit."

Striding into the hall, he snatched open the door. Ailsa. Whatever she wanted, he'd have to tell her. It was the only way to stop the pearl hunters massacring the mussels.

He stood back to let her in. "Maggie, go upstairs," he called.

As the bairn started up the steps, he led the way into the kitchen, and closed the door carefully behind them. "Take a seat. There's something you need to know."

Slowly she sat down, pulled her skirt over her knees and started fiddling with the coiled wire holding the pages of her pad together.

"Cameron's pearl," he said, arms folded. "The one he found. It's cultured."

She was clicking her pen on and off, just staring at him.

He nodded at her pad. "You haven't written it down. You need to write it down."

She didn't move.

"God knows how it got into that shell, but that's beside the point. They're destroying everything. The pearl hunters. You've got to tell them they're wasting their time. Something that big just isn't out there. Certainly not of that perfection."

Why wasn't she saying anything?

He took a step towards the table. "It's not a natural pearl. Don't you understand? Someone took what I'm guessing was an Akoya oyster out of the sea, shoved a bead inside, then put it back so the oyster would cover it with a layer of nacre just like any other irritant that

222

got into its shell. Then, after two to three years, they hauled it out again. Where's the beauty in that?"

Swinging her foot back and forth.

"Someone on the other side of the world."

Swinging even faster.

"They'll all clear off if you put it in the paper. You'll save the mussels. Can't you see?"

She ran her tongue along her bottom lip. "I know."

"What? You know what?"

"That the pearl's cultured," she said evenly. "Someone called me this morning."

Stugly. It had to be Stugly.

"Any idea how it came to be in a Scottish mussel?"

He shrugged then waggled his hand in the direction of the Isla. "Just tell everyone it's cultured so they go home."

"I hear you punched Cameron Wallace in the Victoria Arms on Saturday night."

"You're not going to print that, are you?" he said, horrified.

"Did that have something to do with it? Cameron Wallace says he knows nothing about it. I've just spoken to his brother too. Says the same thing."

The fridge spluttered into life and started a low grumble.

Why was she looking at him like that? He'd told her things. He thought she was on his side. Pals, almost. "You don't think I had anything to do with it, do you?"

Silence. Except for the sound of tiny feet pounding up the stairs.

Slumped at the table in his hut, eyes on the marbled sky, he jumped as the handle turned. Elspeth stood in the doorway in that new pink skirt she'd bought for work. He could tell by the way she was looking at him that she knew what he'd done to Cameron. "Is he OK?"

She leant against the doorpost. "A broken nose and two black eyes."

"I'll apologise."

Her gaze settled somewhere on the floor. "I heard the pearl is cultured."

Silence. The table felt rough underneath his fingers.

"You didn't notice anything when you saw it?"

Somewhere, from a nearby garden, came the urgent start of a lawnmower.

"I . . ." It was useless. He could barely hear himself. The question hung between them as everything else got pushed out with the noise.

"I never saw it close up," he said, filling the gap when the racket stopped. "Even if I had . . ." He shook his shoulders. "I saw it drop out of a mussel."

"There's something I need to tell you."

He didn't like the sound of it, whatever it was.

There was a guttural roar as the mower came to life again next to the fence, and their eyes found each other through the din. With a decisive bang, Elspeth closed the door behind her, and stood, back against the wall hung with cobwebs.

His stomach was getting tighter the longer she didn't say anything. She was going to leave him. Finally.

A scraggy cough as she cleared her throat.

She lifted her eyes to him. "There's no better father on this earth. I know it wasn't you."

The siren for the morning tea break wailed so desperately, for a moment Brodie wondered whether someone had managed to escape. Feet squashed and itchy in the late Christine's boots, he fought through the herd of navy coats charging down the corridor. He had to see the paper. He'd lain awake all night wondering what Ailsa had written, jumping each time Elspeth moaned in her sleep.

As he erupted through the double doors of the canteen, Doreen and Moira raised their heads from a copy of the *Chronicle* lying on the table, and studied him with the penetrating gaze of jurors. He turned to leave, but a stream of workers blocked his exit. Others were clustering around the two women, straining to see what they were looking at.

"Says here that eighty-thousand-pound river pearl is a fake," said Doreen.

"'Expert claims huge Scottish gem that sparked the world's biggest pearl rush is cultured and worth only a few hundred pounds,'" read Moira, sounding baffled.

He sat down and inspected the blue threads on his cuff.

"Cultured?" came a voice from the tea queue. "How the hell did it get there?"

"Some chancer must have put it in the shell," said the woman from reception sitting at a table with a mug.

"'All three men who were there when the pearl was discovered have denied any knowledge of it,'" read

Doreen. "'Cameron Wallace, who claimed he found the pearl, his brother Mungo, who owns Nether Isla's chip shop, the Frying Scotsman, and Brodie McBride, Scotland's last full-time professional pearl fisher, who now works in the town's jam factory, Jolly Jams.'"

Someone poked him in the back. "What's all this, Brodie?"

It was the lady stirrer.

He shrugged. "I couldn't tell you."

"Was it Cameron?" came a voice from the corner. "Is that why you punched his lights out?"

"Of course it was Cameron," said Stugly, stepping forward. "He was in a real hurry to buy my cafe. Funny that."

"Why the hell would Cameron put a cultured pearl inside a mussel shell?" said a woman he'd never seen before. "He's loaded."

Moira shrugged. "Maybe it was Mungo."

His chair clattered over as he got to his feet. "Mungo would never do something like that."

"Must have been someone who needed the money," said a tall woman with a large nose he recognised from labelling.

Why were they all staring at him? "I know absolutely nothing about it." The ridiculous thing was that he even sounded guilty.

"Truth is like a worm," said Doreen, arms folded. "It always burrows out."

Ignoring the customer waiting to be served, she wiped the menu again, seeing the first time she and Brodie met. It wasn't long after he'd arrived at Nether Isla, when he was eleven and she was nine. She'd spotted him pearling alone in the Isla as she sat on a branch, hiding from her father and his temper. Her eyes didn't leave him for a moment. She'd never seen anyone so absorbed, it was as if the rest of the world no longer existed. Each day after school she returned to search for him along the river, and would study him from the safety of the leaves. Weeks later, anxious to see his pearls, she came and crouched next to him as he was opening shells on the bank. The autumn wind then snatched the leaves from the trees, surrounding them in a blizzard of gold.

Brodie never said a word, didn't turn his head, and when she thought he hadn't even noticed she was there, he silently handed her a misshaped white pearl with a pink hue. "Uneven ones like that one are called baroque pearls. Barrels look like barrels, balls look like balls and teardrops look like teardrops." Later, somewhere amid their friendship, love grew. She couldn't help it, someone like that. And she'd kept that pearl, her most-treasured possession, in her jewellery box all these thirty-two years.

"Where's Cameron Wallace?"

A man in jeans and a Led Zeppelin T-shirt was standing in the doorway with a rolled-up copy of the *Chronicle*. She hadn't even had a chance to go out and buy one yet.

"Where is he?" He started walking towards her.

"He's not in."

227

"Hiding, is he?" He held up the front page of the paper to the customers. "You do all know that you're wasting your time, don't you? It's cultured."

A woman with sunburnt shoulders snatched it from him and started reading.

"I've been up here ever since that man claimed he found it," he said, taking another step towards her. "Spent a fortune on petrol getting up here, the hotel doubled its prices, and I've had to eat out every night. That man needs to reimburse me. With interest."

"You'll have to leave. He's not here."

"In which case I'll have a full breakfast on the house while I'm waiting." The chair squealed against the polished boards as he pulled it out.

"Who says it was him, anyway?" said the woman still holding the paper. "Says here he denies it. It could have been one of the other two. His brother. Or that professional pearl fisher."

"Bet it was the pearl fisher," said a man with a Fife accent at the table next to her. "I'd put money on it. Cameron Wallace has just come back from the Middle East. He's an engineer. He'd be loaded. That pearl fisher was the only full-timer left. The pearls are running out. He's got a wife and kid. There's your motivation."

"Bet the wife was in on it too," said the woman, tossing the paper on the table in disgust. She turned to her. "What do you reckon, love?"

Abertawe was looking at him from the same spot on top of the grey filing cabinet. Brodie shifted in his seat.

228

"I don't want to keep you from those two ladies for too long, so I'll get straight to the point," said Dewi, hands clasped together on his desk like a child in prayer. He leant forward with a frown. "Are you trying to grow a moustache?"

"Thought you were going to get to the point."

Dewi's gaze wandered to the blinds. "You'd think people would have better things to do than gossip, like get on with their work for instance."

"What have you called me in for?"

From his desk drawer Dewi drew out a long grey sock with a hole at the heel as if mice had ravished it. He held it up between his fingers, where it swung gently. "I think one of your socks might have blown off your washing line into our garden. Recognise it?"

He rubbed his palms down his thighs. "I've got to get back to work."

Leaving the sock draped along the front of his desk, Dewi ran a hand along his naked head. "Since that story in the *Chronicle* this morning, we've had a large number of calls from journalists, which I'm going to have to return. Several were from overseas."

Brodie crossed his legs.

"I will, of course, defend you to the hilt," he said, pointing at him with a paper clip. "I'm not for a moment saying it was you. But if it were you, now's the time to admit it. We'll figure something out. We could tell them that something affected your judgement. What's that thing you catch from riverbanks?" He looked at the ceiling, then jabbed the mangled clip at him. "Weil's disease! That's it."

He shook his head. "It wasn't me."

"Fifteen years ago we were supplying the middles for Jammie Dodgers." He opened his arms. "Look at us now. Six jams, three preserves and one Dundee marmalade. Exports to fifty-two markets including Japan, America, Australia and, for some reason I've never been able to fathom, the Vatican. That's a long way to fall."

"It wasn't me."

He lifted the receiver and waggled it at him. "I'm about to get on this phone, and tell the world you had nothing to do with that cultured pearl. Is there any reason why I shouldn't?"

The man's head was starting to glisten.

"It wasn't me."

Dewi gave him the same triumphant smile that appeared over the fence whenever Wales beat Scotland at rugby. "Just as I thought," he said, returning the receiver. Round the desk he strode, sounding as if he were off to the Calgary Stampede. "Why don't you and Elspeth come round tomorrow night and join us in the hot tub? As long as you observe the 'No Speedos' rule, of course. I wouldn't want to scare the horses."

The changing room fell silent as soon as he walked in. All he wanted was to sit in his hut and shut out the world. As he struggled to prise off his boots, he glanced out of the window. A huddle of people was standing at the gates like relatives waiting for prisoners to be released. A number of them were wearing suits and dresses, while others, more casually dressed, were carrying small rucksacks. He knew that combination. They were journalists and photographers. He ducked down. The only way out was through those gates. If he kept his hairnet on, maybe they wouldn't recognise him.

He loitered by the door, then silently joined the next batch of workers as they left. Hands deep in his pockets and head lowered, he kept to the back. If he could just get out of the gates, and up the road, he'd be all right. He could run from there.

"Is Brodie McBride on his way out?" came a shout.

A woman in the group glanced at him. It was one of the tasters. The really short one. She wasn't going to denounce him, was she?

"In about half an hour," she called.

As they passed through the gate, he felt their eyes on him. He couldn't believe he'd decided to keep his stupid hairnet on. He was the only person wearing one. The journalists would all be staring at him, wondering who the idiot was.

Almost at the top of the road, he heard a shout, followed by footsteps. He cast off his net and started to sprint, not stopping until he reached home. Just as he was about to close the front door, a high-heeled navy shoe appeared, preventing it from moving.

"Are you Brodie McBride?"

Still panting, he peered round the door. A woman in a tightly fitting blue polka-dot dress and gold earrings was looking at him like she wanted to kick him in the shins. Which paper was *she* from?

"I'm not speaking to the press." He tried to shut the door again, but the slender foot was still there.

"It's about your daughter," she said, more insistent.

Something collapsed inside him. "What's happened to her?"

"Her picture was in the *Scotsman* with the story about that auction. I recognised her."

"Where is she?" He looked up and down the road. There was no sign of her.

"She paid in cash. Two hundred and eighty-five pounds."

"Who did?"

She took another step towards him. "I thought that poor bairn was lost."

"Who are you? How do you know Maggie?"

"She told me she wanted that pearl for her grandmother." She tucked her blonde hair behind her ear. "A birthday present from you, so she said."

The sound of footsteps made him turn. Two men were running towards him. "My mother's dead."

She pointed a sharp fingernail at him. "Then I heard on the radio this morning that that huge river pearl is cultured, and I realised what you were up to. Fancy making your daughter do your dirty work. What sort of father are you? Two other people are under suspicion for what you did. You'd better come clean, or I'm going to the papers. I don't want anyone thinking I was in on it."

As she headed to her car, still glaring at him, he swiftly locked the door and stood with his back to it. She'd said that Maggie had bought a pearl from her.

But she only had seven pounds fifty in her savings account.

The bell rang.

She must have got the money from somewhere. But where? Stolen it? Why would she do that? To prove something to him? That she was good enough at pearling? And then Cameron found the cultured pearl by mistake.

A bang on the door followed by another ring.

But why didn't she think she was good enough? It just didn't make any sense.

Two bangs, much louder this time.

Whatever the reason, it was his fault. Maggie wouldn't steal some money, then plant a cultured pearl in a river mussel for no reason.

The letter box rattled then two fingers jabbed him in the leg. Into the living room he fled and threw the curtains closed, plunging the room into darkness. Someone was knocking on the window now as if they were about to break in. He would just have to tell everyone who it was. It was the only way out. For a moment he looked at his silty reflection in the mirror above the fire, petrified of what he was about to start. He then reached for the phone and started dialling Ailsa's number, feeling a nail pierce his heart.

CHAPTER
FOURTEEN

The curdling in his stomach that had kept him awake since dawn was getting even worse as he reached the bottom step. He paused, a hand on the smooth banister, listening to the friendly clatter of breakfast. By the end of the morning, when the paper came out, everyone would know. Nothing would ever be the same again.

From the kitchen doorway he took it all in. Elspeth was pouring tea from a brown pot, a protective finger on the lid. What would she think when she found out? Maggie, still just a kid in her yellow pyjamas with fairies on them, was reading the back of a Rice Krispies packet as she ate. He'd done the right thing telling the *Chronicle*. The right thing for everyone.

As he took his place at the table, Elspeth filled his mug, then passed him the milk jug. There was something comforting about the rule of no milk bottles on the table. That was what happened in families, you made up rules and lived by them.

"New teapot?" he said.

"I found it in one of the charity shops on the high street. Bleached it."

Maggie's eyes were still on the back of the cereal packet, just like his had been when trying to avoid Aunt Agnes.

"Up to anything nice today?" he asked her.

A shake of the head. She didn't even look at him. Couldn't she be in a good mood this one last breakfast together before everything turned awful? Unable to eat, he stared at the stranger's teapot.

"Don't worry, Brodie," said Elspeth, putting her slice of toast onto his plate. "It'll come out that it wasn't you. Fancy not knowing that a cultured oyster pearl has a bead inside." She stroked Maggie's head. "As I explained last night, if anyone says that Dad was behind it, just ignore them."

The bairn shovelled in a huge mouthful.

"Why don't you show Dad that painting you did for him? The special one of the three of us with the purple glitter. I put it on the coffee table in the living room to dry."

Slowly she slid off her seat and headed out in her battered sheepskin slippers. Heart lifting, he followed her. He'd keep this painting forever. Maybe even get it framed. From the doorway, he could see a big piece of green paper with something sparkling on it. He was going to love it, he knew. Maggie stopped in the middle of the room, a frown forming as she watched Fake Frank approach the frayed ends of the TV aerial cable nose first.

"Don't let him chew it," he warned. "He's got to get out of the habit."

But the creature gave it a bored sniff, then bounded off towards the wastepaper basket.

An almighty wail sounded, then Maggie pointed to the animal. "Frankenstein!"

Something wasn't right. The cafe blinds were still drawn and they were due to open any minute. Elspeth tried the door. It was locked, and she hadn't brought her key. Hearing voices from inside, she knocked on the glass. A couple of fingers appeared and prised open the blind. What was Mungo doing here at this time of the morning?

He locked the door behind her, then stood scratching the back of his neck. Cameron and Alpina were sitting at a table bearing the remains of breakfast. Alpina wasn't wearing her chef's hat or her pinny.

"Aren't we opening?"

"Sit down," said Cameron, pulling out the chair next to him.

She didn't move. "Is it because of yesterday?" There had been furious people coming in all day. At one stage Rev Maxwell had had to hold someone back from trying to punch Cameron. As if he needed his nose breaking again. There'd been at least five people looking for Brodie.

"It isn't just here," said Alpina, fiddling with the pepper pot. "They keep coming into the chippy and accusing Mungo. I don't know how anyone could think he did it. Or Cameron."

She felt a flare of anger. "Are you trying to say that it was Brodie?"

Mungo took a seat. "Then there were all the journalists asking questions. I had to shut the chippy early yesterday. Couldn't stand it."

"It might take a while," said Alpina, running a short, stout finger across something yellow on her plate and licking it, "but they'll find out who did it."

"But what about all my regulars? They won't come in any more, thinking I did it."

Alpina pointed at him. "People will always want a battered sausage, Mungo. It's the way of the world."

"When will we reopen?" said Elspeth.

Cameron patted the seat next to him. "Have some breakfast. I'll make it."

She stayed where she was. "We're not closing down, are we?"

"You'll get paid for the next two months. Both of you."

She shifted her weight. Two months' wages. How would they manage the bills once that was spent?

"Someone's got a lot to answer for," said Alpina, tapping a teaspoon on the table. "Ruining two businesses."

"It would certainly help if Brodie confessed, I can tell you that," said Cameron, leaning back and lacing his fingers behind his head.

She slung her handbag on the table. "I don't know how you two can just sit there saying that Brodie stuck a cultured pearl inside a mussel. It's the last thing he'd do. Surely *you* don't think it was him, do you, Mungo?"

He looked as if he didn't know what to say.

She felt a hand on her shoulder. "I know it's a lot to take in," said Cameron, standing next to her. "But you're going to have to face it sometime, Elspeth. People change, especially in difficult circumstances. He's not exactly rational. Look what he did to me."

She shrugged him off. "It wasn't him."

There was a thump on the door.

"Just ignore it," said Mungo, lowering his head to the table. "They'll go away."

A second bang.

"We're closed," shouted Cameron.

"Is Cameron Wallace there?" said the voice.

"No," called Alpina.

"I'll move Mum to Fiona's for a few days," said Cameron. "There were journalists knocking on her door all day yesterday. Fiona's got guests leaving like rats deserting a sinking ship."

Eventually, the racket outside stopped, and Alpina pushed back her plate. "I'm going to get the paper to see what they're saying now."

Once he'd locked the door behind her, Mungo picked up the phone. "Better cancel my order for all that haddock. If they'll let me."

As the kitchen half-doors swung closed Cameron turned to Elspeth. "How are you bearing up in all of this?"

She blinked, her eyes suddenly filling. No one had asked her that. No one.

"It can't be easy for you," he said, his warm fingers rubbing the back of her hand like everything would be all right.

She couldn't remember the last time someone had touched her. Not like that.

". . . being stuck in the middle like this."

She stood up. "I'm not in the middle. I'm with Brodie."

"You're in early," said Doreen, a smear of lilac lipstick on both front teeth.

He pulled on a pair of gloves. "Early bird catches the aphid."

Silence.

"Are you all right, Brodie?" said Moira, her tiny water vole's eyes on him. "You look a bit peely-wally."

"Right as rain." He scooped more raspberries towards him, his gloved fingers already stained as if he'd just stuck a knife in someone. How was Maggie going to take it?

Doreen patted him tenderly on the arm. "Don't listen to what people are saying. It's a conspiracy started by that lot in labelling. They'll be laughing on the other side of their faces when it comes out that Cameron Wallace did it. As I said, the truth eventually burrows out."

Moira's teeth glowed like margarine in the artificial light. "Pity you didn't hit him harder while you had the chance. They were interviewing people from Blairgowrie on the *Nine O'clock News* last night. They reckoned half the residents of Nether Isla were in on it. God knows what people will be saying about us in the *Chronicle*."

He lowered his head. "You shouldn't believe everything you read in the papers."

The sharp rap on the door made Elspeth flinch.

"We're closed," shouted Mungo, coming back from the kitchen. He sat dejected on the counter. "They said it was too bloody late to cancel the order."

"It's going to be like this all day," said Cameron nervously. "We should go somewhere else. It might get nasty."

There was another brutal knock, followed by a rattle of the door handle.

"It's me, stupid," called Alpina. "Open the bleedin' door."

After unlocking it, Mungo stepped aside, but Alpina didn't move.

"Quick," said Mungo. "In case someone tries to come in."

Clutching the *Chronicle*, Alpina just stood there. "They've found out who did it."

Elspeth got to her feet. "Who?"

"They admitted it and everything." She was shaking her head, like it was too much to take in.

She raised her voice. "Who was it?"

"The whole of the Co-op was talking about it. I couldn't get out."

"Who was it?" Taking a step forward, she tried to grab the paper, but Alpina wouldn't let go.

There was a horrible pause.

"Brodie."

240

He jumped as the mournful siren for the morning tea break sounded. Already? It usually took ages. Slowly he peeled off his gloves. There was no way he was going to the canteen. He'd stand outside and try and clear the static in his head from not having slept.

As the changing-room door banged abruptly behind him a group of smokers immediately fell silent. One of them let out a long, poisonous cloud of smoke that engulfed him, then tapped off her ash, her eyes still on him. He fled back through the door. He just wanted today to hurry up and be over, then he could go home and be with the only two people who mattered.

After wandering the corridors, he stood staring at the relentless cardboard walls and industrial grey carpet ahead. Where the hell was he? From behind came the low sound of voices. Two men in white coats were striding towards him. Management. He took the first turning, but he could still hear them. They seemed to be getting closer. The nearest handle felt cold as he seized it, and he quickly shut the door behind him. His chest pinched as he turned. The canteen.

"Why did you do it, Brodie?"

It was Andy Brady from school, getting to his feet.

"Do what?" It was all he could think of.

Andy snatched a copy of the *Chronicle* from a nearby table, where a crowd of people had been reading it, and held it up. There, in the stark lettering of a gravestone, was the headline: THE ASTONISHING CONFESSION OF SCOTLAND'S LAST PEARL FISHER.

More heads were turning.

"How could you have done such a wicked thing as that?" said the lady stirrer, standing up.

As a crowd started to gather in front of him he took a step backwards, feeling for the door handle.

"What I can't believe is how you stood here yesterday and told us all that it wasn't you," said Doreen. "You let everyone think it was one of the others. Why did you lie to us?"

A swallow. She seemed so disappointed in him.

"The whole world is looking at Nether Isla thinking we're a bunch of fraudsters because of you," said Moira. "You should never have been given a job here."

"It's not just Nether Isla," shouted the man from accounts who'd promised to sort out his tax code. "Think of all the damage he's done to Scotland. People will be talking about it for years."

"Are you sure it was you?"

Stugly, wanting it to be Cameron.

There were jeers of derision as everyone seemed to be getting closer. He tried to take another step back, but his heels hit the door.

"We could go out of business and lose our jobs, all because of him," said a tall, thin woman with blue glasses.

They all hated him

"At least say something, Brodie."

He couldn't tell who was speaking any more. It was all coming at him.

"I'm sorry." He sounded ridiculous.

"Is that all you've got to say?"

242

"After all you've done," said Doreen. "I don't think that's good enough."

"Poor Elspeth," said Moira.

He'd done it for her, and for Maggie. For both of them.

"She didn't know, did she?" said Andy.

He pointed at them as he turned the handle. "Don't any of you bring her into this. She knew nothing about it."

"Dewi would like a word," said the woman from reception, appearing next to him at the sorting table.

Thank God for that. He couldn't stand the silent treatment any more. Since the tea break Moira and Doreen had been shooting him looks even more arctic than the fruit he was searching. At least Dewi didn't detest him. He'd take up his offer of joining him in the hot tub tonight and bring round a couple of bottles of wine. He didn't even mind if it was fondue again.

Settled in the same chair as yesterday, Brodie watched as Dewi studied his stapler. When the man still hadn't uttered a word, Brodie tentatively picked up the voluminous grey sock that was still heaped at the front of the desk.

"Think this *is* mine actually," he said, examining it. "I recognise the hole."

Tiny hands clasped over his stomach, Dewi started twisting back and forth in his leather chair. "This can't go on."

"I'll get some new clothes pegs."

"I just don't understand it."

243

A shrug. "It's been windy."

"You sat there yesterday and swore blind it wasn't you. I stuck up for you on live television."

"It wasn't until I found the other one this morning that I realised it was mine."

Dewi picked up a pen and started swinging it between two fingers. "I still can't figure out why the hell you did it."

"It just happened. You peg out a sock, and you expect it to still be there when you go back for it."

"Journalists have been ringing all morning. Even the Yanks have got their knickers in a twist. Twice CNN have called for an interview — America's our biggest export market."

Silence.

"You do understand what this means?"

Brodie held up his hands. "Absolutely."

Slowly Dewi rose to his feet. "By the way, Shona's just rung about the hot tub."

He raised his eyebrows. "Oh yes?"

"Better hold off on the whole thing. Something to do with the balance of the chemicals not being right."

"I couldn't have come anyway," he said, swatting away the very notion. "I've only got Speedos." He stood and grabbed the door handle.

"Brodie," said Dewi, coming round the side of his desk with a smile. The man must have had a change of heart. Now he wouldn't have to tell Elspeth that he'd lost his job on top of everything else. Everything was going to be all right.

244

"Here," said Dewi, reaching out a hand. "You forgot your sock."

With a green paper towel he carefully wiped the dead woman's boots, then placed them back on the rack, toes and heels neatly together. Alone for the first time, fingers fumbling as he tried to undo the buttons of his navy coat, he noticed a white cardigan on his peg. He picked it up, moved it down one, then hung up his coat. How was he going to explain all of this to Elspeth?

A snatch of breeze brought with it the familiar scent of pines as he stepped out. Instinctively, he raised his eyes, surveying the sky for approaching weather. Just lacy smudges of cloud. Everything would work itself out. He'd go home and make some cauliflower cheese for this evening, and when Elspeth was back from work they'd all go for a walk in the woods like they used to. He'd see if Maggie still remembered the calls of the birds. If Elspeth still did.

"There he is! By the door."

Standing outside the gate were even more journalists than yesterday. Some had TV cameras hoisted on their shoulders, others were aiming great long lenses at him.

"Brodie!"

"Why'd ya do it?"

"Was it for the money?"

"Did your family know?"

The heavy door slammed behind him as he hurried down the corridor. There had to be another way out. Eventually he found himself passing the development kitchen and he stopped. He could climb through the window and scale the back fence. If he cut across the fields he'd be home with a beer in his hand before that lot outside had even realised he'd left.

He pressed an ear against the door. No one. After checking both directions, he punched in the code and turned the handle. It wouldn't open. He tried again. It still wouldn't. He must have remembered it wrongly. Finally, on the third attempt, he stepped in.

With both hands he pulled up the blind then slithered out of the window. There was a shout. Someone with a camera was running towards him. One of the photographers must have slipped through the main gate. They were all coming now, feet thundering like camp guards pursuing an escaped prisoner of war. He sprinted to the fence, and as he scrambled up all he could hear were cameras firing at him like gunshot.

Her toes sore in her cramped wellies after running all the way, Maggie hobbled into the library, her rucksack heavy with books. You could hide behind a shelf all afternoon here and no one would find you. Not Frankenstein with his stupid shiny eyes, not the people who had been ringing the doorbell all day, and not the police who would definitely arrest her once they'd found out what she'd done.

"Saw you in the paper the other day." The massive mole by Bald Eagle's mouth moved as she spoke.

Maggie stared at the librarian's dark, curly hair. Everyone said she wore a wig, but she'd never been able to see the join.

246

"That's your father, isn't it? The professional pearl fisher."

"I want to renew the one on the top." She pushed her pile of books across the desk towards her.

Bald Eagle snapped them open to the first page. "Overdue. All of them. You'll have to pay a fine."

"I haven't got any money."

"You must have some pocket money."

"Already spent it."

"What on?"

"Pickled onion crisps."

As if trying to crush an earwig, Bald Eagle started stamping the books. "I'm afraid you won't be able to borrow any more until the fine is paid."

"But I haven't finished *Little Women*. You need to reissue it."

"It's against the rules."

She had to finish that book. "But what about Beth?"

"Please keep your voice down."

"She's got scarlet fever. She might die any minute. Her mum and dad aren't there."

"If you don't lower your voice, I'll have to ask you to leave. There are always consequences to our actions. Your father can tell you all about that."

Stupid woman. Why was she going on about Dad all the time? She grabbed her bag, walked over to the children's books, and tugged out another copy. Sitting crossed-legged in the Military History section, with her back against the World War II shelf, she found the page she'd got to last night, and lowered her head.

After a moment something made her look up. There was a pair of hairy man's legs next to her. Samantha Grey's dad was choosing a book. The witch wasn't with him, was she? She got to her feet, but it was too late. There she was with her horrible long hair and green eyes suddenly in her face.

"You're about to cry."

"Am not."

"Are." She poked her face. "Your cheeks are all red. What are you reading?"

She held up the novel. "Beth's got scarlet fever."

"She gets better."

Maggie smiled.

"You should read the next one, *Good Wives*. She dies in that one."

Without a word, she put the book back on the nearest shelf.

Samantha Grey rested a hand on her hip. "It's not real, you know."

"Didn't say it was."

"Thought you must have been upset about your dad."

There was the sound of heels and Bald Eagle appeared at the end of the shelf. "You two girls, keep your voices down. I'm not going to tell you again."

They watched in silence as she walked away.

With a sly smile, Samantha Grey turned back to her. "They'll definitely arrest him this time."

"He didn't try to murder Cameron Wallace. It's a lie."

"For putting that oyster pearl in a mussel shell and trying to convince everyone that it came out of the Isla, dummy."

"It wasn't my dad."

She prodded her on the chest. "Then why is his ugly face in the paper admitting he did it?"

It was horrible. "It wasn't him."

"Was. He said so. And now everyone hates him. But not as much as they hate you." She leant towards her. "Spazza!"

Her empty rucksack jumped about on her back as she ran down the high street. She couldn't see properly she was crying so much. It wasn't true what Samantha Grey had said. Dad couldn't have admitted it — he didn't do it. And why did Bald Eagle have to ban her from the library? It was Samantha Grey who'd shouted that horrible word, not her.

"Maggie!"

She stopped, chest heaving as she tried to find the familiar voice.

"Where have you been?" said Mum, standing outside the General Store with her shopping bag. "Thought you were going to Mrs Wallace's today."

"Nowhere."

Mum cupped her hand against her cheek. "What's wrong?"

"Nothing."

"Has anyone said anything to you? About Dad?"

She shook her head.

"We'll just pop in here for some bread, then we can go home. I've got the rest of the day off. We can stay indoors, away from everyone. Do some jigsaws."

As the two of them stepped inside, the customers talking to Alice's mum at the counter fell silent. Mum grabbed her hand, led her down one of the aisles and picked up a loaf.

"You've got the wrong one."

"Doesn't matter." Mum started heading for the till.

"It's brown."

"We need to get out of here."

"But we always have the white one."

"It's time to go home."

The customers parted, and, without a word, Mum put the bread on the counter. Why did everyone have to stare at them?

"What was Brodie thinking, Elspeth?" said Alice's mum. "I've got a shop full of stock I've just ordered. I'll never shift it. Everyone's leaving."

Mum hunted through the coins in her purse, then handed over a five-pound note.

"He must have given a reason."

Silence.

She was still just holding the money, while Mum looked at the floor.

"You didn't know all this time, did you, Elspeth? I hope to God you didn't. I'm probably going to have to sell this place."

"Keep the change, Nessa." Reaching for her hand, Mum headed for the door.

They were almost at the end of the high street when the man with the horrible beard who made coffins hurried over from the other side of the road.

"Not at work?" he said to Mum.

It was a stupid question because she was here, standing in front of him.

"I've got the day off."

"Heard the cafe's closed down."

"Opening again tomorrow, actually, with a new menu."

"And you'll still be there?"

Mum frowned. "Why wouldn't I be?"

"Just wondering."

"I haven't been sacked, if that's what you mean."

Now two women walking towards them were staring and whispering.

"Must have been a terrible shock."

"If you're trying to find out whether I knew or not, Alan, I didn't. Is that what people are saying? That I knew all along?"

She wanted to go home.

He held up his palms. "Wasn't me."

"How ridiculous. They'll be insisting that Maggie did it next. Who was saying it? That I must have known."

She pulled on Mum's hand, but she wouldn't move.

He rocked his head from side to side. "It was more like you *might* have known. And they've never even met you, so forget about it."

"Who?"

He shrugged. "Just some of the journalists who've been in." He took a step back. "Don't look at me like that, Elspeth, I stood up for you."

Dusk was slipping through the trees, and the smell of fermented earth was even stronger now that it was raining. It was that tacky sort of drizzle that hung in the air like damp cobwebs. He'd have to go home, despite not having worked out what he was going to say to Elspeth. He could still recall that very first time he saw her hiding barefoot in the trees as he fished the Isla, her hair billowing in the wind. For what seemed like weeks he pretended not to have seen her in case she left him. When, eventually, she came to sit by him, he was so delighted he was initially unable to speak. Something happened inside and he gave her the white baroque pearl with the pink tint he'd just found. Never had he seen anyone so taken with a pearl. He didn't believe in love at first sight. It was ridiculous. So how come he couldn't remember a time when he'd never loved her?

About to emerge from the woods, he stopped, sensing something was wrong. He looked back, trying to work out what it was. It was the unsettling silence. The woodpecker must have found its mate.

Having checked to see that there weren't any reporters outside the house, he darted down the street. The front door firmly closed behind him, he breathed out. He'd go and change out of his wet clothes and warm up in a bath. Hopefully there was some of that nice bubble bath left.

252

"I've got something to say," said Elspeth, walking stiffly out of the kitchen.

She didn't need to. There were two suitcases at the bottom of the stairs.

"Alpina said we could stay with her for a while."

"Why would we want to do that?"

"Maggie and me, I mean."

He shivered. "Just the two of you?"

"In the loft conversion."

"When are you coming back?" The diamond had slipped round her finger again.

"There's milk in the fridge."

"You'll be back in a couple of days, won't you?"

She put a hand on the banister. "They keep knocking on the door. Ringing the bell. Phoning. It's not fair on the bairn. She hasn't stopped crying."

"Wouldn't it be better if I came with you? All three of us together."

"Bin day's Thursday."

Something caught his eye. Maggie was coming down the stairs in those crazy tiger slippers he'd bought her and not seen for months. Surely she didn't want to go. "Maggie?"

Wouldn't even look at him.

"What about Frankenstein? Why don't you take him with you?"

Eyes still on the floor.

"Maybe you'll grow to love him."

Bending her knees, Elspeth picked up the cases. "There's no love without honesty."

"Don't go."

"You know where we'll be."

As she came towards him, brushing against the coats on the rack, he bent forward for a kiss. But she didn't stop. He could smell her perfume. It was the happy one she'd bought herself. At least he presumed she'd bought it. Maggie trailed after her, still in those mad slippers.

"Don't go, Elspeth."

"You've got their number."

"Please don't leave me."

The door thumped uselessly as she attempted to pull it shut behind them. She tried once more, but still it wouldn't close. He held his breath as the door opened wider this time, then failed once more to shut. Over and over, hope coming and going, light blooming and withering. The final bang ricocheted down his back, and all that was left was the frightful sound of them walking away from him.

CHAPTER
FIFTEEN

At the sound of the doorbell Brodie woke, his mouth tasting like the bottom of the bin. Unsure of the time, he turned to see whether Elspeth was still asleep. That was the worst bit, waking up and remembering. Each morning he'd be struck again by the ruthless shard of grief. Abandoned. Left. Discarded. Whichever way he put it, the horror was just the same.

The bell rang again, and still he didn't move. It had been five days since they'd left, and never once had he been out of the house or answered the door. The only time he'd picked the phone up was to speak to them. And even then everything was different. They were just four streets away, yet it felt as though they were on the other side of the world. Maggie could just about get her words out. As for Elspeth, he hadn't dared bring up when they were coming back. As long as he didn't ask, she couldn't tell him never.

Finally he sat up, toes searching for the comfort of his slippers. They'd gone, too. With a hitch of his pyjama bottoms, he wandered into Maggie's room. There was her small wooden desk where she used to do her homework. Above it was the shelf with her books from when she was little. He took down Richard

Scarry's *What Do People Do All Day?* and studied the drawings. Maggie had once pointed out the owl optician, the lion doctor and the rabbit beautician, and wondered where the pearl fisher was. Hanging forgotten on the back of the door was her furry cream dressing gown. Was she cold at Mungo and Alpina's? He bent down and looked into the doll's house, all its tiny occupants safely tucked up in their own beds. He'd kept it round at Dewi and Shona's until it was her birthday. As he straightened, he noticed something missing from her chest of drawers. She'd taken her jewellery box. It had all her seed pearls in it. Elspeth must have told her they were never coming back.

In his last clean shirt, and the trousers that had been consigned to gardening, he trudged downstairs and lifted the lid of the bread bin. Just crumbs and an empty bag. Its florets now the colour of soot, he batted aside the cauliflower in the fridge. There was nothing left in here either. As he turned, his foot hit the empty bottles clustered around the bin, and they skidded wildly across the floor. He couldn't have drunk that much in five days. It was impossible.

Slouched at the table with a spoon and can of tuna, he eyed Elspeth's napkin with its silver ring engraved with her mother's initials. Adjacent to it was Maggie's wooden ring, painted with a puffin, which they'd bought on the Isle of Skye. If he'd known it was to be their last holiday he wouldn't have read his book, or gone for a walk when he needed to be alone.

Swallowing an oily mouthful, he stared ahead. He'd done the right thing taking the blame. He couldn't have had the papers branding Maggie a thief. A fraudster even. The whole world knowing what she'd done. The bairn would never have recovered from it. She had enough stacked against her as it was.

He loaded his spoon. And then there was Elspeth. He couldn't have put her through it either. She'd have found a way of blaming herself, the way she did for Maggie having been born with only half an arm. It wouldn't have been right. The bairn was the light of her life. Of his. The girl they'd named Margaret as it came from the Latin word for pearl.

Up on his bare feet, he opened a drawer and bundled away their napkins. He scratched at his uncombed hair. Now the table looked even worse. With a desperate scrabble he put them back out again. Hands hanging by his sides, he stared at the pointless place settings. Something furry brushed against his toes and he started. For some reason Fake Frank was now glimmering with purple glitter. How could he look after that thing when he couldn't even look after himself? The creature hung limply as he tucked it under his arm and screwed his feet into his shoes by the door.

"When are we going home?" Maggie slumped onto the bed and stared at her tiger slippers. Nothing was the same without Dad. She hated it here. The duvet cover didn't even have flying hippos on, and there hadn't been any Rice Krispies for breakfast yet again. Mum had cooked her French beans from the Co-op, but they were horrid.

"You've already asked me that once this morning," said Mum, sounding like everything was normal. "Come over here and I'll do your hair."

Sitting on the blue stool at the dressing table, she studied Mum in the mirror. She didn't like it here either. At night Maggie could hear her in bed next to her pretending she wasn't crying. Why didn't they just go home if she hated it here too? Neither of them had seen Dad for five days. She'd counted. Earlier this morning when Mum was in the shower, and Alpina was hanging out the washing, she'd run home, but Dad didn't answer the door. She'd tried her key, but it wouldn't turn, and she couldn't even look in as all the curtains were drawn.

"But we can't stay here forever."

Mum started brushing her hair. "Like I said, it's just for a while. Then we'll make a plan."

"What about Dad?" She might never see him again.

The bristles started moving faster against her head.

"Why is everyone saying he did it?"

The brush stopped. "He spoke to that reporter from the *Chronicle* and then all the other papers picked up the story. And the radio and television. He did the right thing. You have to own up when you've done something wrong. Cameron and Mungo could both have lost their businesses. Lost their houses even."

"But what happens if it wasn't him?"

She was looking at her like she'd just said the silliest thing in the world. "Why would he admit to doing something he hadn't done?"

Silence.

258

"What's wrong? You look worried."

"Nothing."

"Plaits or bunches?"

"Hate both."

"I'd like to bring this back," said Brodie, depositing Fake Frank next to the till.

The assistant held his gaze with her black-rimmed eyes. "And why might that be?"

"It doesn't chew the TV aerial cable."

She stopped fiddling with her nose ring.

"If there's one thing I can't stand in a rabbit, it's piety," he said.

"What about the Easter Bunny?"

"That's the one exception."

From the cage next to him a solitary lovebird started up a high-pitched squeak that reminded him of a baby's toy being repeatedly stamped on.

She picked up the fraudster and started stroking his head. "I don't see what the problem is. He's really cute."

"Exactly! Where's the anarchy? The moustache? All the greats have a moustache. Einstein. Nietzsche. Lemmy."

"Hitler had a moustache," she said sulkily. The creature started scrabbling up her shoulder and she set him down again. "I can't take him back."

He ran a hand down his brittle cheek. "Why not?"

"He's covered in purple glitter."

"It washes off."

"It might not."

"Just tell everyone he's going through his glam-rock phase. They'll understand. We've all been there."

She shook her head. "You'll have to exchange him for something else."

"Something else? I can't look after a pet, that's the whole point."

"How's about a goldfish? Two for one. Offer ends tomorrow."

He leant forward, both palms on the counter. "So now you bring out the goldfish? It's all too late for goldfish, don't you see?" His voice was getting louder. "We came in and specifically asked for a goldfish and you didn't have any, so we got Frank. She fell for Frank big time, but Frank went and did a runner. Then *she* left. And I'm stuck with this interloper."

"You're frightening the terrapins."

For a moment he stared out of the window. "Can't you just take it?" He was almost pleading. "I don't even want my money back."

"Have you got your receipt?"

He shook his head. Just take the goddamn rabbit.

"We'll need the receipt."

"But you must remember us coming in," he cried, shaking his outstretched hands at her. "The girl with scruffy blonde hair and sunflower shorts. Chose the weirdest-looking rabbit in Christendom."

There was a pause..

"I remember you," she said evenly. "And your daughter. She not with you today?"

"No." He looked at his feet.

"Saw you both in the paper."

Appalled, he raised his head. So everyone knew. "I'd better go."

She traced the counter with her fingertips. "I had a bet with my boyfriend that it wasn't you. Lost thirty quid."

Even the lovebird fell silent.

From his pocket, he pulled out three ten-pound notes and dropped them on the counter. She looked at them, seeming confused. He hoisted Fake Frank under his armpit, and walked out, not listening to what she was trying to tell him from the doorway.

"Freedom," Brodie announced as he opened the passenger door, revealing the tempting fields behind him.

Eyes fixed on the glove compartment, Fake Frank remained on the seat.

"Look at that." He stood to one side and pointed to the verge, a nice juicy green one just outside Perth. "Buttercups and everything."

The only thing that moved was his nose.

"Off you go. It's a lot better out there than our living-room carpet."

He still didn't move.

"It's freedom I'm offering you — what everyone wants. A chance to leave all the crap behind."

The creature turned his back on him, exposing his tail.

He nodded at the fields, trimmed with hedges, disappearing over the horizon. "Think of all the lady rabbits out there. As much sex as you want."

Nothing.

"They're going to love you. Even the woman in the shop thought you were cute."

The thing hopped over to the driver's seat, leaving behind a round deposit.

"Right, that's it." He burrowed his fingers around the animal's warm belly, and hauled him out. Onto the verge he marched, and set him down next to a tasty-looking weed. He ran back to the car, the wheels skidding loudly on the loose stones as he pulled away. Buffeted by a passing lorry, he glanced in the mirror. The daft thing hadn't even moved.

Alice was supposed to be her best friend, but every time she'd been round to see her since Dad was all over the newspapers, Alice's mum had told her she wasn't there. Hesitantly, she pushed open the door and stood at the counter piled with cakes and loaves of bread with half-price stickers on them. It wasn't as if they'd have to keep out of the way of the customers any more. There weren't any.

"Is Alice here?"

Alice's mum lowered her crochet. "Heard you and your mother have moved out."

"We're having a holiday in Auntie Alpina's new loft conversion."

"A holiday? Is that what you call it?"

Silence.

"How's your father?"

She scratched her thigh. "On holiday too."

"Lost his job at the jammie is what they're saying."

"Is Alice here?"

"Did he say why he did it, Maggie? That's what I can't understand. Everyone's convinced it was for the money."

From behind the shelves came the sound of tins being moved. She followed the noise, and there was Alice in her yellow-and-white-checked dress holding a brown feather duster. Why didn't she look pleased to see her?

She offered a smile. "Fancy doing something?"

The feathers continued to flick back and forth across the cans of mushy peas. "Like what?"

"Anything."

"The rain's on again."

"We could go up the Tolbooth," she whispered. "See if those robbers left the money in there after we left."

"There's isn't any money there," Alice hissed back. "There never was. In fact I had even less money after going as I had to buy a new pair of flip-flops." She moved down to the tins of sweetcorn.

"If you've called round," she said, following her, "and no one answered, it's because we're not there."

"I haven't."

Silence.

"My mum met this man," said Alice, still not looking at her as she flicked. "One of the pearl hunters. I thought he was going to be my new dad."

She fingered the edge of her shorts. "You can't get a new dad that soon."

"Can." Alice straightened the tins of soup. "You can have a new one whenever your mum finds one that's better than your real dad."

Mum wasn't going to do that, was she? Maggie didn't want another dad. She loved the one she had. "What's he like?"

"He went home three days ago with the rest of them."

"Maybe he'll come back."

"She's still waiting for him to call."

She tried to smile. "Will you send me a postcard from Spain?"

"We're not going any more. It's too expensive." The duster came to a halt. "Why did he have to do it?"

"Who?"

"Your dad."

She swallowed. "It wasn't him."

"Of course it was him, silly." She was shouting now, almost crying. "He said he put the stupid thing in the shell. And now we're on our own again and we can't even go to Spain. He's ruined everything."

For God's sake. As the sign for Nether Isla came into view Brodie stabbed his foot on the brake. The car rocked from side to side as he reversed into the entrance of a field. Wheels slithered as he pulled out, and he headed back the way he'd been coming for the last eighteen sodding minutes.

If only he'd leave. Elspeth watched the last customer wipe his mouth on the back of his hand. He must have finished by now. He'd already pressed his finger into the constellation of crumbs on his plate and licked it. What was he waiting for? She wanted to get out of here.

264

People were still coming in to clap Cameron on the back and tell him they'd known all along it wasn't him. What were they trying to imply? That they'd always had Brodie marked down as a cheat?

Elbows on the counter, she rested her cheeks on her fists. It was all still so difficult to believe, but she'd found that little suede bag, the type jewellers use, in the washing machine. It must have been what they'd put the cultured pearl in. How could she have got Brodie so wrong after all these years? She'd been such a fool. Was there anything else that he'd been lying about? That journalist who'd been in his hut. The one with the cleavage and the hair. Was there anything going on with her? All those times when he'd been away for the night at the shells . . .

Finally the customer picked up the bill, leant back, and dug a hand into his pocket. After counting out the coins, he arranged them in a Tower of Pisa next to his plate and got up. As she stood by the door to hasten him out, he stopped and tucked in the back of his shirt.

"That business with the pearl. I can't help wondering whether the wee girl had something to do with it," he said. "You know the one I mean? The one with the false arm who was in the paper. Maybe they were working together, father and daughter. They use handicapped children in India to get money out of people. Just a thought. Anyway, I've got to be going. You have a good evening. The sun's out."

She didn't know where she was going. Somewhere. Anywhere but here. Maggie was round at Alice's, so there was no need to go back to Alpina's straight away. They'd have to leave that place soon and find somewhere else. There were only so many of Alpina's snipey comments she could stand.

She kept her eyes on the pavement as she passed the remains of the abbey. That was where Brodie had first kissed her, as they lay among the noisy fallen leaves and the red sandstone arches. Maybe it was all her fault. But all she'd done was point out that the pearls were getting scarcer as he just didn't seem to get it. How could she feel so guilty about it and angry with him at the same time?

A light breeze tossed her hair as she placed her hands on the warm wall of the bridge, and looked down at the Isla. It was here that Brodie had first told her that he loved her. He'd written it on the riverbed with stones, and she felt so elated she couldn't help taking his hand. He hadn't included her name, but she knew it was meant for her — he went bright red. For weeks she came every day to see it, and just stood there imagining their future. There was no trace of it now. A swollen white Co-op bag was caught in a branch reaching into the water, and bobbing next to it was a lurid red Coke can.

Her flat work shoes slipping on what was now mud, she staggered down to the water's edge. She glanced at the path running under the bridge, seeing them all sitting there opening their shells during the storm, and the pearl falling into Cameron's hand, much to everyone's astonishment. Especially Brodie's. To think that she'd gone to his hut and reassured him that she knew he had nothing to do with it. So much for everything he'd said that time in the kitchen about there being magic in the world.

A bird with a white breast settled on a branch ahead of her as she made her way downstream. Brodie would have known its name. Was this it, then, after almost twenty years? Too defeated to carry on, she sat down wanting to forget it all, but was besieged by memories she no longer trusted. The times they'd shared in the fisherman's hut when they were young, exploring each other. Walking hand in hand along this very path newly married, talking about how many children they'd have. That snowy Saturday afternoon, fat flakes flying horizontally, when she'd conceived Maggie on the living-room floor. The family picnics up in the Cairngorms, picking blaeberries and throwing the ones they didn't eat at each other.

"Wasn't sure which way you went."

Shielding her eyes, she looked up.

"Mind if I join you?" said Cameron, sitting down. "I saw you on the bridge as I was driving past. Thought you might want some company."

It had been a week since she'd stood in front of him and that journalist and insisted it wasn't Brodie, and she was still too embarrassed to look at him properly.

"I'm sorry he didn't admit it earlier."

"It would have been helpful."

She turned to him then. At least his eyes were less bloodshot. "Has he apologised? For any of it?"

"I'm afraid not. It must have been quite a shock for you, your husband doing something like that."

267

She watched the sun fire copper on the water. "I'll never understand it. He always hated cultured pearls."

"People change, as I said before. At least you've moved out. You don't want to end up like some Tory MP's wife standing at a five-bar gate in support of her errant husband while the rest of the world looks on in disgust." His hand rested lightly on her knee. "As a friend of yours, I suggest you don't let it drag on any longer. Announce your decision and cut your ties. Otherwise you and Maggie are going to go through hell living here. People won't forget."

She got to her feet. "I'd better go."

"There's something I've been wanting to ask you."

"I've got to get some food in for tonight."

"For years," he said, standing. "I just never did."

"The bairn'll be home soon." She stared at her muddy shoes.

"I've always wondered why that letter wasn't enough. What more I could have done to have kept you."

She looked up. "What letter?"

"It put me right off, getting no reply. That's why I never tried to get you back when you left me. I just presumed —"

"What letter?"

"It took me ages to write it. It was the first one I'd ever sent a girl."

"What letter?"

"The one in which I told you how much you meant to me. You must have got it. I put it through the door myself at your parents' house. It was during the Easter holidays."

Silence.

"Unless they didn't give it to you." He frowned. "But I always thought your parents liked me."

Furious, she shook her head. "Alpina."

It was here, definitely. He remembered the way the branches curved over the road as if trying to reach those on the other side. And that was the field with the solitary oak at the top. Standing on the verge, he turned in a circle. There was still no sign of Fake Frank. He squinted at the road, hardly able to look. Nothing squashed. So he'd done it after all. Taken his chance and run for it.

The engine protested as, foot down, he headed back the way he'd come. All that worry for nothing, thinking that short-haired numbskull was too domesticated — or thick — to survive in the wild. That if he didn't hurry he'd find him reduced to a flat furry pancake on the tarmac, and it would be all his fault. He was probably down a burrow at this very moment with some velvet-eared pal. What a waste of petrol. Like he didn't have enough on his plate.

As he cleared the brow of the hill, wondering whether he could cut the black bits off the cauliflower, something darted out the side of the road. There was a terrible squeal and an acrid smell of burning as he fought to bring the car to a stop. Finally still, he remained where he was, hands stuck to the wheel. It wasn't a child, was it? There were houses on either side of the road with bikes outside. A kid could easily have run out. They were fast, children, you had to keep an eye on them. Somehow he managed to open the door and stagger round to the front of the car. He shouldn't have been going so fast, especially over a hill. What a moron he was. Finally he lowered his eyes. Whiskers fluttering rakishly, Fake Frank was just sitting there as if waiting for a travelling dentist.

Back in Nether Isla, parked outside the Co-op, his tongue slickened at the smell of freshly baked bread. There was nothing in the house for supper, but he still couldn't face going in. Everyone would just stare at him, the man who'd kicked the town to death when it had just got on its feet. It had been bad enough when everyone was shouting at him in the canteen. He'd felt sick with guilt, even though it wasn't even him. The car shuddered as he turned the key. The Victoria would be empty at this time of day. After a few pints and the crossword, he'd go to the garage in Blairgowrie and get one of those tinned steak and kidney puddings. Reduced, hopefully.

As he walked into the pub, with its reassuring smell of stale beer, Mungo was hunched at their table by the fire cupping a glass in both hands. Even better. "Can I get you a drink?"

There was a rattle of ice cubes as Mungo raised his tumbler. "Got one."

Whisky. A double by the looks of it. And it wasn't his first either, he could tell by his voice. "Fancy another?"

"Be off in a minute."

"That's the first time you've ever turned down a free drink."

270

Mungo wiped his lips on the back of his hand. "Don't need any haddock, do you?"

He paused. "We could do some training."

A shake of the head.

"'Fidelity, Bravery, Integrity' is the motto of which organisation?"

"Integrity?" He almost scoffed. "Not in the mood."

"What about a game of Cluedo?"

"Nah."

"I'll let you be Miss Scarlett."

Mungo took another swig.

"Come on, Mungo, you love being Miss Scarlett, and I've never asked why. That's what pals are for."

He lurched back. "I still can't believe it was you. I'd sooner think it was Cameron."

That.

"I've known you since we were eleven. Makes you wonder who you can trust."

"You can still trust me."

"I just don't get it. I'm not exactly cashed-up myself, but I'd have lent you what you needed. Borrowed it from somewhere." He looked like he was about to cry.

"Come on, Mungo. I'm exactly the same person I've always been."

Those eyebrows came down.

"All that time people thinking it was me. You should have heard what they were saying. I was even thinking of moving away."

Trying to smile, he took a step towards him. "Remember when they sat us next to each other the first morning I arrived at school, and we took the ham

271

out of my sandwiches, stuck it underneath Miss Forbes's desk, and waited for it to drop on her lap?"

"All that speculation in the papers," said Mungo, staring at the beer mat he'd started to shred into tiny pieces. "Those carefully worded sentences that weren't quite libellous, but which clearly meant I'd got nowhere in life and the chippy was about to go bust. They even found out how much rent I owed on it."

"Remember that time we painted the chippy, and you tried to use my hair as a brush?"

"I even wondered whether Mum thought it was me at one point. She certainly didn't think it was you."

"Does she still make that treacle tart we used to have when I came round for tea after school?"

With a jerk of his head Mungo drained his glass and stood up. "I'm off. Cooking Maggie barbecued spare ribs to cheer her up. It's her favourite, in case you've forgotten. Did you ever think of her in all this? Or Elspeth?"

Silence, followed by the sound of his best pal walking out on him. For a moment he stood looking at the slammed door.

"The usual, please," he said, approaching the bar.

Alan turned a page of the *Scotsman*.

"A pint, when you're ready."

"Listen, Brodie," he said, slowly folding the paper. "People aren't very happy."

"What's new?"

Alan scratched at the rusty whiskers on his neck. "It's a tricky situation, what with everything that's happened."

272

"You just have to stick a glass underneath that tap."

Shaking his head like it was the last thing he was going to do.

"You're not barring me, are you?"

He held up his hands. "Good Lord, no! You're one of my best customers . . . I'm just saying that, for the moment, it's best you don't come in. Nothing to do with me, I've done very well out of it all. It's just that everyone's a bit . . . We need time for people's knickers to untwist, if you get my drift."

"But what about the quiz? I'm team captain. How will they manage without me?"

"They'll find another one. Cameron, most probably. But the more pressing concern is the tab." He opened a ring file and ran a warty finger down a column of figures. "It currently stands at two hundred and thirty-one pounds and twenty-seven pence."

It was so ridiculous he smiled. "I haven't got that sort of money."

"So what are you going to do about it?"

He shrugged. "The car. It's all I've got."

"That bean can on wheels?" he said, incredulous. "You'd have to pay someone to take it off your hands."

The only sound was the tips of Alan's fingers on the counter.

Without a word he left. Several minutes later he returned and parked Fake Frank on the bar, his fur shimmering in the afternoon light.

"What am I meant to do with that?" said Alan, stepping back. "Stick it on the menu?"

He didn't turn as he made for the door. "It's all I've got left."

In the unlit living room, pink velvet curtains tightly closed, the unbearable silence was pierced by the muffled shrieks of a television. Dewi and Shona would be watching it snuggled up together with a bottle of wine. His stomach rumbled low and long as he fiddled with the threads on the armrest, trying to avoid looking at Elspeth's Taj Mahal that had started to lean on top of the bookshelf.

At least he still had the shells. Now that the pearl hunters were gone he'd go tomorrow and see what was left. There'd be something at that little spot in the Laxford. It had been a month since Cameron had found the pearl. Something had to go right sooner or later, surely? The law of averages and all that.

The bell rang, making him jump. Without thinking, he got up to answer it. It wasn't until the sun was ablaze in the hall that he realised what he was doing. But it was too late by then. Ailsa was on the step eager to come in.

He shielded his eyes against the light. "I'm a bit busy."

"I tried calling, but nobody answered."

"I'm rushed off my feet." He ran a hand down the back of his unwashed hair.

"I was wondering if you knew yet."

"Why don't you come back when I've got more time? Maybe in a week or so. Or a month."

"You've no idea, have you?"

"I haven't got any milk."

"Is it OK if we talk inside?" As she moved towards him, he stepped out of the way. She wasn't meant to be in here. No one was. He trailed after her into the kitchen, listening to more empties toppling over and spinning across the floor.

"Do you mind if I open the blind?" she said, already hauling it up. "It's really dark in here."

She stared at the encrusted pots and smeared dishes stacked around the sink.

What must she think of him? He heaved the bin outside to get rid of the smell.

"Have a seat," he said.

She didn't move.

"I'd offer you a cup of tea, but as I explained, there's no milk." He noticed one of his shirt buttons was undone and he did it up, fingers fumbling.

Silence.

"I've got half a can of tuna. Only opened it at lunchtime. Fancy some tuna?"

There was the sound of things being shunted around her bag, and she fished out her notepad.

He backed up against the fridge. "I'm not talking about it. The pearl. To anyone. I've said my bit."

"I heard you lost your job. I'm sorry," she said, eyes on the carnage around the sink again.

"Doesn't matter. I'm going back to the shells tomorrow. Full-time. The only one left, remember?" He tried to smile.

She just looked at him.

He pointed to the hut. "I'll show you on the map where I'm going. There's this great little colony in the Laxford. Bet no one's tried it."

Her gaze drifted uneasily out of the window, then returned. "The story's going in tomorrow. I'm just after a few quotes, if you wouldn't mind." She looked at her watch. "I'll have to phone them through."

Hunting for the radio, he picked his way through the piles of washing that hadn't yet made their way into the machine. "Do you know what the forecast is for tomorrow?"

"Brodie."

"It'll be sunny, I bet." He almost laughed, already seeing the mussels half buried in the gravel, tips ajar.

"They've banned it. Pearl-fishing. It's all over."

CHAPTER
SIXTEEN

That was it. Brodie snapped on the bedside lamp, and hurled back the hot bedcovers. It still wasn't even dawn, but he had to know. Whichever way he looked at it, what Ailsa had said just didn't make sense. She must have made a mistake. How could they ban pearl-fishing? With immediate effect, she'd claimed. Some idiot had got their wires crossed. He'd tried to tell her yesterday, but she just wouldn't have it.

It would only take about two and a half hours to get to Inverness. Less if he ignored the speed limits. Dr Kerr would know what was going on. He'd get him to call Ailsa and put her straight. As he pulled out, he glanced up at the window of Mrs Wallace's spare room. It was in darkness, like all the others in the street. Had Cameron been invited round for Mungo's spare ribs last night, and stayed over?

The muddy light was lifting by the time he spotted the Scottish Natural Heritage sign in front of an ugly modern building, a red-and-white-striped barrier blocking the entrance to the car park. He pulled up on double yellow lines, and stood leaning against his car, trying to work out which was Dr Kerr's office. In a few hours the man would arrive for work, and everything would be cleared up. After he'd seen him, he'd try a river or a pretty burn while he was up here. Thankfully his pearling stick and boat were still on the roof rack. He'd ring Elspeth when he got back and tell her how many pearls he'd found. Then he'd convince her everything was going to be all right, and he'd ask her to come home.

Just before nine, he drew up in front of the barrier, and waited, fingers tapping, for the attendant in a voluminous yellow jacket and black peaked cap to approach.

"I've come to see Dr Kerr."

"You look familiar," said the man, grey stubble running rampant over his chins. "What's the name?"

"McBride."

A finger with a dirty plaster ran down a list on a clipboard. "Your name's not down. You'll have to make an appointment."

"Dr Kerr knows who I am."

"He knows who the Queen is too, but she'd still have to make an appointment." He jerked his thumb. "You'll have to move. The vehicle behind you needs to get in."

"I'll only be a couple of minutes."

"You're causing an obstruction. It's the chief executive."

"I just need to speak to him." He revved the engine. "Someone's got it all wrong."

"I know you." He wagged his finger at him! "You're that pearl fisher who was in the papers. You're a disgrace to this country."

There was a high-pitched whine as he reversed into the approaching traffic, and, ignoring the indignant honks, drove off round the block. He didn't have time for all this. It was after nine. Dr Kerr would be sitting at his desk by now. As he approached the entrance again, a white car passed below the barrier, which then started to descend. Aiming for the diminishing gap, he pressed his foot down. Someone, somewhere, was shouting. A frightful scraping sound came from the roof, like the world was being ripped in two. It was only when he came to a stop across two parking spaces that he dared to look in the mirror. The remains of his boat, made in the McBride tradition, were littering the ground like a shipwrecked coffin.

He launched himself through the doors, and scanned the list of names next to the lift. Again and again his fist hit the button. Come on! When there was still no indication of it coming, he darted up the stairs, taking them two at a time. Turning in circles on the third floor, he spotted a sign to room 314, and the grey corridor filled with the sound of his thudding feet.

As he opened the door, Dr Kerr was on the phone, fingering his neat beard.

"They've got it all wrong," he said, striding to his desk.

"Just a minute." Dr Kerr put a hand over the mouthpiece.

"The *Perth & Kinross Chronicle*. They've got it all wrong."

He looked bewildered. "We don't get it up here."

"That reporter came to see me. Ailsa."

"This isn't a good time." Dr Kerr was still holding the smothered receiver. "Why don't you ring me later?"

"She's got it into her head that they've banned pearling. With immediate effect."

His gaze fell to his diary. "Or come back tomorrow. I'll be less busy tomorrow."

"The woman said pearl mussels have been granted full protection under the Wildlife and Countryside Act. You need to tell her it's not true. There's going to be a story about it in the paper this morning."

"Actually, the day after would be better."

Brodie reached out a finger and disconnected the call.

Slowly Dr Kerr put down the receiver. "You've got your pyjama top on," he said evenly.

He lowered his eyes. It was the one with the red-and-blue checks. There was something on the lapel. A grey tuna flake.

"Why don't you take a seat?" Dr Kerr helped himself to a Polo.

He took a step closer. "I've got her number. You've got to call her. She'll write a correction."

The phone rang and Dr Kerr's hand shot out. "Yes. He's here." He was on his feet, peering out of the window. "Jesus, I see what you mean . . . No, don't get them involved . . . I've known him for years, that's why . . . There's no need to call them . . . Because I'll handle it . . . Yes, quite sure . . . I'm perfectly aware of that."

The receiver rattled back into place and Dr Kerr sank into his seat. He stared at something on the edge of his desk for a moment. "It had to be with immediate effect. In case there was a last-minute run on the pearls. You know what people are like."

He leant towards him, knocking over a pen holder. "People have been pearl-fishing in this country since before Julius Caesar pitched up."

"Take a seat, Brodie," he said, inching back on his chair.

He stayed where he was.

"The surveys we've conducted over the last three years have been desperate. You know how bad the situation is just as well as I do. Pearl mussels in Scotland have been becoming extinct by an average of two rivers every year since 1970." He nodded to a map on the wall pierced with coloured pins. "Mussels are no longer found in twenty-six of the sixty-nine Scottish rivers that supported populations."

Brodie stared at the map, then back at Dr Kerr.

"There are now only eight rivers with any signs of juvenile mussels and only three where numbers are healthy. Three. As for England and Wales, they only have one river each with healthy reproducing populations. I don't even know why I'm telling you all this. We've discussed it often enough."

He held out his palms, incredulous. "But what about the Royal Charter of 1642? The one that grants Scottish commoners the right to fish for pearls?"

Sitting there in silence like he hadn't just announced the end of the world.

"What's a ban going to do?" He could feel himself beginning to lose it. "It's already against the law to kill or injure pearl mussels, but no one cares. You've seen all the piles of open shells on the banks."

Dr Kerr scooted his chair back further. "Now it's illegal to intentionally or recklessly kill, injure, take or disturb freshwater pearl mussels or to damage their habitat. Anyone doing so will be prosecuted."

It was so ludicrous he smiled. "If you catch them."

"There'll be no point taking them. You'll only be able to sell pearls collected before today, and then only if you have a licence from the Scottish Executive."

"Why can't they just keep things as they are?" He was yelling now, trying to make him see how idiotic it all was. "The pearl rush is over. Everyone's gone. It's just me." Surely he could see that?

Dr Kerr got to his feet. "I still can't work out why you put a cultured oyster pearl inside a mussel and thought you'd get away with it. I've known you all my working life. Stupidly, I told everyone it must have been one of the others. You do know how much damage it's caused? I felt physically sick when I saw the state of the Isla. And that was just one river."

"But the pearl rush is over," he said slowly, so Dr Kerr would get it. "They've all gone home."

He tossed his pen onto his desk. "It wasn't anything to do with it. They just brought the ban forward by a few months. It was going to happen anyway. And it's not just pearl mussels. Basking sharks and bluebells are also being given protection."

282

"Bluebells?" His laugh was loud and ugly. "My family hasn't been picking flowers for five generations."

"Take it up with the government. The Department of Environment. We don't make the law."

He could hear the mint clicking against his teeth. "How long? How long are they banning it for?"

Dr Kerr raised his eyebrows. "I'd say at least three."

"Three years." He looked at the floor. "I suppose it could be worse."

"Decades, Brodie. And that's for the populations to recover significantly enough for any relaxation of the ban to even be considered."

"I'll be dead by then," he said, almost to himself.

The phone started ringing.

"I'll show you out."

Something went limp inside. He reached for the armrests and lowered himself down. So Ailsa was right. It *was* all over.

"Nobody ever manages to find their way out of this place," said Dr Kerr, coming round the desk. "Everywhere looks the same."

He slumped back. He'd never be able go to the shells again. Or finish the necklace.

"I'd better get on. Call people back."

He'd never see a riverbed again. Feel the thrill of opening a shell.

"Are you all right? Do you need a glass of water?"

What was he now, if he wasn't a pearl fisher? Someone should open a window. How were you meant to breathe in this place? A hand grabbed his elbow as he tried to stand.

"Maybe you should sit a bit longer."

"I've got to get out of here."

Somehow he found the door handle, and he started down the corridor.

"Brodie!"

He kept on walking.

"Are you OK?"

He didn't turn.

"Brodie! What are you going to do now?"

Couldn't possibly tell him.

Maggie pressed the bell yet again. It was the third time she'd been round since they'd gone to stay with Uncle Mungo and Auntie Alpina, and Dad hadn't answered the door once. Each time she'd tried to open it with her key, but it must have been locked from the inside. He'd better hurry up as she didn't want anyone to see her. All day she'd been hiding in the woods from the police.

As she waited, stomach rumbling, she looked around for Dad's car. There it was. He'd taken his boat off the roof rack. Feeling hopeful, she got out her key. Maybe he was having a snooze, and that was why he couldn't hear her ringing. The door opened.

"Dad?" She stepped into the darkened hall.

After a moment she ran into the living room and threw back the curtains. Not even useless Frankenstein. He must be at the table reading the paper. She trod carefully to the kitchen window and raised the blind. There were bottles lying all over the floor, which was covered in drops of red wine, like a nosebleed. He hadn't done the washing-up. Through the open window she could smell the bin standing outside, overflowing with tins and brown vegetables.

Must be on the toilet. Up the steps she pounded, ready to knock, but the bathroom door was wide open. Several grey socks, scrunched up like nests, were scattered on the floor. You were meant to use the laundry basket.

Asleep then. She gently pushed Mum and Dad's door so as not to wake him. It was empty. He hadn't even made the bed. She sniffed inside one of the mugs on his bedside table. Red wine.

She knew where he'd be. He'd be looking at the ledgers in his hut with a cup of tea, planning a trip to the shells now that everyone had left. Maybe he'd let her go with him. Her feet slipped on the stairs as she tore down them and ran out into the garden, the shaggy grass tickling her feet in her sandals. Her heart lifted at the sight of the door standing ajar. Smiling, she stepped in.

It was horrible. Someone had torn the map and all the articles about Dad off the walls and ripped them into little pieces. She nudged at them with her toe. It was like a dog had been at them. And look what they'd done to the ledgers. They were lying open at funny angles on the floor, as if they'd been thrown. No one was allowed to take them off the shelves apart from Dad.

Her foot struck something. It was a snapped piece of Grandpa's pearling stick. Another bit was over there in the corner. How could anyone have done that? You had to ask permission to touch it.

Back in the hall, she sat on the bottom step, chin on her knees as she waited. After waiting some more, she took from her pocket a piece of newspaper with half of Dad's face on it. The other half was lost. Eventually she stood up, no longer hungry. He just wasn't coming back.

She looked Alpina straight in the eye as she passed her the ketchup. It had been a whole day since Cameron had told her about the letter, and still she hadn't found the right moment to bring it up.

"Hardly any left," said Alpina, as she squeezed red curls over her chips, both hands gripping the plastic bottle.

"That's because we've had haddock and chips three times this week already," said Maggie.

She shot her a look. "It's lovely, thank you, Mungo." She hated being here night after night in someone else's dining room. Even if they were family.

Mungo reached for the salt. "We should be through all the haddock by Christmas."

"If we live that long," said Cameron, tunnelling into his batter like a miner after gold. He speared a piece of white flesh.

"What are *you* doing for Christmas, Elspeth?"

It was one of those typical Alpina questions. One that landed straight in the heart. "It's only August."

"You're more than welcome to spend it here with us is what I'm saying. The two of you."

She stared at her knife. Was it just her and Maggie from now on then? She'd never imagined it ending like this. Never.

"For some reason there's a rabbit hopping around the Victoria looking like it's on its way to a disco," said Cameron. "Must be some kind of alternative mouser."

"Has he got a moustache?" said Maggie, eyes wide.

"We've talked about that," she said. "When bad things happen, and there's nothing you can do about it, you just have to accept it." She nodded at the bairn's untouched plate. "Eat up."

In the silence Elspeth tapped at her batter with her fork. Was *she* supposed to accept that her marriage was over?

"Please can I have some ketchup?" said Maggie.

"Offer it to the others first. It's impolite to finish it off without asking if anyone else wants some."

"Speaking of the Victoria, have you heard from Brodie?" said Alpina, herding peas into the curve of her fork.

Another one. Did she work them all out beforehand? She could see her now with that awful perm picking up the letter from the mat, studying the writing on the envelope, then putting it in her pocket to read in her bedroom.

"I couldn't get through the last time I called."

"He's probably drowning his sorrows with that rabbit," said Alpina, her mouth full. "It's not every day they ban pearl-fishing."

Why did she have to say that? She hadn't had time to tell Maggie yet.

The bairn looked at her like she didn't get it.

"Having said that," said Alpina, wagging her empty fork at her, "he won't be in the Victoria. Fiona said Alan's barred him."

"What's she taking about, Mum?"

She paused, searching for the words. "People aren't allowed to go pearling any more."

"Why not?"

"There aren't enough mussels left. The species might become extinct."

"What's extinct?"

"When something runs out."

"But what about Dad?"

"He'll have to wait until there are more of them."

"When will that be?"

"Might never happen," said Alpina, a reluctant splatter of ketchup landing on her plate. "Not in our generation."

The bairn was doing that thing with her mouth when she was trying not to cry.

"What do you think Brodie will do now?" said Cameron.

They were all looking at her.

"He'll manage." She tried a smile.

Alpina reached for the vinegar. "He should never have planted that pearl."

Mungo dropped his cutlery. "I'm sick to death of hearing about it. Can you just shut up"

"Here, Alpina, why don't you have some more ketchup?" she said, offering her the bottle. "You've only had two servings."

"But I haven't had any," wailed Maggie.

288

"You should hear what the bowling club's been saying about him," said Alpina. "They all know he's my brother-in-law."

"Why don't you finish it off?" She could hear the edge in her voice as she held it out to her again. "You haven't taken enough. Go on, take what's not rightfully yours."

"I was hoping to get on the committee next year. They might not have me now, all because of him."

"Just take the goddamn ketchup!"

Alpina ducked as the bottle spun past her, hit the mantelpiece and clattered to the floor. A smear of red, like a squashed insect, remained on the wall.

Silence.

"No, thank you, Elspeth," said Alpina curtly. "I've had sufficient."

Maggie started kicking the table.

She stood up. "I'll make some tea."

As the kettle rumbled into life, she stood at the window, biting the edge of her little finger.

"I shouldn't have told you. About the letter," said Cameron, suddenly by her side. "Sorry."

"It'll sort itself out."

"Would it have made a difference?"

She didn't turn.

"The letter," he said. "If Alpina hadn't taken it."

She couldn't think straight, so much had happened. "I'm going to find somewhere else for Maggie and me. We can't stay here forever."

A hand rubbed the small of her back, lingering in the intimate bit where it dipped. "Stay at my place, both of you. I'm moving in next week. You'll like it. It's got views of the Isla. It'll be strange living on my own again."

The kettle was starting to shriek.

"There's plenty of space. Maggie can pick her room."

She kept her eyes on the firs as they caressed the sky in the wind.

"Happiness doesn't just turn up on the doorstep with the milk," he said, giving her back another small rub. "You have to change something. You said it yourself to Maggie — bad things happen and you have to move on."

She shifted her weight.

"And if you must know, the contents of that letter still stand, though I think I would put it a bit more eloquently these days."

There was a click, and the racket subsided.

She looked at him then, standing there trying to make it all better. For her and for Maggie. Those brown eyes again. He really meant it, she could tell.

The early-morning mist writhed in his headlights as the foxgloves lurched back and forth in the verge like dead man's bells. Pitched forward, he wound down the window to help him concentrate, but it was useless. He kept seeing the same nightmare that had always woken him. The one when he was trying to reach Dad, but those frightful fingers, white, bloated and urgent, kept sinking away. Not matter how many times he'd dreamt it, the look in those retreating eyes always said the same thing: your fault.

The Cairngorms, hunched and dark, were now all around him, and he pressed on. Hours later, a mile away from the village that had once been home, he finally sat back feeling strangely becalmed. It was as if a storm had passed, the damage had been wreaked, and it was all too late for anything as laughable as hope. As always, he turned off at the junction and crossed the small bridge over the darkened Carron, leaving it far behind.

Alone now, except for the trees, he glanced around. It was the first time he'd been here for thirty-four years. Eventually he spotted the Oykel slipping silently to a better place. It was this river, according to Dad's ledger, that had thrown so many lovely cream balls. He'd always refused to fish it after his childhood was bagged up and put out with the bins.

As he followed it, he watched the water dancing over rocks as if nothing had happened. Anxious not to miss the right spot, he slowed. The last time he'd gone there was to try and find an answer after that horrendous conversation with Mum in the kitchen. It took him half a day to cycle there, tyres slipping in spiteful spiralling snow. Convinced he'd find a note, he'd picked up all those frigid rocks and searched underneath them. What a little idiot he'd been.

It had to be here somewhere. It was one of the first questions he'd asked Mum: where in the Oykel?

"After the third bend," she'd said, carefully hanging a red-and-white-checked tea towel on the oven handle to dry. "Where the gap in the trees is. The one that looks like God has reached down and parted them. Near the pearl colony."

Here. He stamped on the brake, and pulled into the side of the road. Back sore from the drive, he staggered towards the bank, feeling the bounce of the grass. Standing at the water's edge, a faint breeze coming at him, he ran a hand down his face, feeling the sting of his bristles. It was here all right. He remembered that trunk bending towards the water as if trying to drink it. His chest rose as he inhaled. Nothing. It was nonsense that you could tell a river by its scent. It was just another ridiculous story he'd told Maggie about Dad to fill the gap that he'd left. He'd spent his life telling *himself* stories, like the one about Dad giving him the tin in which he kept Elspeth's pearls, and that it had belonged to his great-great-grandpa. Dad hadn't given it to him, he'd found it knocking around a charity shop. Nor had Dad told him that pearls got their pink tinge during stunning sunrises, the same way that they became white if they opened their shells when it snowed. He'd made it all up, just like Dad taking him to the woods to find a piece of hazel and teaching him how to whittle it into a pearling stick. The hideous truth was that he couldn't remember a thing about Dad. Not a single thing. He had no recollection of him even taking him pearling. All his memories had been wiped the moment he learnt that Dad had jumped into this stretch of the Oykel, huge stones strapped to his boots, then sunk numb and noiseless through the murk to the riverbed.

He lowered himself onto the grass, feeling the creeping damp of a spent shower. The irony was that, try as he might, he couldn't forget the inglorious details of finding out what Dad had done and everything that happened afterwards. He'd been standing next to the tinned faggots in the corner shop, trying to remember what Mum had sent him for, still unable to believe Dad was dead. Angus Buchanan, the red-headed kid in the year above, then rounded the aisle, unwrapping a Twix.

"Why did your dad kill himself?" he said, a big spot on his chin.

"Didn't. He drowned while pearling in the Oykel." Mum had told him that morning, three days after he'd gone missing.

He took a bite. "Did," he said, mouth full. "My neighbour found his car while walking her dog and told the police. I went to watch the action. When the diver pulled your dad out he had a piece of weed hanging from his mouth and rocks tied to his boots with rope."

"Liar."

He ran home while the rest of the world carried on as if everything were normal. Standing in the furthest corner of the kitchen, he repeated what Angus Buchanan had just told him, while Mum, in that green flowery pinny she always wore, made meringues, even though only Dad ate them.

Heels against the skirting board, willing her to say it wasn't true, he watched as she continued to pass a fat sunny yoke between two brown eggshells, each time tipping out the viscous white into the glass bowl below, where it swung against the sides.

"Your father didn't tie the rocks on with rope," she said, sounding like she was in another country. "He used belts. Not sure whose."

"Why did he do it?" His voice was small, like someone else was speaking.

A crack as she broke another egg against the side of the bowl. "He didn't bother to explain himself. Everyone knows that if you kill yourself you're meant to leave a note."

The etiquette of suicide.

She then grabbed a whisk and pointed it at him, a smear of sugar streaked across her cheek like crushed diamonds.

"If anyone asks, your father died of a stroke."

Despite what Mum had said, for a week he watched the Kyle from his bedroom, waiting for Dad to come back. When he did, he was screwed inside a coffin at the front of the church, a minuscule white flower arrangement resting on top like a hat that was too small. Only the couple from next door came round after the funeral, each clutching a tray with enough sandwiches and sausage rolls to feed every household all the way to Dad's lonely grave. The four of them sat in a pitiful row on the sofa keeping the other seats free, lifting their heads hopefully at any sound from the road. Afterwards, as he shovelled the food into the bin, he still couldn't understand why no one else had come. It wasn't until years later that he realised it must have been because they simply didn't know what to say.

294

Once the neighbours had gone, Mum tore up the house that she'd just taken three hours to tidy "looking for a note from your father". Empty-handed, she then gazed round the living room, and started tossing out all of Dad's things, as well as the empty bottles she'd missed the first time. Feeling the cold of the snow through his slippers, he ran outside to save what he could from the shed. He hid all the ledgers and Dad's stick and cap under his bed. Never once did he tell Mum they were there, and at night he'd read the books with his torch, telling himself that Dad had gone pearling in Russia.

The empty beer cans scattered loudly across the dusty floorboards of the Tolbooth as Maggie kicked them aside with her welly. Sitting among the feathers, curled and white like angel wings, she wiped the rain from her forehead. She'd keep hiding in here so the police wouldn't find her. It was drier than the woods and safer than the library. The horrible sleeping bag was gone, thankfully, so no one would disturb her.

From her rucksack she took out the bag of sultanas she'd found in one of Auntie Alpina's cupboards, and pierced a finger through the plastic. She took a mouthful, but her tummy hurt again. Where was Dad? He wasn't going to become a tramp now that he didn't have a job, was he? The one with the dog didn't have a house and probably never saw his children. Maybe Dad had already gone off with his sleeping bag somewhere and she'd never see him again. It would be horrible.

As she stood at the window, a fat pigeon flapping furiously rose up from the trees, and headed for the hills. The biggest one was the tummy of a giant who'd dropped down dead from fright after trying to steal the tail of a fox that suddenly woke up. Dad had told her that story when she was little to teach her it was wrong to take things that weren't hers. She should never have pinched that money. Everything was much, much worse than before and it was all her fault. Her fingers reached for her dress pocket, and she checked inside her bead purse to see if she had enough money to try and make it all better. Rucksack jiggling on her back, she scurried down the broken stairs, leaving the sultanas behind in case the tramp ever came back and was hungry.

He lifted his eyes from his boots and gazed at the cloud-smeared sky. He'd never wanted to go to Nether Isla to live with Aunt Agnes. Eleven by then, he'd stopped following Mum to the loo in case she never came back. He was managing all the shopping, cooking and cleaning, and if anyone at school mentioned Dad a thump always shut them up. Mum must have thought sending him a hundred and fifty miles south would do him good. Get him away from the gossip and the reproaches from Dad's other relatives. The day he had to leave, he hid in the pantry behind a sack of potatoes sprouting tiny green umbrellas. But she heard him when his foot went to sleep and he moved.

"When will I be able to come home?" he asked, standing up.

"In a few months. I'll be better by then. Come and fetch you."

296

But no matter how long he stood at his bedroom window at Aunt Agnes's lonely place, she never turned up. Like Dad, she mustn't have wanted him either.

Pinpricks of rain stung his cheeks. For thirty-four years he'd been wondering why Dad had thought death was a better option than being with him. It had been getting worse in the last year as he approached the same age Dad had been when he killed himself. Much worse. He couldn't get the question out of his head, except when he was face down in a river hunting for a pearl. It was the only time when the noise would stop completely, and he no longer told himself that if Dad had loved him, he wouldn't have done it.

Feeling uneasy, Elspeth stepped into the hall. It seemed odd coming home after all this time, especially not having seen Brodie. She'd tried to call when the ban was all over the papers yesterday, but couldn't get through. It was silly to worry, but she just wanted to know that he was all right. She'd better be quick — she'd told Cameron she had an errand to run, and would be back in ten minutes.

Something was different. The smell for one thing. It was the pine floor cleaner she used for the kitchen. Brodie never washed the floor. That wasn't all. Someone had taken up the carpet on the stairs, revealing the pale green underlay. She picked up an invoice from the bottom step. A stairs and landing carpet was going to be laid next week, and the word "Paid" had been stamped on it in red letters. Her name was down as the contact, and that was the cafe's phone number. How on earth could he afford this?

A burst of music came from behind the living-room door. Brodie must have finally fixed the cable to the aerial and was watching the television. But as she entered, the only thing in his armchair was the old cushion, which was strangely plumped up. Nor was he in the kitchen, which was so tidy even the washing-up liquid was out of sight. Why had he left his watch on the windowsill? She opened the fridge. Cheese. Lots of it.

Outside the back door was a heap of black bin bags pooled with rainwater. Her fingers fumbled as she untied one. It was full of ridiculously neat squares of the ruined carpet. Must have taken him ages. None of this was making any sense.

The door to his hut was closed. Was he in there then? Hesitantly she walked towards it, eyeing the faded quote he'd painted over the door years ago: "*And Britain's ancient shores great pearls produce*" — *Marbodus, Bishop of Rennes, circa 1070*. She stood in the doorway, trying to understand it all. Still confused, she took a step forward, keeping a hold of the handle to steady herself. Ghostly squares of new-looking wood covered the walls where the newspaper cuttings and map used to be, their abandoned nails ginger with rust. The table had been cleared of his scales, all the mugs and glasses, as well as the photo of her and Maggie boiling a kettle on a little camping stove at Loch Lomond one Boxing Day.

All the empty bottles were gone. In their place, tucked tidily underneath the table, was a cardboard box. The brown parcel tape squealed as she ripped it back. The ledgers. His father's tweed cap. Her hand delved further. Bits of snapped pearling stick, their vulnerable white insides exposed. The photo of her and Maggie, wisps of orange duster caught in the frame. Hardly daring to look, she tugged at the table drawer until it opened. His emergency amber pearl was gone.

Then she ran.

Back through the kitchen she fled, and up the stairs, the unfamiliar underlay unsettling her further. Not daring to enter, she stopped at their bedroom door. Then slowly, with her fingertips, she pushed it open. The bed was so perfectly made it was as if house-keeping had done it. There were no clothes strewn across the floor, and the books on his bedside table were all facing the same way. Had he moved out and gone to live with someone?

There was something on her pillow. She took a step towards it. It was a flat, red box, its leather worn, on top of which was a pale blue envelope bearing her name. That was Brodie's writing. She didn't like the look of any of this. What did he have to tell her that he couldn't say in person? She lifted the brass clasp and then the lid. Inside was an exquisite circle of white pearls, as round as river pearls got, with a delicate pink glow. They were exactly the same colour as the baroque pearl he'd given her before they'd even spoken. She groped for the letter with its words too fragile to be spoken, and tore it open. Just one sentence of his looping handwriting stretched across the page. *For Elspeth McBride, collected with love since the day of our marriage, 6 October 1979.* Underneath was his signature and the date. She raised her head, trying to understand. The window was open, as if a bird had flown away.

The rocks felt comforting as he grabbed them and stuffed them into his jacket pockets. More. He needed more. Once they were full, he shuffled to the edge of the bank. He was in a trap, whichever way he looked at it. All he had to do was lower himself in and he'd be out of it. Elspeth and Maggie would be free of him. They'd be much better off on their own. He closed his eyes. He might see Dad again. But how would he recognise him? Didn't even know what his own father looked like. With a final breath he leant towards the beckoning water.

CHAPTER
SEVENTEEN

Red clover. He could definitely smell it. It was the scent Hebridean fishermen once followed to guide them back to land on misty days. Brodie opened his eyes to the water with its patches of light, flickering like mirrors. Head tilted back, he took a deep breath. There was something else with it. Polished silver. So he'd been right all along: all rivers did smell different. He'd assumed it was just another story about Dad that he'd invented for Maggie to reassure himself that the man had even existed.

How would the bairn feel if he went through with it? He could see her now sitting on a bed in Alpina's loft conversion, while Elspeth tried to find words for the unspeakable. Elspeth would be wearing something that Maggie would never be able to forget, an excruciating colour snapshot that would keep coming back to her in those evil hours when the rest of the world slept. The bairn would blame herself for the rest of her life. And what about Elspeth? She'd be better off without him, he knew that, but Dad's death had reduced Mum to a shrunken ghost. The only time she left the house was to go to work at the laundrette. He'd had to bring his invented meals on a tray to her bedroom. How many times had he sat on the other side of the door asking God not to let anything happen to her? He had to remind her that her hair needed washing, and he'd do it for her in the sink with a cup, hating it when shampoo got in her eyes. He couldn't do that to Elspeth. To either of them. That was thing about suicide — you happily cruised to oblivion, but the poisonous wake you left behind never stopped contaminating everyone else.

There was a stagger as he got to his feet and grappled in his pockets. He hurled the stones far into the Oykel, the sharp smacks sending a green-shank into startled flight. When it was all over, he wiped his slick forehead with the back of his wrist, watching the ripples rocking against the bank. Finally they smoothed out and the river filled with smuts of cloud again. The idiocy of it all. Dad. Him.

Hands clamped to the wheel, he followed the road not knowing where he was going, and found himself crossing back over the Carron. He paused at the junction. To the right stretched the road heading back south. The other, curving left, led to the village. He hadn't dared go back for thirty-two years.

Within minutes the vast bridge was in front of him, and below it the mighty Kyle was sliding, polished as a pew, to the sea. Slowing down, he scanned the hill. It was that house up there at the end of the terrace. It looked much smaller than he'd remembered it.

Hesitantly, he passed through streets of grey-stone cottages, built to withstand the cruellest of winters, unable to believe it was all still here. Stomach twisting, he parked opposite the house, then made himself look.

That window there had been his bedroom. Someone had since double-glazed it. He could remember the bitter draught against his chin resting on the cracked white sill as he watched the Kyle, still convinced months after the funeral that Dad would eventually come back from Russia.

His fingers scrabbled for the handle, and he got out. His back to the house, he stared at the careless Kyle. What was he now that no one wanted him?

"Rain's stopped."

Some old bloke in tartan slippers and a checked shirt was standing next to him. With any luck he'd go away.

"Aye." He faced the river again.

"I never get sick of looking at it."

He kept quiet, hoping the man would get the message.

"You'd wonder where all that water comes from."

What would Elspeth be doing now? Working in the cafe with Cameron, no doubt. Talking about old times. And Maggie? Playing with Alice probably.

"Saw you in the paper."

Appalled, he stared at him, a stranger all the way up here in the northern Highlands.

"It gave me a bit of a start, I can tell you."

He swallowed. It would be like this for the rest of his life. He'd never get away from it. Never.

"We couldn't believe it."

He stabbed at the ground with his toes.

"I said to Jean you look so much like him. Though you're much taller than he was, of course."

He raised his head. "Than who?"

"Your father."

A thump to the heart.

"Jean saw you looking at your old house. Said I should run out and say hello before we missed you. I did tell her I had my slippers on, but she said it didn't matter."

It was him, the next-door neighbour, his nose and ears bigger with age. What was he called?

What's-his-name squinted at the sky, hair the colour of the herding clouds. "There's the rain on again. You'll come in for a cup of tea, I hope? Jean said I was to warn you there weren't any biscuits. 'For the love of God, there's Brodie McBride,' she said. 'And you've just had the last custard cream.'"

"You'd better take off those boots. You know what Jean's like about the house," said the old fellow when they reached the front door. "Where have you been to get all muddy like that?"

Silently he left them on the hall mat, and in his worst socks, brown and pitted, he padded after him into the living room. Standing at the window with its view of the road was a woman in a yellow cardigan, her hair a series of small cresting waves. Her fingers were toying with the end of a blue handkerchief poking out of her sleeve as she looked at him.

"Gordon's explained about the biscuit situation, I hope, Brodie." She then bent her head and fled past him in pink nylon slippers. "I'll make some tea."

Gordon, that was his name. The old man was staring at the empty doorway as if he'd just spotted a rare bird.

"Not often you see Jean lost for words. Last time was when she sent me out for some Brussels sprouts and I came back with a sink plunger." He gestured to the armchair. "Make yourself at home, lad. You know where everything is."

Hands on the armrests, he sank much further than he expected while taking in the suddenly familiar china figurines in the wall cabinet, the picture of the stag over the gas fire, and the *Radio Times* lying on the coffee table between them. From somewhere came the low rumble of a kettle beginning to boil, and the frantic opening and closing of cupboards.

"I expect the place is a bit different from how you remember it," said Gordon, settled on the sofa. He leant towards the open door. "When did we change the wallpaper, hen?"

"1981."

"1981," he repeated with a nod of satisfaction. "Jean's choice. Likes yellow and orange."

Brodie studied the pattern.

"And the telly." He pointed. "That's new. When did we get the new telly, hen?"

"1988," came the reply over the hysterical kettle.

He raised his voice even more. "We've still got the receipt, haven't we?"

"It's in the drawer."

Happily he pointed to the sideboard. "It's in the drawer."

Searching for a thread, Brodie fingered the end of the armchair.

After the silence came a tinkling from the hall. Jean appeared with a tray bearing a pink tea set, the pot bulging snuggly in a knitted green cosy. In the middle stood a chocolate cake covered with candles. With a perilous rattle, she lowered the tray onto the coffee table, then perched on the edge of the sofa.

Gordon frowned at the cake. "It's got my name on."

"It's for your birthday, that's why." She poured out the tea. "Is it still one sugar, Brodie?"

All he could manage was a nod before reaching for the cup.

Gordon was blinking. "For the last seventy-eight years my birthday has been on August the 20th, Jean. Today is August the 19th."

The knife hovered above the cake. "I'll get you another one for tomorrow. Brodie's come home." She glanced at him as if to check that he was still there.

"You should come back more often, lad." Gordon smiled as he offered her a plate. "Never had two birthday cakes before."

The knife clattered as she put it down. "Before we go any further, Brodie, I want you to know something. The reason why I never said goodbye . . ." Her voice failed and she covered her mouth with the tips of her crooked fingers.

Silence.

"The reason why I never said goodbye is because we didn't know you were going. Your mother . . . she didn't tell us."

306

Gordon rested his empty plate on his knees. "Catriona wasn't at all well, hen. You remember what it was like."

"We assumed you'd be coming back. I asked her over the fence. I'll never forget it. She was pegging out some tea towels that hadn't even been washed. She said you'd gone to stay with your auntie in Nether Isla for a few months."

He took a sip of tea.

"We had all your balls that had come into the garden," said Gordon. "I put them in the shed so you could have them when you came back. They kept rolling around whenever I took out the mower."

"But you still didn't come back, and then Catriona died and we thought we'd see you at the funeral. It had been such a long time since you'd left. Hadn't it, Gordon?"

He nodded solemnly. "Two years and three months. Shortly after, I'm sorry to say, I had to throw your balls out. Lost all their air."

Brodie ran his palms down his trousers. "I didn't know."

"About the balls?" said Gordon.

"He means the funeral," said Jean, twisting the end of her handkerchief.

"Aunt Agnes didn't tell me Mum had died until four months later." A heart attack, she'd informed him as he was going up to get his bath, her hand resting casually on the banister as if reminding him to not to take too much hot water.

"Some blamed poor Catriona for . . . what happened," said Jean. "Especially your father's side of the family. Thought she'd driven him to it, or she should have been able to prevent it. I suppose blaming someone was the only way they could understand it. Some things just don't make sense, and folk don't like that."

He tilted back his head. "Aunt Agnes . . . she never spoke about Dad. Didn't even have his picture on the mantelpiece. He was her only brother." He paused as he looked at the floor. "It was like he'd never existed."

There was a long silence.

"Are we going to light the candles?" said Gordon.

She cut a large slice and passed it to Brodie. "You should have stayed with us when Catriona couldn't cope with the shock of it all. We said that when we eventually realised you were never coming back, didn't we, Gordon? The spare room."

"Aye, the spare room." His voice faltered.

"We should have said it right at the beginning when it was clear Catriona wasn't right. But we didn't want to interfere."

"Didn't want to interfere." Gordon clutched his vacant plate. "So we had you round as much as we could."

"We never did have one of our own."

Lost somewhere, Gordon lowered his head.

"We missed you." From her sleeve she pulled out her handkerchief and gripped it.

"Oh aye." His voice was muffled, like it didn't want to come out.

Brodie prodded at the chocolate icing with his fork. "Big piece, Gordon?"

"None for me thanks, Jean."

Suddenly he was aware of a ticking sound. In the corner stood a grandfather clock, a pink-cheeked moon on the dial. He could remember clambering onto something and winding it up with Gordon.

"Comfy, Brodie?" Gordon said.

He nodded, patting the armrests.

"Your father had exactly the same chair. Liked mine so much he bought one himself. 1962, wasn't it, hen?"

She shook her head. "1964. The year he . . . Jim needed something comfortable for his back when it became too bad for him to go to the shells any more. He used to sit in it by the window just staring at the Kyle. You could see him when you walked past. Catriona said the view became a torment to him. All those rivers upstream with pearls in them."

He shifted in his seat.

"That was when Catriona started working in the laundrette to bring in some money," said Gordon. "Sometimes I slipped Jim a fiver to help out."

She turned to him. "You never said."

"The man was my best friend. There was the bairn to think of . . . Maybe if I'd given him more, there wouldn't have been all that bother with the necklace." He looked at the patch of green carpet between his feet. "I've always regretted not giving him more. But I didn't want it going on the whisky. You know how bad it got, hen."

She fingered the neck of her blouse. "You don't drink, do you, Brodie?" She sounded hopeful.

He took a noisy gulp of tea.

"Catriona thought someone had stolen it," said Gordon. "You remember it, Brodie? The string of cream pearls she always wore. Jim gave it to her on their fourteenth wedding anniversary. Found them all himself. Something to do with a family tradition."

He knew all too well about the tradition. Mum had told him about it when they walked back home from Dad's funeral, and she spotted a woman wearing her necklace.

Jean cut into her cake with her fork, then put it down again. "Catriona called the police, as anyone would if their jewellery went missing. They even came to interview us. I think that short one thought *we'd* taken it."

Gordon shook his head. "We hadn't."

"Then Catriona saw Freya Thompson wearing her necklace in the high street. Comes running round here telling me she thinks Jim's having an affair. I tried to calm her down, but she wouldn't have it. She knocked on the woman's door and had words."

He closed his mouth.

"Turns out Jim had sold it to Freya's husband. You remember him. He was the doctor who used to have the practice next to the post office."

Gordon rubbed the side of his face. "Must have needed some money for the drink."

"Of course, Catriona confronted him. Wanted to know why Freya had it. Not long afterwards Jim . . ." She stared at her hands.

310

"Pour Brodie some more tea, hen. The poor man looks parched."

He couldn't lift his cup.

"I still don't know why he did it." Gordon nodded at the armchair. "I've sat there for more than thirty years wondering."

Shoulders hunched, he slid his hands between his knees. "I . . . I should have done something to stop him."

"You?" said Gordon, incredulous. "What could you have done? You were just a bairn. If anyone should have done something, it should have been me."

"Nonsense, Gordon," said Jean, patting his leg. "I've told you not to blame yourself."

He leant forward, knees still gripping his hands, unable to look at them. "I've never been able to . . . I can't remember anything about him." The hideous truth just came out.

"Jim?" she said. "God rest his soul, he was the nicest man you'd ever meet. There aren't many people Gordon would give a fiver to."

He shook his white head. "Always liked a chat over the fence when he was doing the garden."

Jean raised an eyebrow. "Jim struggled to see over that fence."

"He wasn't as tall as Brodie, that's for sure. He never did take my advice about that lawn of his. Moss. Riddled with it. We should have a photo of it somewhere."

"The moss?"

"The garden, hen. He was always so proud of it."

"Not as proud as he was of you, Brodie," she said, smiling at him. "He was happiest at the shells with you and your mother. You were only four when he first took you. I remember you coming back with a yellow one the size of a freckle that you'd found in the Shin. You were wearing that wee green jumper your mother knitted. The same wool she used for my tea cosy. Your father always said you were going to be the best pearl fisher in the family."

A sound came out of him, something between a sob and a wail. He stared at his lap, trying to hold it all in.

Someone blew their nose.

"I'll go and dig out that photo," said Gordon.

The sound of feet going upstairs. Exhausted, he rested his head on the back of the chair.

"It's a long drive back," said Jean eventually. "You should stay the night. There's the spare room."

Gordon returned with a red photograph album. "On top of the wardrobe, as I suspected."

"Brodie should stay the night, shouldn't he, Gordon?"

"Oh aye," he said, as if it made perfect sense. "The spare room."

"Your mitten's in the drawer of the bedside table."

Gordon sat down and put a hand on her knee. "It wasn't his, hen," he said gently. "We discussed it at the time."

"It was lying on the pavement outside the house after he'd left." She sounded indignant. "Whose else would it be?"

"Some bairn who was walking past. You picked it up days later."

She turned to him. "It's in the drawer, Brodie, still waiting for you. All washed."

He couldn't speak, even if he'd known what to say.

The stiff grey pages, covered with small black-and-white photographs, turned noisily as Gordon hunted through them.

All he could feel was his heart.

"There!" Gordon rested the album on the table and swivelled it towards him.

He didn't know which photograph he was meant to be looking at. One showed a woman standing on a lawn, holding a basket. Another was of the same woman standing behind a garden bench. Sitting on it was some man in a cap next to a wee boy.

A finger with a slight quiver tapped it.

"I'd forgotten about that one," said Gordon. "You can see his blackcurrant bushes in the background. The new people dug them out."

Brodie stared.

The finger tapped again. "That's Jim, there. Sitting next to you. Your mother used to cut your hair. That's her standing behind you both. She didn't say much. Shy, you could say. But she was good-natured, wasn't she?"

"That she was. Always gave me a jar of blackcurrant jam whenever she made some."

"You haven't given me any cake, Jean."

With both hands Brodie pulled the album greedily towards him. At the back of the photograph stood a rough-looking shed and a row of blackcurrant bushes, netted to keep off the birds. Mum, the breeze lifting her hair, was smiling as she shielded her eyes from the sun. Him, sitting there with his tiny legs stuck out of those shorts. Dad, in his tweed cap, had his arm round his shoulders, pulling him close. There was his little hand resting on Dad's thigh, finding comfort. Something happened at the back of his throat, and his vision instantly blurred. Finally, he remembered.

Puddles of white light glowed below the curtains, and he turned in the unfamiliar single bed to see the time. No clock. Pushing back the covers, he got to his feet. His heap of clothes on the wicker chair had been replaced by a folded navy dressing gown. He shouldered it on, grabbed the unopened toothbrush that had been placed on top of it, and inched open the door. The landing smelt of bacon as he slunk across it to the bathroom with its foreign fluffy pink mats. Standing under the shower, eyes closed and sopping hair in his face, his stomach turned. He couldn't believe what he'd almost done to Elspeth and Maggie yesterday.

"It's after eleven, Brodie boy," said Gordon cheerfully, sitting at the kitchen table, a blob of shaving foam on his ear and something shiny combed through his hair. "You must have slept like the dead."

There was a whiff of lily of the valley as Jean kissed him on the cheek and placed her hand on his arm. "Your clothes are in the machine. There was mud up the back of your trousers. I don't want your family thinking we didn't look after you when you go home."

Home ? He didn't have a home. Not without Elspeth and Maggie. He pulled out a chair.

"Thought I was never going to get my breakfast. Jean said I had to wait, even if it was my birthday. You can dish it up now, hen. Let's hope the scrambled eggs aren't as hard as bullets. I'll never pass them."

Clutching a wooden spoon, Jean turned from the stove. "Brodie doesn't want to know about your constipation. Pass him the paper."

He took it from Gordon and placed it still folded on the table between them. He'd had enough of newspapers to last him a lifetime. "Happy, birthday."

"It's going to be my best one ever." Beaming, he pointed to the clock on the wall with his knife. "I know that for a fact and it's only seven minutes past eleven. Be your birthday soon."

He stared at the bottle of brown sauce. Maggie had made him a cake out of modelling clay not knowing if he'd be back from the shells to eat a real one.

"I did black pudding and tattie scones as well," said Jean, lowering a cooked breakfast onto each mat. She untied her pinny and sat down. "Thought I'd push the boat out, considering who's here." Her eyes almost disappeared as she gave him another smile.

"It just gets better and better," said Gordon. "Help yourself to ketchup, Brodie, I know how much you like it. We didn't mention all that business about the pearl yesterday, as we were too pleased to see you. Isn't that right, hen?"

Head lowered, he started cutting his bacon. Couldn't they just carry on being pleased to see him?

"You're always welcome in this house, Brodie. Whatever you've done. I always said to Gordon there was more to it than met the eye."

"She did. We're . . . We just feel . . ."

There was a clatter as Jean put down her knife and fork. "What Gordon's trying to say is that we're both very proud of you."

Gordon nodded. "There's not many like you, my boy. Not many who's been through what you have, then done what you've done. I was always worried about what would become of you. Shouldn't have been."

"Pass him the *Scotsman*. He's no idea what you're talking about."

Gordon offered it to him again, and reluctantly he unfolded it. Maggie. Smiling on the front page. She was sitting on the stone wall of the bridge in her sunflower shorts, the Isla stretching out behind her. What the hell had happened now? He'd only been away a day.

"'Pearl Fisher's Daughter Planted Pearl to Save Parents' Marriage,'" said Jean, tapping on the headline.

Brodie stared at the words. To save their marriage? Is that why she'd done it? He still didn't understand. "But how do they know it was her?"

"She told them," said Jean triumphantly.

"But why would she do that?"

They were both looking at him like he was thick or something.

"Because she couldn't stand everyone thinking it was you, you great numpty," said Gordon. "It says you must

316

have confessed to it once you realised it was your daughter. You didn't want her to get into trouble."

"That's right, isn't it, Brodie?" she said eagerly.

He nodded. It was all too much to take in.

"Course it is, Jean, that's the beauty of it all." Gordon beamed again. "They both sacrificed themselves for each other."

"You should have seen them in the baker's this morning when I told them I was washing your socks."

"But the money. Where did she get the money to buy the cultured pearl?"

"I'm afraid she stole it," said Jean. "Money for the gardener she found hidden in a cupboard in a woman's house. A Mrs Campbell."

He covered his face with his hands.

"But Maggie went to see her and the woman's accepted her apology," said Gordon.

Someone put their hand on his arm and he looked up. He could feel Jean's worried fingers through the dressing gown's sleeve.

"You haven't got marriage troubles, have you, Brodie?"

He looked at his untouched food.

"I see."

"She's the only thing that matters," he said. "Both of them. Elspeth and Maggie."

"Does Elspeth know that?" said Gordon, leaning forward.

"You do tell her, don't you?"

He shook his head. How could he tell her? Everyone he'd loved had left him.

"Love's flighty," said Jean. "People like to know it's still there."

The pair were looking at him like it was the most obvious thing in the world.

Gordon nodded at the paper. "Says they haven't been able to reach you for a comment. Didn't you tell anyone where you were going?"

Jean reached for the salt. "The man was coming home, Gordon. That's what he was doing. Coming home."

Legs stiff from the journey, he hobbled as quickly as he could to the house. He'd been such an idiot. The key slid around the lock as he tried to get it in. Eventually it found its way inside and he pushed against the door, picking up the newspapers as they caught underneath it. He had to tell her.

"There you are."

He straightened.

"I hope you didn't mind," said Ailsa, one bare leg reaching out of her car parked opposite the house. "I couldn't reach you."

"Didn't mind what?"

She walked towards him, smiling in that way that suggested it would always be summer. "I took Maggie to see Mrs Campbell when she came to tell me what she'd done. Thought things would come across much better if she'd apologised."

"That was your idea?" he said, still clutching the papers.

"Tricky woman, Mrs Campbell. I had to pay her back to get her on side. Maggie must have called the *Scotsman* afterwards. And there was me thinking I had an exclusive. That's some kid you've got."

"How much was it?"

"Three hundred and twenty quid." She smiled again.

He ran a hand through his hair. "I'll give it back to you. Somehow."

"Don't worry, the editor did." She leant a shoulder against the door frame, her diamond earring catching in the light. "She's hoping you'll give us your first interview. Everyone thinks you're a hero, taking the blame like that to save your daughter."

"There's something I need to do. Immediately." He tossed the papers onto the hall table.

"I thought maybe we could go to the pub," she said, pointing her pad in its direction. "Do the interview there."

He raised his chin. "I don't drink."

She seemed confused. "Since when?"

"Today."

A shrug. "Then have a Coke. What's that green woolly thing?"

He pushed his mitten deeper into his pocket.

"We could go and get some lunch," she said, brightening. "That new French place in Perth. I'll put it on expenses."

It had been years since a woman had looked at him like that. Years. "I've got to do something. We'll do it on the phone. I'll call you."

"I'm sorry," he said. He couldn't believe that he actually meant it.

Filling the coffee machine with water, Cameron glanced over his shoulder. That white plaster thing was still stuck across the bridge of his nose.

"For hitting you. I shouldn't have."

He waited as Cameron, one hand on his hip, continued pouring with the ease of a man who'd won his war. Had Elspeth already gone back to him? He'd driven as fast as he could.

"Where is she? Elspeth."

"Popped out."

Still pouring, not even bothering to look at him.

"Tell her I'll be waiting for her."

Was he about to tell him he hadn't got a chance? That if he hadn't been such a rotten husband she wouldn't have left him?

Slowly, he turned and just looked at him. "Where?"

"She'll know."

Underneath their rowan, heavy with blood-red berries, Brodie looked at this watch. It had been more than two hours. Maybe Cameron hadn't passed on his message. A breeze started crinkling the surface of the Isla. What if Cameron had passed on the message, and she had no idea where he meant? Worse still would be if she knew precisely where he meant, but she'd decided not to come.

He'd give them the house, of course. Somehow he'd find a job, and rent a bedsit nearby. Close enough to see both of them. Just a glimpse of Elspeth would do, even if she were with Cameron.

"It's been ages."

Elspeth. Wearing a summer dress with cherries printed all over it. He'd never seen it before.

"Dr Kerr came in just now looking for you."

He must have wanted paying for that barrier he'd bust.

"He was wondering whether you'd work for him as a consultant on his conservation project, seeing as though you know the rivers so well. That's his card."

With both hands he took it, but the surge of excitement died as soon as he raised his eyes. Did *she* want him, though? That was the only thing he cared about.

"Where have you been?" She sat down next to him, hugging her knees tightly. "Everyone's wondering. Dewi's desperate to give you your job back. And you should have seen Mungo. The poor man burst into tears when he saw the paper. He's the first person I've ever seen cry with happiness."

He studied the water flashing white as it bounced over the rocks. "I put some yellow roses on Dad's grave this morning." There was no other way of saying it. Not now. "He drowned himself in the Oykel thirty-four years ago."

All he could hear was the Isla. He knew what was coming next.

"But I thought he died of a stroke."

"That's what I always told people. Mum didn't want people thinking he was mad. He wasn't."

321

Silence.

"There was the stigma of it." Please God, let her understand.

"Why did he do it?" Her voice was barely there.

It was the same question he'd been asking himself since he was nine. A lifetime spent mourning and blaming himself. "I'll never know for certain. Just have to live with the not knowing."

"I'm so sorry."

A cloud skated across the sun, turning it silver.

"The pearls . . ." He still couldn't look at her. "It wasn't how I was planning to give them to you. I started collecting them when we got married. It's a family tradition. I wanted to give them to you already strung, but I never found the big one. The one for the middle."

"I never knew who they were for." She sounded far off, somewhere in the past. "That was the awful thing."

"Who they were for?"

"When I found them."

He looked at her then. "Found them?"

"Last year. When I was doing the vacuuming. That loose floorboard."

"You knew about them?"

"I couldn't work out why you were hiding them. I'd lost my job and we really needed the money. I kept waiting for you to ask me to sell them. When you didn't, I started wondering if they were for someone else. A present."

He couldn't get it straight in his head. "You knew about them and thought I was collecting them for someone else?"

322

She looked bewildered. "It was awful. I couldn't think who she was. How was I to know they were for me? It wasn't as if we were . . ."

"They were for you. Of course they were for you. I remember finding each one."

He studied the branches, the way they'd shifted position over the years to survive in the wind. Unable to bear it any longer, he got to his feet. "I'm useless at this sort of thing, Elspeth. Useless. I always have been. You should have known how I really felt, and it's my stupid fault for not having shown you. Or told you." He started pacing. "I love you, Elspeth. Every bit of you. The fact that you think carving the Taj Mahal out of a piece of Cheddar is perfectly sane. Your smell. How I feel at home just looking at you. The way you are with Maggie. Look how wonderful she is. It's all because of you." His chest heaved. It was all too late. "I don't know what to do. I just don't know what to do."

She lowered her head. He'd lost her, he knew it. Why had he been such an idiot?

"The drinking. I've stopped. From today. I'm going to get some help and do it properly." He raised both hands. "You don't have to believe me. I don't expect you to. God knows I've said it often enough. But you'll see. I'm sorry I put you through it. I'm ashamed. It wasn't good enough. *I* wasn't good enough."

She was fiddling with a piece of grass. What was she thinking? That it made no difference, she was leaving him anyway? He couldn't bear it.

His back to her, he gazed at the Isla hurrying away from him. "I can't even say that no one could ever love you as much as I do, because it's rubbish. Utter rubbish. Any man would adore you." He paused. "How could they not?" It came out as a strangled whisper.

She didn't reply.

"If you want to be with Cameron . . ."

Still nothing.

He turned back to what he could see of her. "Just let me love you." What was the point of anything if he didn't have her? He wiped his stupid cheek.

Up on her feet, she brushed the back of her new dress. Something lurched inside. This was it, she was leaving him. There was nothing more he could do. He'd said it all, and it hadn't been enough.

She looked up at him, eyes as blue as harebells. "You're right, Brodie, about what you said before. There *is* magic in the world." She reached for his hand and held it like she'd never let it go. "It's you. And only you. Come home where you belong. With us."

"Go on ahead if you want," said Mum, standing with all their stuff in Uncle Mungo's hall. "Dad'll be there. I've just got to thank Alpina."

As soon as she was out of the door she started to run. She was going the fastest she'd ever gone — way faster than anyone in the Olympics. Feet slapping in her tiger slippers, she was just about to pass Samantha Grey's house when she stopped. There she was, sitting on the sofa in a pink T-shirt watching the television and drinking a can of Irn-Bru. She could call her whatever she liked, she didn't care any more because now she was famous. Ailsa, the

324

journalist she'd gone to see on the bus, said what she'd done was so amazing someone should make a film of it. She'd already told Alice, who was all happy again as the pearl hunter was coming to see her mum at the weekend. Alice had said she'd like to be in the film too. Someone would do their hair and make-up properly. Wouldn't end up looking like a bog brush. She knocked on the window. As the witch turned, she leant forward and stuck her tongue out as far as it would go, still covered in cheesy Wotsits, hopefully.

A bunch of people was standing outside their front door. They must be reporters wanting to speak to Dad again. She managed to push past them as they shouted her name and slid her key into the lock. There he was, standing in the hall with his lovely wizard's hair, as if he'd been waiting for her all this time. As he lifted her up, she pressed her nose into his neck, and all she could smell was home.

The leather box balanced on her lap, he watched as Elspeth lifted the tarnished brass catch, and raised the lid. There they were, seventy-three glorious white pearls with an exquisite pink blush, finally strung. He'd waited for this moment almost two decades. It had been worth it, every second, just to see this look on her face. Her finger traced the uneven one in the middle. It was the very first pearl he'd given her, even more striking for its imperfection.

"They're all so beautiful," she said, her voice uneven.

Maggie, sitting on the other side of him on the sofa, leant across to see, her mouth covered in chocolate birthday cake. "I love it."

"Will you put it on me?" Elspeth asked, turning her back.

His throat tightened as he opened the clasp, and reached underneath the soft warm hair that had covered his chest all night. For what seemed like ages, she stood in front of the mirror above the fire, fingertips skimming the necklace.

"I've been thinking," she said, settled back next to him. "I'd like to open a pearl museum in Nether Isla. It would explain how the monks used to fish for them and how your family has been making a living from them for five generations. There could be a section on your conversation work with Dr Kerr. People would come from all over now that the town's on the map. The ledgers could be open at certain pages so people could read them. We could display your glass and even your dad's cap."

Unable to speak for a moment, he swallowed. "Together. We'll do it together."

His eyes travelled back to his birthday present. He'd come down this morning to find the black-and-white photograph Gordon and Jean had given him hanging on the wall next to the others. The very best of surprises. Framed in gold were Mum, Dad and him in the garden with the blackcurrant bushes behind them netted to keep off the birds. Mum, the breeze lifting her hair, was smiling, and Dad, in his tatty tweed cap, was pulling him closer. There was his tiny hand resting on Dad's thigh, finding comfort.

He reached for the hand he would always hold. "Mine must have seemed a wonky kind of love, Elspeth. I see that now. But inside it never faltered. God knows yours is the only song I wish to sing. I shall sing it to the wind, and my love for you will be heard forever."

Author's note

Pearl-fishing was banned in the UK in 1998 when the pearl mussel was given full legal protection. It is an offence, under the Wildlife and Countryside Act 1981, to intentionally or recklessly kill, injure, take or disturb freshwater pearl mussels or to damage their habitat. This means that it is illegal to catch the mussels in order to look for any pearls that they might contain. Any suspicious activity in or near a river that may contain pearl mussels should be reported to the police as soon as possible.

It is illegal to possess mussels or pearls collected since 1998, as well as to sell, or advertise for sale, freshwater pearl mussels or their pearls unless done under licence from the Scottish government.

The law was changed when the effect of over-fishing, water pollution and engineering works in rivers threatened the survival of the freshwater pearl mussel. It remains one of the most critically endangered molluscs in the world.

Acknowledgements

I would like to thank Ann Goodburn, a family friend, for showing me her necklace of Scottish river pearls after I'd been pearl-diving in Bahrain. It was the inspiration for this novel. I'm extremely grateful to the retired Scottish pearl fishers who kindly agreed to speak to me — Bill Abernethy, Essie Stewart, Eddie Davies and Sheila Stewart. My sincere thanks also to pearl-mussel experts Dr Mark Young and Fred Woodward; jewellers and specialists in Scottish river pearls Cairncross of Perth; pearl jewellery specialist Chrissie Douglas of Coleman Douglas Pearls; Mackays, the jam producers in Arbroath; local historian Margaret Laing; and Sheila Thomson.

Utmost thanks to all at Vintage, especially Beth Coates and Áine Mulkeen, and, of course, to my lovely agent, Gráinne Fox, whose countless talents include knowing precisely when a large gin and tonic is called for.

I'm indebted to Henry Sutton, of the University of East Anglia, whose mania for point of view I hope not to have stoked with these pages. A number of readers were thoughtful enough to post messages of encouragement and gratitude on my website while I was writing this, which I greatly appreciated. The very great kindness of my fictional next-door neighbours was inspired by that of my own, whose many generosities include passing breakfast over the fence when I returned from a three-year absence in the Middle East. I should perhaps point out that the slightly annoying hot tub with the disco lights mentioned here was in *my* garden. The contraption was such a strange and wondrous sight in the badlands of south-east London that I kept being buzzed by the police helicopter.

Other titles published by Ulverscroft:

ONE SUMMER IN VENICE

Nicky Pellegrino

When Addolorata Martinelli lands in Venice, alone in one of the world's most romantic cities, she sets herself a challenge. One list, ten secrets to happiness. The problem is, she knows her list should be full already. She has everything she thought she wanted — her own restaurant, a husband, a child — back home in London. But lately it's all been threatening to come apart at the seams. Now, with no one to accompany her, she hopes Venice will help her find the answers. Wandering through the tangled maze of streets and canals, Addolorata must work out what happened to the person she used to be. And with the help of food, music and some accidental new friends, she realises her list has more than a few surprises.

THE FIRST PHONE CALL FROM HEAVEN

Mitch Albom

In the small town of Coldwater, Michigan, a handful of bereaved residents start receiving phone calls from beyond the grave. Some call it a miracle; others are convinced it's a hoax. Regardless of opinion, one thing is certain: Coldwater is now on the map. People are flocking to this tiny, remote town to be part of this amazing phenomenon . . . Sully Harding's wife died while he was in prison, and he now cares for his young son — who carries around a toy cell phone, believing his mommy is going to call him from heaven. But Sully soon discovers some curious facts: the calls only come in on a Friday, and each recipient happens to have the same cell phone plan. Something isn't adding up, and Sully is determined to keep digging until he uncovers the truth . . .

READER, I MARRIED HIM

Tracy Chevalier

Commissioned to celebrate Charlotte Brontë's bicentenary year in 2016, this collection of original stories by today's finest women writers draws inspiration from a line in *Jane Eyre*. A bohemian wedding party takes an unexpected turn for the bride and her daughter . . . A family trip to a Texan waterpark prompts a life-changing decision . . . Mr Rochester reveals a long-kept secret . . . Jane's married life after the original novel ends is explored . . . A new mother encounters an old lover after her daily swim, and inexplicably lies to him . . . A fitness instructor teaches teenage boys how to handle a pit bull terrier by telling them Jane Eyre's story. These tales, and more, salute the lasting relevance of Brontë's famous novel and its themes of love, compromise and self-determination.

A PROPER FAMILY HOLIDAY

Chrissie Manby

Sisters Chelsea and Ronnie Benson haven't spoken to each other in two years. When their mother announces she wants the whole family to go on a week-long holiday in Lanzarote for her sixtieth birthday, both dread the excursion for different reasons. Sophisticated singleton Chelsea, a fashion journalist, would rather not revisit the "chips with everything" world she left behind when she moved to London. Ronnie, now a mother of two, is feeling fat and frumpy: the last thing she wants is to strip down to a swimsuit alongside her super-thin, super-chic sis. The week begins badly and gets worse, as underlying tensions and secrets are exposed. And then their mother drops a bombshell on the group. Will the holiday bring the sisters closer, or blow the Benson family apart?